DARK HORSES

DARK HORSES

John W. Russell

Library of Congress Number:		2001119185
ISBN #:	Hardcover	1-4010-3465-9
	Softcover	1-4010-3464-0

This is a work of fiction. Names, characters, places and incidents either are the product of the author's imagination or are used fictitiously, and any resemblance to any actual persons, living or dead, events, or locales is entirely coincidental.

This book was printed in the United States of America.

To order additional copies of this book, contact:
Xlibris Corporation
1-888-7-XLIBRIS
www.Xlibris.com
Orders@Xlibris.com

DEDICATION

The loveliest creature on God's earth,
Though man contrived its regal birth,
The wisest tongues have always said,
It is the noble Thoroughbred!

PROLOGUE

In the failing light of evening, a large motor yacht eased away from its dock, powerful engines quietly throbbing as it slowly made headway out onto Long Island Sound. All eighty odd feet of it were illuminated from lights below decks, but the only sign of life was a single individual high up upon the bridge. As he steered the yacht past the shore lights that gradually faded into the summer haze, the barely visible figure switched on navigation lights and pushed the throttles forward to maximum power. The yacht surged forward, the sound of the engines increasing to a full-blown roar.

A brief smile flicked across the man's face as he enjoyed the implied sense of power that the vessel transmitted; he was certain that the next few hours were not going to be entirely unpleasant. Dumping the body that lay below decks was not going to be the highlight of the evening, but considering his contempt for the victim and the finality of his association with him, there would be no regrets about seeing him go over the side.

The girl was another matter altogether. She was beautiful and, at last, completely at his mercy. He knew that when he released her that she would come out fighting; he admired her spirit. But since she would be unaware of the demise of the other fellow, he was sure that he would be able to convince her that he meant no harm, at least until he was finished with her. He hoped that would not be too soon. He fantasized for a moment about the possibility of spending the remainder of the weekend anchored somewhere off the New York shore, indulging his desire before he killed her. He refused to contemplate how he would do that, thinking that it was to his credit that he had never killed a woman before.

Checking the radar screen on the instrument panel, he could see that there were no other boats within five miles on his present easterly heading, so he would have at least fifteen minutes to go below and get rid of his old friend. Switching the steering mechanism onto autopilot and taking one last look to reassure himself that there were no other vessels in sight, and whistling a cheerful tune, he proceeded to go below.

CHAPTER 1

A year earlier and an ocean away, an old but venerable sports car roared through winding roads, the driver's fair hair blowing in waves, framing a young and beautiful face. She felt the fast car an extension of herself, dangerous but always in control; she took pleasure in the summer sun and flashing dappled shadows cast by the overhanging trees. This was the English countryside of Suffolk that she loved so much, the land of her childhood and the birthplace of Thoroughbred horse racing.

Winning and losing were a familiar part of her experience as a jockey, but life and death, the one taken for granted and the other unthinkable, escaped the sublime sensibility of her youth. Within the confines of her world, however, that would soon change.

The engine howled a protest when shifted down through the gears to slow the little car. At a more moderate pace, it wound around the clock tower of Newmarket and threaded its way along the high street of the ancient town. She waved back to a pair of stable lads coming out of the Red Lion, a favorite hangout of the locals. Although not on intimate terms, the boys who rode work with her regarded her with almost reverential respect whenever she came to their racing stables.

The car slowed sufficiently for her to appreciate once again the history and timelessness of Newmarket. The ancient town must not have changed too much, she thought, since King Charles II would dally here with his mistresses in the middle of the 17th century. She was amused at the thought of the portly monarch, fancying himself as a jockey, vainly attempting to dazzle his escorts. She wondered how gratuitous his competitors had been in

1671 and 1674 when they followed him to the finish line in the Newmarket Town Plate, now the oldest race in England.

More than three hundred years had elapsed since then, but the narrow winding streets still passed racing stables with ancient Georgian and Elizabethan mansions, towering edifices behind Baroque wrought-iron gates that each day spilled long processions of horses out onto the gallops.

Now slowed by the steady stream of race day traffic, the little car left the main street and headed out onto the Cambridge road before turning into the vast parking fields of Newmarket Racecourse. Steering between rows of cars and up to the jockeys' entrance, she parked, and vaulted out.

Dressed casually for the warm summer weather, she wore knee length tan Bermuda shorts, sandals, and pale yellow polo shirt revealing a boyish, athletic frame. She was tall for a jockey, but her fine bones gave her a weight advantage over most of her male rivals. Her clear, wide, blue-gray eyes, golden skin and quick smile could have taken her to the world of fashion as easily as the rough and tumble world of a race rider.

Carrying a leather bag slung over her shoulder containing her tack, she showed her badge to the guard on duty and passed through the security gate leading to the jockeys' room.

"Afternoon Miss Kent," the clerk of scales greeted her as she went through the front door into the weighing room. "You're on two today, and one's a cert," he said, implying that one of her mounts was a certainty to win.

"No such thing as a cert Mr. Stubblefield, but wish me luck all the same," she replied, smiling.

She spun around as Eddie Handley, another jockey, gave her a gentle whack on the rump with a whip. She regarded him through narrowing, suspicious eyes.

"How the hell did you get under me for Dantes today, Fiona?" he scowled, and then broke into a friendly grin. "You must have worked old Rand over pretty hard."

"Come on Eddie, you know better than that, I hardly know

the man," she countered, relieved at his good humor. "Perhaps he just wanted to get weight off the horse. It's in awfully light. You couldn't make the weight?"

"No, not by a long shot, but you owe me one. I talked Rand into giving you the mount."

She threw her arms around him and kissed him. Then, quickly, she slid her arm behind his neck and playfully slipped a headlock on him. He enjoyed the moment, making no attempt to struggle.

"Okay, Eddie, now you've got to tell me how to ride him."

"Just don't fall off!" he croaked.

"But seriously Fi," he continued as she released him. "He has one little habit that you can ignore. He likes to run with his tongue flopping out on the right side. Just don't pay any attention and don't try to shift the bit in his mouth. You'll do just fine."

"Thanks Eddie, I'll remember that."

Fiona picked up the racing silks that her trainers had left for her and went down a narrow hallway into the changing room for women jockeys. The room was adjacent to that of their male counterparts, but a fraction of the size. There was a small bathroom with a shower, three lockers and a bench where saddles, number cloths and weight pads that made up the correct weight for the riders could all be laid out.

She unpacked her bag and placed her saddle with its two elastic girths upon the bench, adjusting the leather straps of the aluminum stirrups to the correct length. While she was working, she appreciated the skill of the craftsmen who produced the diminutive racing saddles. They were hand stitched, fine pigskin and glove leather stretched over a willow and aluminum frame, and although not the most comfortable seat, they were immensely strong. Beneath the saddle, Fiona placed the leather and felt saddle pad that had side pockets in which one-pound sheets of lead could be placed to make up the assigned weight for the race.

She then stripped down to sheer underwear over which she pulled on britches, boots, and finally the racing colors. Carrying her saddle and weight pad, she went back into the weighing room where the clerk of scales weighed her with the tack, making up the correct weight with the appropriate amount of lead for her first race.

"You're very lucky to be this light without having to starve yourself," Stubblefield remarked as he checked the scales. He was old and stooped, and leaning unnecessarily close, peered myopically over Fiona's shoulder at the numbers on the scales.

"I know, I can eat like a horse. You wouldn't want to feed me."

"Yes I would, anytime," the old man wheezed.

An hour later Fiona joined the procession of jockeys into the walking ring adjacent to the saddling paddock. She was dressed in crisp white britches tucked into highly polished, black boots, with gold and scarlet silks matching the helmet that she swung carelessly in one hand, a short whip in the other. She was always self-conscious in racing colors; her lithe figure and her graceful walk, a subtle confluence of feminism and athleticism, invariably drew stares from much of the public.

Fiona approached trainer Timothy Rand, a tall figure dressed in a dark gray business suite with binoculars slung over his shoulder, waiting in the middle of the parade ring with his owner, Adrian Harrington. The latter, in impeccably tailored navy blue blazer and gray flannel slacks, white shirt and military striped tie, was strikingly good-looking. Tall as the man that stood beside him, his slim frame and deep tan suggested that he was athletic and spent much of his time outdoors. In his early thirties, he had dark well groomed but stylishly long hair combed back from a high forehead above a straight nose and intense brown eyes, generous mouth and a strong jaw. Fiona was immediately struck by his appearance as he bowed slightly and offered a broad, friendly smile.

Rand introduced him. "Fiona, I don't think you've met Viscount Harrington."

"It's my pleasure. I'm delighted that you're riding Dantes for us today," Harrington greeted her.

"I'm flattered that Mr. Rand has asked me," was all that Fiona could offer. She was increasingly self-conscious, affected by

Harrington's palpable charm. She turned her attention to the trainer who proceeded to give her riding instructions.

"You have the rail side, Fiona, and plenty of speed, so just steady him along without fighting him for the first six furlongs," Rand explained. "He's very generous but only a two-year-old and a little green, so be quiet with him."

Fiona nodded. "Yes, sir."

"If something outruns you early," Rand continued, "be patient, but give yourself room for the last couple of furlongs, he'll finish well. Did Eddie tell you about his tongue?"

"Yes, sir, he did. He said not to worry," she replied pulling on her helmet, her brow slightly knitted in a frown of concentration. "That's all he told me."

"Well he's easy to ride, you'll have no problem."

Rand nodded and gave her a leg up onto the tiny racing saddle, giving Dantes a reassuring pat on the neck as he did so.

She liked Rand, but having respect for him and being anxious to follow his instructions, combined with the undeniably engaging presence of his owner, gave her a twinge of anxiety. She murmured under her breath, more to herself than to the horse: "Don't make a mess of it!"

Dantes was led out onto the course where his attending groom turned him loose. He cantered off down the course with Fiona leaning hard against the bit to restrain him. This was a moment that she always enjoyed; the tremendous power of a straining Thoroughbred, transmitting an almost sensual strength from his rippling muscles, her own muscles taut to maintain control. Her silks chattered as the wind rushed past, and in spite of her almost transparently thin colors and britches, she was already perspiring, as much from nerves as from exertion.

It took almost all of her strength to pull Dantes up into a walk as they approached the start, joining the other fifteen runners. It was here that they had a chance to walk in a large circle and get their wind back before being loaded into the starting stalls. As they started to load, Fiona, with trembling fingers, adjusted the chinstrap to her helmet and pulled down her goggles.

For the hundredth time, the question of why she competed in a dangerous sport, traditionally the domain of men, flashed through her mind. She never tired of the exhilaration that left no room for fear. She loved the sound of thundering hooves, the crescendo of thousands of cheering spectators, the color and the pageantry, and the power of a magnificent Thoroughbred. The years that she had spent at university seemed mundane compared to her life as a jockey, and although she had appreciated the school and those carefree days, she was obsessed even then by the love of horses and the excitement of racing.

After the last few horses were loaded into the starting gate, there was some shouting of jockeys and handlers, and then suddenly a momentary calm. An instant later, the gates crashed open and sixteen horses lunged into action. Fiona's heart was always pounding at this moment. In spite of her having ridden over fifty races, there was always that rush of adrenaline.

Dantes broke well and galloped away in third place with two other horses merely a length ahead and to Fiona's left. She glanced over and saw that Eddie Handley was on one of the leaders, his horse going well.

The field was bunched for the first three-quarters of a mile, with the two leaders slipping over to the right-side rails and in front of Dantes. He continued to gallop along, alternating between third and fourth place, with several horses lapped on his left flank. It was a straight mile course, and although all the horses were in dangerously close quarters, there was only occasional contact between them. Fiona's confidence increased with every stride. She ignored the high-pitched yells of a couple of jockeys shouting for racing room, each hoping to move through any opening they could find.

With only a quarter of a mile to go, Fiona saw a small space between Handley's horse and the other leader in front of her. Dantes was pulling hard now, and as Fiona eased the pressure on the bit, he surged forward. Handley, pushing his mount along, glanced over his shoulder, saw Fiona moving closer and gradually moved out to give her racing room. That was the opening that Dantes needed. Quickening his stride with little effort, he pulled Fiona to the lead as both Handley and the rider on the rail horse gave their mounts a slap with the whip to urge them on.

By the time they reached the furlong mark, the result was no longer in doubt; Dantes was drawing away. Fiona was down, crouching low, pushing hard against Dantes' neck in rhythm with each stride. His mane lashed across her face as he thundered towards the finish line under the roar of the crowd. She was barely aware of the crescendo of sound as she peered through the flying mane, concentrating upon keeping her mount straight. She had no need for the whip, but kept pushing, pushing, pushing, stride after stride. Finally, as they crossed the finish line, she rose up, and breathing hard from exertion, gave Dantes a well-earned pat on the neck. She looked back over her shoulder to see that Handley had finished second, beaten several lengths but with the remainder of the field straggling far behind.

With her remaining strength, Fiona was able to slow Dantes down to a trot and finally a walk, turning him around to join the other tired horses. She reached up and with a huge sigh of relief, pushed her goggles up onto her helmet. Dantes jogged back to the entrance of the unsaddling enclosure, Fiona waving to Handley as they passed.

"Thanks Eddie," she called over. "You didn't have to do that."

He flicked her off with a finger and a grin. "Now you owe me two!"

She rode the sweating Dantes up to his groom who, with a pat on his neck and a "Well done, Fiona!" led him through the crowd into the winner's enclosure. Fiona kicked her feet out of the stirrups and slid to the ground. She reached up to unbuckle the girths, and pulled off the saddle amid a swarm of congratulations.

"Good job Fiona, well done," Rand greeted her with the hint of a smile. "Go and weigh in, we'll wait for you here."

Amongst the bustle and excitement, everyone talking at once and laughing congratulations, she turned, saddle in hand, and trotted into the weighing room.

"Well done young lady," grinned the old clerk of scales as she stepped up to be weighed. Then in a loud voice, making the official announcement for the stewards and all to hear: "Weighed in, weighed in!"

Fiona relieved of her saddle but still flushed with exertion, hurried outside to meet the trainer and Adrian Harrington, the latter standing some distance away from the festivities. After the ceremony in the winning enclosure, Rand and Fiona walked over to join the owner.

"Thank you. I'm delighted and most impressed," Harrington beamed, shaking her hand. "Congratulations."

"It's my pleasure. I hope we can do it again."

"Yes, of course, I hope so too, but I must leave that up to Mr. Rand," glancing over at the trainer.

Harrington was evidently well schooled in racing protocol, his reserve prompting the appropriate response. Trainers made those decisions.

"Would you join us for a drink to celebrate?" he continued. "We'll be in the bar."

"Yes, please do," Rand pitched in.

"I'm so sorry," Fiona apologized. "I haven't brought clothes suitable for the members enclosure, and I do have another race to ride. I'd love to join you another time."

"You promise?" Harrington looked hopeful.

"Thank you, yes. I'd look forward to it," she smiled.

"Fiona, stop by my stables sometime when you have a chance" Rand said as she turned to leave for the jockeys' room.

"Yes sir, I'll be there in the morning."

The two men retreated to the bar for the traditional celebration. After vintage champagne was served and a toast was struck, they discussed the merits and future of Dantes. Adrian Harrington, however, was quick to change the subject.

"How long have you known Fiona Kent?"

"Not long, I'd met her at the races a couple of times with mutual friends of ours," Rand replied. "But I've watched her ride, and she's damn good."

"Somehow she doesn't fit my perception of a jockey," the younger man chuckled, shaking his head and topping off their glasses.

"I've known her parents for many years; they're charming people," Rand continued by way of explanation. "When we were in college, her father and I were on the national sailing team. Haven't seen much of him over the years but we have bumped into each other on a few occasions since then. Lovely family."

"Would you mind if I got her phone number off you and gave her a call? I really would like to show my appreciation."

"No of course not, ring my office in the morning," Rand smiled. "Perhaps it's more than merely appreciation, though."

"Perhaps," Harrington said thoughtfully. "Cheers!"

Before departing, both Harrington and Rand watched Fiona's second mount of the afternoon, which was neither talented nor inspired, and with demonstrative contempt for her exhortations, galloped along ineffectually in the middle of a small field of horses. Fiona consoled the disappointed owners with a cheerful smile and an opinion that "perhaps the horse would make a splendid jumper," and fled.

She returned to the changing room, oblivious to the male jockeys running around in various stages of undress. She had seen it many times before, but on the first occasion or two had reacted with curiosity mixed with embarrassment.

Now she passed their quarters without a glance, preoccupied with thoughts concerning Adrian Harrington. She wondered if his overt formal mannerism suggested that his interest in her was more than incidental or whether he was just bloody boring. She admitted that she would like to find out; on the surface he was attractive and engaging.

CHAPTER 2

Early dawn of the following day found Fiona riding out with a string of Timothy Rand's horses on Newmarket Heath. Her first stop upon arriving at the stable was to visit Dantes. Standing in his stall with straw bedding up to his knees, he was a portrait of contentment. When Fiona came to the door he turned and ambled over to her, the natural response of a friendly, curious, intelligent animal. When he pushed his warm muzzle, soft as velvet, against her face, sniffing, searching for a familiar scent, Fiona wondered if he recognized her as the person that had ridden him in his last race.

"You were wonderful, old boy," she whispered.

Half an hour later, a string of twenty horses in single file, walked out of Rand's Stable yard and headed towards the gallops on one of the many trails threading their way through the town. Fiona, mounted on a large bay horse and dressed in an oilskin rain jacket over sweater and riding britches, protection against the unseasonably cold morning, chatted and joked with the other riders. Upon reaching the gallops, the head-lad who was well mounted on a large gray hack, gave the riders their instructions.

"Fiona, you're going to work up the hill head-an'-head with Tommy over there. Get that old horse warmed up a bit and then go a half mile, well in hand," he called. "When you've finished, the boss wants to see you in his office. Off you go."

Just as the wind picked up and a threatening summer storm erupted, Fiona worked her horse in company with its stable mate, driving rain stinging her face as they sped up the gallop. She was chilled and wet despite her foul-weather gear by the time they had finished their work and ridden back to the stable-yard. The ritual of unsaddling her horse and rubbing him down was mercifully relegated to a stable lad.

Fiona wondered what was in store for her when she joined Timothy Rand in his study, but thawing out beside a roaring fire with cold hands wrapped around a steaming cup of tea was a welcome relief from the driving rain outside.

Rand languished in a large leather chair behind a mahogany desk cluttered with sporting newspapers, racing calendars, and magazines devoted to the equine world. It was an inviting, wood paneled room with large French windows that opened out onto a trellised rose garden, flagstone paths meandering through flowerbeds and ornamental trees.

The rain continued to rattle against the windows, sheltering those within the room and bringing a sense of intimacy that would perhaps have been less palpable in a different setting. The maid had quietly closed the door behind her after producing a tray of buttered toast, marmalade, hot tea and coffee.

"You know Fiona, your father and I have known each other from our days together at Hamden," Rand began. "We haven't seen much of each other over the last several years, but we have maintained a cordial friendship."

"I know that, sir. Father always spoke fondly of you as he followed your success in racing."

"I hope you're not offended when I tell you that I have the same concern for you as if you were my own daughter," he continued. "You probably know that Rachel and I have never had any children and over the years I became so totally involved in caring for racehorses that I have neglected some of my responsibilities to her."

He swiveled his chair around without getting up, looking out through the window at the driving rain. "Actually we were unable to have children but we probably should have adopted a child. I know Rachel would have liked that, but of course it's now too late," he added almost inaudibly, reminiscing to himself as much as a remark to his audience.

Not knowing how to respond, Fiona sat quietly sipping her tea, while Rand gazed silently out into the garden. She was uncomfortable, not only because of the intimacy that Rand was showing toward her, but also by the maudlin reflection of his marital life.

"I appreciate your interest in my career," she said finally, wishing to change the subject. "It was very kind of you to give me the ride on Dantes. I'd look forward to riding out for you any morning that I can."

"That's good of you to offer Fiona, I'll ask you more often," Rand replied as if gathering his thoughts again. He turned back toward her and poured himself a second cup of coffee. "A little more tea? Toast?"

Fiona declined and shifted her gaze to the fire.

Rand sipped his coffee and continued. "Viscount Harrington asked if he might give you a call, and with your permission, I shall give him your telephone number. What do you think of him?"

Fiona frowned and continued to stare into the fire, uncertain as to how she should answer.

"Of course I really don't know him. He seems charming," she replied at length. "Is he always so extraordinarily polite?"

"Ah, yes, that's Harrington," Rand replied with a smile.

He put his cup down and shuffling through mounds of papers, found a well charred briar pipe, which he proceeded to stuff with tobacco, tamping it down with a thumb. He lit it, producing a large cloud of pungent smoke, and threw the flaming match into the fire.

"I think he may be a little in awe of you," he continued with an artful smile. "He's actually led a relatively reclusive life, living much of the time abroad, educated in boarding schools and tutors, you know.

"His father, Sir Harold Harrington, was knighted for his stint in the Foreign Service at the beginning of the cold war. The old man was abroad for much of his career while attached to British

Intelligence. I think, frankly, it was a strange sort of childhood for Adrian."

After a long pause he added, "Perhaps I shouldn't tell you this, but I trust your discretion. His father, toward the end of the cold war, was posted to only a minor position in a South American Embassy because of some questionable dealings he had previously conducted with foreign diplomats. Some sort of political impropriety I suppose, no one seems to know, but those in government that did, kept it very close to their vest, perhaps to save their own skins. Anyway, he fell out of favor and was posted somewhere out of sight where eventually he drank himself into the grave.

"The estate, which had been in the family for over two hundred years, fell into disrepair by the time Sir Harry died, and was sold to pay inheritance taxes. I think Adrian was about twenty by then and his inheritance was relatively modest. Perhaps in deference to Sir Harry's contributions throughout the cold war and the winds of political change, Adrian was granted the title of Viscount."

"Is his mother still alive?" Fiona inquired.

"I'm afraid not. By all accounts, she was very beautiful, but I don't know much about her other than she was French and much younger than Sir Harry. When she was only a child, her parents were active in the French resistance in the Second World War, during the German occupation of France. It was at a post-war diplomatic function in Paris, sometime in the early sixties I suppose, that Adrian's father met her, where they apparently fell in love. She gave up a promising acting career to live with him. They were never married and had only one child, Adrian, before she was tragically killed in an automobile accident in Monte Carlo. She was reportedly in the company of another man when it happened. However, that may have been merely malicious gossip, but that and grieving over her death probably contributed to Sir Harry's eventual decline."

"How awful," Fiona interjected, "How old was Adrian when she died?"

"Oh, he was very young, perhaps three or four I suppose. He probably never knew his mother, really. His father didn't recover from the shock, took to drinking heavily, and never married. Adrian was raised largely by servants since no other family members felt inclined to care for an illegitimate child. I think it was a few years after this all happened that his father fell into disfavor with the powers of the government and was pretty much sent into exile. It's quite a sad story, you know."

"It is, yes," Fiona said after a thoughtful pause. "He seems to have overcome quite a lot. But I would look forward to meeting him again."

"Yes, well I'm sure you will."

Fiona, still uncertain as to how she should react, and despite her respect for Rand, hoped the visit would end, realizing it had been intended as a sort of briefing and perhaps a warning concerning Adrian Harrington. Between the gloom of the wind and rain pelting down outside and the melancholy story of the Harrington family, she was beginning to sink into a depression uncharacteristic of her usual buoyant disposition. She searched for an excuse to leave.

Rand got up, came around the desk, knocked his pipe out against the fireplace and stood warming his hands with his back to the fire. He looked over toward Fiona, perhaps, Fiona feared, reading her thoughts.

"Well, Fiona, you see that Harrington may come with some baggage also, and I want you to be careful. I don't know much about his most recent life but it is rumored that he is a spender of some renown, living quite lavishly. He has always paid his training fees to me though, and he's had some success with a couple of fairly nice horses."

"What business is he in?" Fiona asked.

"I'm not sure, exactly," Rand replied with some hesitation. "I know that he travels to Central and South America quite a lot, but really don't know what he does precisely. I believe he works for British Intelligence or something, just as his father did. I don't know if he has investments abroad, but judging by his lifestyle, he appears to have some considerable income. I feel compelled to tell you this because I'm very fond of you. I value your friendship and that of your parents."

Fiona smiled gratefully as she stood up and thanked him. "I do appreciate your concern. I really don't think I have much to worry about."

She held her hand out to him. He took it, and searching her face, suspected that he also had little to worry about. He was pleased for her father, his old friend, Peter Kent.

She drove slowly home in the driving rain, wondering what, if anything, the future and any association with Adrian Harrington would bring. Would he call her? Should she even encourage an association with what may turn out to be an impossibly complex man? She admitted to herself that he was intriguing and attractive, but wondered why she should be depressed over the life story of a virtual stranger.

Perhaps, she finally concluded, it was nothing more than the appalling summer weather that had brought about her gloomy frame of mind. By the time that she had pulled into the driveway of her little cottage, her refuge above the Vale of Aylesbury, she had decided that intriguing or not, Adrian Harrington would not complicate her life.

She picked up her mail as she entered through the front door, and after skimming through it, dropped it unread onto a hall table and went into the bedroom. She stripped off her still damp clothes intending to luxuriate in a long, hot bath. She stood naked before her dressing room mirror, and with self-effacing humor, critically debated whether her slim body was that of an athlete or just skinny. "Skinny," she concluded with a shrug. "I bet he thinks I'm skinny, too."

Minutes later, sliding into the bath through aromatic steam, she reflected upon her years at university, and the boys she had met during those years. They were mostly just attractive, uncomplicated, curious boys, quite unlike her perception of Adrian

Harrington. Those relationships never developed beyond the occasional party. With the exception of two memorable incidents, exploring each other in the back seat of a car or furtively kissing upon a crowded beach was the sum of her intimate experiences. Those had been carefree days with few responsibilities, but since her interests now focused upon her riding, social connections were few and even more casual. Her attitude had never changed from that of an extroverted, fun-loving child that had been gifted but unspoiled, yet she wondered what it would be like now to have a serious relationship with anyone.

As she bathed, she became acutely aware of her own sexuality that stirred an innate desire to have more contact with men than the amiable associations that she had had in the past.

She reflected upon the two school pals that had slept with her. Allen, the tall, gregarious Devonshire boy, the darling of the school and the scrumhalf of the university rugby eleven, was the first. He never stopped laughing, even when he had slipped up behind her one evening and slid his hands beneath her tee shirt and onto her breasts. She had slapped him hard, and kicked him, but he laughed it off, kissing her and holding her until she stopped struggling. Her anger abated, she had returned his kisses. On the way home that evening, after too many glasses of wine at a local pub, they stopped by a small stream where they made love on a blanket in dark shadows beneath a willow tree.

"I want to show you a trick an old poacher taught me, how to tickle trout," he had said, parking the car off the road on the bank of the stream.

She laughed and said, "Rubbish, it's too dark, and anyway you can't do that."

He had pulled a blanket and her out of the car, ignoring her objections. He easily picked her up, threatening to throw her into the stream, but held onto her as they both, laughing, fell upon the blanket. He rolled on top of her and pressed his body hard against her. She had resisted for a moment, then closed her eyes and pulled him toward her. Kissing her, he whispered, "I lied. You're the trout."

He had slipped her underwear down from under her summer dress and unbuttoned himself enough to be able to enter her, the first time that any man had ever done so. She felt the momentary pain, but then he waited for her response without moving. She remembered how she had caught her breath and then whispered, "Don't stop Allan, I want you."

It was the following winter, not long after Allan had graduated and left Fiona with memories of uncertain emotions that a riding companion had taken her at the end of a day of fox hunting. They had ridden to hounds that day, and after an early dinner at another local pub he had taken her to his house in the village. His parents were abroad, vacationing in Spain while he was on Easter holidays from school. Although he and Fiona had known each other since they were pre-pubescent pony clubbers, they were both approaching twenty, and only then had their friendship developed to a point where it was anything more than casual.

She kept a change of clothes in her car, and was soaking in a bath when he brought a glass of wine to the bathroom door.

"May I come in? I've brought you a little something to warm you up," he had called.

"I suppose so, since you probably will anyway and the door doesn't lock."

He sat on the edge of the bath, a bottle in one hand and a glass of port in the other.

"Best vintage. Dad'll be furious if he finds out I wasted this stuff without a conquest," he said and bending over her, held the glass to her lips.

She had laughed at him, took a sip, and said, "I think he's going to be furious then."

Then, acting upon impulse, she reached up, grabbed him by his tie and pulled him head first into the bath, shirt, britches, riding boots and all. He came up spluttering, pouring the red wine over her and into the foaming bathwater but saving the bottle. He lay there on top of her as they kissed. Without getting out of the bath, they took off his clothes, bit-by-bit, methodically alternating a garment with a kiss and each of them taking a drink from the bottle for each garment discarded, laughing the entire time. They eventually surrendered to the influence of good wine and the carnal desire flooding within them.

Both occasions had been intense experiences, but had not led to any lasting commitment. They had been largely encounters of self-indulgence, and although she remembered without regret, she wondered if that was going to be the most that she would find in the bed of any man.

CHAPTER 3

Albert, the doorman at Adrian Harrington's fashionable London apartment, greeted him with the usual, "Welcome home, sir, that was a short trip."

For some reason this unvarying salutation always annoyed Adrian. His trips abroad were invariably short and he was intolerant of mundane chatter, but more probably his irritability stemmed from the fact that these excursions were exhausting and occasionally exposed him to considerable danger. He often returned to London weary and emotionally drained, and rarely acknowledged Albert's polite greeting.

He let himself into the flat on the third floor, dropped his overnight bag in the middle of the room, and made an immediate bee-line to the bar to pour himself a large single malt whiskey, no ice. He opened a cabinet and turned on a stereo player, flooding Mozart into the exquisitely furnished suite. Picking up the mail that the housekeeper had left on the bar and flipping through it with little interest, he kicked off his shoes, loosened his tie, and collapsed into a comfortable wingback chair.

He took a large gulp of scotch, his mind drifting away in the security of his surroundings, knowing that at least for the time being he was safe. Except for the occasional sip of his drink, he made no attempt to move for a long time. Finally, empty glass in hand, he went to the bar, poured another scotch, picked up the phone and dialed a number.

"'ello, Molter 'ere," said a Cockney voice.

"Max, I have some good news for you. I managed to make all the arrangements with our man in Amsterdam, and I need you to make contact with him tomorrow night. He will be coming in to

13263-RUSS

Filey harbor and we need to get this business completed as soon as possible."

"Bli'me, that's a bit short."

"I know, but it's urgent, he can't hang around."

"Awright, don't you worry, I'll be up there with the lorry tomorrow afternoon."

"Thanks Max, you're a gem, I'll be in touch."

Adrian rang off, closed his eyes for a moment, then wearily ran a hand through his hair and looked at his wristwatch. It was only eight in the evening, so after taking another sip of his drink, he scanned his phone book and dialed a different number.

It was answered after half a dozen rings.

"Hello?"

"Miss Kent?"

"Yes."

"This is Adrian Harrington, am I calling too late?"

"Oh, this is Fiona, of course not. I'm glad you called."

If he could read anything at all into her voice, he believed she meant it.

"I was wondering if you are racing tomorrow, and if not, I'd very much like to take you to lunch."

"I'm riding one at York tomorrow. I'm sorry, I'm afraid I have to leave quite early," she apologized.

"York?" He hesitated for a moment. "That is a coincidence, I have some business up in Yorkshire that I could take care of tomorrow after the races. May I join you and drive you up there?"

"Yes, of course, that would be lovely. I'm in the three o'clock, though, we'd have to leave here quite early in the morning."

"That'd be no problem at all," he said. "But I'd like to spend a few minutes with someone on the way home. If we did that and stopped for dinner, we'd get back pretty late. Would you mind?"

She paused. She hardly relished the thought of staying up late at night, least of all with someone she hardly knew. But she did want to see him again, she decided, and he would at least be doing all the driving.

"No, I don't mind, as long as you don't mind the driving."

"Sure, my pleasure. Where do you live?"

"Just outside the village of Winslow, about ten miles west of the M-1." She gave him the address.

"I'll pick you up at seven," he promised and rang off. He could kill two birds with one stone, he mused. He could swing by and pick Fiona up on the way north and take care of his business on the way back. If it got too late returning home, perhaps she would agree to a warm bed somewhere along the way. The two drinks and the prospect of a cheerful day with a beautiful companion brightened him up immensely. Humming a few bars of Mozart, he tackled with renewed interest the dinner his housekeeper had left in the oven. His meal finished, he poured another drink, took a long shower, and turned in for the night.

The following morning, Adrian's dark green, luxury sports coupe left the suburbs of London and flashed along the M-1 motorway, heading north at high speed. An hour later, by the pale light of early dawn, it pulled up in front of Fiona's cottage. She was already up, dressed and waiting in the kitchen, a cup of coffee in hand. Declining an invitation to go in, Adrian threw Fiona's riding tack in the back of the car. He held the door for her as she slid in, and as the first hint of the sun crept above the eastern ridge of hills that overlooked the mist-shrouded valley, they were on their way.

The long drive to York took them into the North Country, the green of summer and the purple heather of the moors providing spectacular scenery under the rising sun of a new day.

Fiona felt quite at ease and was enjoying the ride despite Adrian driving at high speed. She complimented him upon his taste in cars; he asked her about her upcoming race. She wanted him to tell her about his travels abroad, which he stepped around carefully, only talking in general terms about the countries, and nothing of what he did.

They stopped for an early lunch at an inn that Adrian was familiar with, just off the motorway. Once they were seated and had ordered, Fiona pressed harder, inquiring into Adrian's personal life.

"Where did you go to school?" she asked. "Was it in England?"

"I wound up at Leeds University, up here in Yorkshire," he replied. "But I went to prep-school in Singapore when my father was attached to the Embassy there. I had private tutors before that."

"Did you like it at Leeds?"

"I enjoyed England. I spent my holidays trotting around South America though. My father was in Columbia after Singapore, and then was later packed off to Brazil, which I liked a lot. I was pretty irresponsible in those days. I liked the nightlife, the beaches and the partying," he smiled.

"Does your father still live there?" Fiona knew the answer, but was curious as to how he would react. She wondered, under the circumstances, if there had ever been a close relationship.

"He died in Rio de Janeiro while I was at school in England," he replied with an indifferent shrug, looking out through a window and showing no emotion whatsoever.

"He drank himself to death," he added with perfect candor.

"Do you miss him?"

"I hardly knew him," Adrian replied. He turned to look directly at her. "Are you always this curious?"

"Only about you."

He laughed. "I'm flattered, but I want to know more about you. How did you ever become a jockey?"

"Well, my parents put me into pony club when I was very small. I think they wanted to keep me off the streets. Don't all parents?"

"Not mine."

"I suppose I was a bit of a tomboy, but I loved horses. I spent my holidays hanging around stables whenever I had the chance."

"And then you became a jockey?"

"I went to university and wound up spending the summer holidays riding out for a local trainer. I liked it so much that after graduation I started with a few rides in amateur and ladies races. Now I ride in open races."

"Timothy Rand said you're very good. Are you?"

Fiona frowned and curled a lip. "Well if you think you want to bet on me today, save your money. I'm not that good." There was a heavy emphasis on "that".

They arrived at York Racecourse by early afternoon and drove into the Members' parking lot. Fiona had enjoyed their lunch and even the drive, her spirits lifted as much by her companion's easy manner as by the warm, sunny day and the spectacular profusion of summer flowers for which York was famous.

They entered the Members' gate where Adrian carried her tack to the jockeys' room, wished her luck, and headed for the bar. The afternoon passed quickly while he enjoyed the races, making a few bets and drifting back and forth from the paddock to the rails where the bookmakers plied their trade. He was in luck, backing a couple of good winners and taking great satisfaction in collecting from the bookies. When the three o'clock race came around, he went down to the walking ring to see Fiona. He watched from a distance as she received her riding instructions before being legged up onto what turned out be a pedantically slow horse. It ran within the middle of the pack for the entire mile and a quarter, Fiona's ineffectual urging resulting in her exhaustion and the animal's obvious indifference.

After the race and a brief discussion with the owners and trainer, she worked up a quick sweat in the steam room; a luxury made available to her but generally reserved for the male jockeys. They reluctantly covered themselves in deference to modesty, but not without a good-natured chorus of teasing. Tired, but refreshed after a cool shower, she dressed and went in search of Adrian in the bar.

Adrian stood up to greet her, not for the first time struck by her unpretentious beauty. The sun streamed through the window, reflecting off the golden highlights of her wet hair. Her liquid eyes crinkled at the corners as she smiled a greeting. He thought it would be very easy to love her.

"I'm sorry I didn't do very well," she apologized, taking the seat that he held for her. "I hope you had a better day."

"Well you can't ride any faster than the horse can run. Anyway, it was fun. I won a couple of bets." He poured her a glass of champagne.

"I'd like to get going as soon as you've relaxed a little," he continued. "I'd like to get together with a chap for a few minutes on the way home. There's a little pub just outside Doncaster where I said I'd meet him. We can stop there and have some dinner if that's okay with you."

"You seem to know all the taverns around here," she teased. "Do you spend a lot of time in them?"

"I did as an errant youth," he admitted, raising his glass with a grin and a toast to the past. "Remember, I was in college not far from here."

They left before the crush of racecourse traffic engulfed them. They headed south away from York towards Leeds, the university town that brought memories but little nostalgia to Adrian. He knew the area well, and Fiona, appreciating not having to drive, relaxed while listening to the typical schoolboy stories.

"I must admit," he said, "I didn't get much out of going to school here. My time was pretty much wasted with parties and sports."

"You really didn't like it much did you?"

"Not much. Although I love England, I found Leeds a pretty dreary place. I would much rather have been back in Rio. I had a lot of close friends there that were attached to the American Embassy. I liked the Americans."

"Do you still have a lot of friends abroad?"

"Not really," Adrian replied hesitantly. "Most of the people I know overseas now are business associates."

"Racing?"

"Oh no." He was emphatic. "No, except for Ireland and France, I don't race abroad."

Fiona wondered again what his business might be, but since he seemed reluctant to discuss that, she let the matter drop.

CHAPTER 4

As promised, the tavern where they stopped was indeed small, with only a single dining room and bar. A bartender who greeted Adrian with indifferent familiarity directed them to a table in a corner. Since it was a warm summer evening, Fiona was happy to be seated by an open window that was framed outside by a trellis laden with roses. The sweet fragrance of the climbing flowers provided relief from the aroma of smoke-impregnated timbers within the ancient room.

They ordered their meal from a sulky teen-age girl who, after an interminable wait, served them tepid Dover sole surrounded by over-cooked vegetables.

"Sorry about that, Fiona. This would hardly be my first choice for gourmet dining but I promised to meet this chap here. It was just convenient for both of us."

"I'm not terribly hungry anyway," Fiona admitted.

They had almost finished their meal when Fiona sensed that Adrian had recognized someone seated behind her at the bar, presumably the person he had intended to meet.

"Your friend's here?" Fiona asked.

"Hardly a friend, but I've got to deal with him. Do you mind waiting? Promise I'll only be a couple of minutes."

Adrian left the table and headed for the bar to meet his acquaintance. Fiona watched with little interest until she noticed that the man Adrian was meeting was an unusually rough looking character who, without a word, simply nodded in acknowledgment of Adrian and followed him out of the bar into the parking lot.

He was a thick set, powerfully built, tough looking character with long, dark, untidy hair and a full beard that did little to disguise a cruel scar running across the bridge of his nose to just below his right ear. He appeared to be about Adrian's age, in his late twenties or early thirties. Dressed in shabby jeans and a military type of jacket, he was a striking contrast, Fiona thought, to Adrian's perfect features and immaculate dress. She wondered what Adrian could have in common with such a coarse looking individual, but since they were on the fringe of England's industrial heartland, she reasoned, perhaps it was not entirely improbable.

It was too dark outside for Fiona to see anyone through the open window. However, moments later, she could hear the murmur of voices somewhere in the vicinity of Adrian's car. While idly sipping her glass of wine she made no conscious effort to listen to their conversation, but after a few minutes of barely audible murmuring, she could not avoid hearing Adrian's voice rising.

"You know we're never going to get together on this so why don't you just piss off. Go back to your people and tell them to bugger off too!"

The other man was mumbling a protest when he was cut off.

"I don't want to hear it!" Adrian was almost shouting. "You'd better stay out of the way, damn you, or there'll be very unfortunate consequences. If you don't want to work with me you can go to hell!"

Adrian was obviously the aggressor in the argument, but Fiona heard the man protesting again, rising anger in his own voice.

"Oh, come off it Hansen," he snarled, "you know I can't go back to my people without something better than that."

"Bugger you, that's your problem!"

"So we don't have a deal, is that final?"

"That's final," Adrian continued in a loud voice but with a more moderate tone. "And you can tell your people that I'm not wasting my time with them any more. They can go to hell, and you too!"

Fiona was stunned. She could not imagine what the outburst was about, and was even more confused as to why Adrian had been referred to as "Hansen". She was certain that there was no one else involved in the argument.

Moments later, Adrian alone returned to the bar. He was flushed and obviously agitated. He took a minute to ask the bartender to settle the bill, but by the time he had joined Fiona at their table, his demeanor had changed dramatically; he was totally composed. Fiona hoped that her own discomfort and embarrassment went unnoticed. She was certain that he was unaware that she had overheard the bitter exchange outside.

"I hope you weren't too disappointed about your dinner," he said with a disarming smile. "I'm sorry to have deserted you. Are you okay?"

"Yes, yes of course," she stammered with a forced smile. "Just a little tired. Can we go?"

It was with some trepidation that Fiona accompanied Adrian out into the dark parking lot but was relieved to find that scar-face was nowhere in sight.

They drove for the next two hours talking very little, both absorbed with their own thoughts. Fiona, tired but more relaxed, eventually started to fall asleep. When he noticed her nodding off, Adrian suggested they find a place to spend the night.

"You look as though you've had enough. Would you like to turn in?" he asked. "I know of a hotel close by."

She was sure he did, and that he probably intended to share a room. Had she not still been uneasy about his acrimonious outburst, she might have found the prospect more appealing.

"Adrian, I must get home, but thank you for the offer. Would you like me to drive?"

"No, of course not." He reached over, took her hand to his lips and kissed it. "You have been the most enchanting company, Fiona. Even wearing men's britches and boots you are exquisite," he laughed quietly.

"Thanks Adrian, I was just getting over feeling pretty silly about that."

"When do you ride your next race?"

"I'm not sure." Fiona was hedging, not wanting to commit herself. "I'll have to look at my calendar, but I'm sure it's not for a couple of days."

"Can I call you?"

"Of course. Give me a call tomorrow and I can let you know."

They drove on for the next half-hour, finally turning off the motorway onto the smaller winding road for the last few miles to Winslow. Fiona was almost asleep when, suddenly, without warning she was jarred awake, her heart pounding as the car skidded with squealing tires, hit the grass verge, and slid to a violent stop.

"What . . . what was that?" She was wide-awake, bolt upright, trying to focus bleary, tired eyes. She could see a blue car several yards in front, coming to a stop and blocking the road.

Adrian, without offering any explanation, viciously jammed his car into gear, spun the steering wheel and turned the car around, and then with tires howling, tore off down the road in the opposite direction.

"The bastard tried to run us off the road," Adrian said as they sped away.

Fiona could only see his profile faintly illuminated by the dim lights of the dash, but she could see the grim set of his jaw.

"Who? Why?"

"I don't know," he replied.

Then, with relief flooding over her, despite the dim light, she could see that he began to smile.

"Maybe my driving pissed them off. Are you okay?"

In the next instant, before she could even reply, he was jamming the brakes on again, bringing the car to another sliding stop. The lights illuminated a van parked sideways across the narrow road, blocking it entirely. Fiona barely had time to see a man starting to get out of the van before Adrian reached across her and threw her door open.

"Get out, get out!" he yelled.

Confused, scared and with heart pounding, Fiona dived out and onto the grass verge as Adrian ran around the back of the car, grabbed her by the arm and started running down the road, away from the van.

"What . . . " Fiona began to protest when she was interrupted by the thud of a gunshot. She heard the bullet ricochet off the road beside her, and then a second that whined overhead.

They both ran with Adrian desperately dragging Fiona by the arm. They had gone only a few yards when they could see the lights of a car coming toward them. It started to slow down as it came around a bend, and with fading hope, Fiona could see enough of it to know that it was the car that had run them off the road. As it was apparently in the line of fire, there were no more shots, but Fiona and Adrian were trapped.

Adrian swerved to the left into the shadows of some bushes and pulled Fiona through a small ditch to a low, stone wall paralleling the road. Fiona, terrified and gasping for breath, scrambled over the wall, still attached to Adrian by his fierce grip.

"Get down! Get down and keep moving, we're going back!" he hissed.

They started back toward the van, Fiona crouching behind the wall and running as best she could.

"Adrian, what's going on?" she panted.

"Quiet, he's coming down the road."

They stopped, Adrian pulling Fiona down beside him, kneeling. They could hear footsteps running down the road, drawing level and then going on by.

The car coming from the opposite direction had skidded to a stop, its door slammed. Then Fiona heard the voices of the men from the two vehicles talking excitedly in a foreign language that she was unable to understand.

"Come on, follow me!" Adrian whispered.

They started crawling away from the voices, staying low behind the wall. They could see the beams of flashlights going up and down the wall, some thirty or forty yards behind them, searching the bushes and the shallow ditch.

They crawled past Adrian's car, past the van, until they were a hundred yards beyond where the two men were searching, well out of range of the flashlights and the car lights. They were in a field, and judging by the rough grass that Fiona had crawled through, she guessed it was probably a pasture. She fervently hoped there were no animals grazing nearby that might take flight and give their position away. After a hundred yards or so, they came to a corner, and even in the dark, Fiona could see that another wall ran across the field, perpendicular to and joining the one that they were crouching behind.

"Come on, let's get on the other side of this. We can follow it away from the road," Adrian whispered.

They scrambled over the wall into another pasture, and bending low, crept away from the road. After going another two hundred yards they stopped, both of them breathing hard, Fiona struggling with bursting lungs not to make any noise. Although they were well away from the road, they could see the light from two flashlights going up and down the ditch, still searching, and each going away from the other. Both men were calling to each other, until finally, one was back at the van and the other at his car.

"They're going to leave," Adrian whispered, apparently understanding what the men were shouting. "We'll just stay here until they've gone."

Fiona sat down, not daring to peer over the wall, her heart pounding in her chest. It seemed an eternity before she heard the door of the van slam, its engine start up, and saw the glow of its lights against the night sky, swing up the road and drive away. A moment later, she saw the lights of the car follow up the road and disappear out of sight.

"Adrian, they were trying to kill us!" Fiona whispered, anger rising in her voice.

"They wanted to rob us." He was speaking very softly.

"Why didn't they take your car?"

He hesitated before replying. "Probably because it's too easy to identify. They wouldn't have got very far before the police would have spotted them. They certainly picked their spot, there isn't a house or a farm anywhere around here."

"What do we do now?" Fiona was still whispering.

"We'll just wait awhile to make sure they don't come back. Are you okay?"

"Oh, sure, I'm just great. At least I'm still alive, I think!" Despite the warm night, she was trembling uncontrollably.

He put his arm around her and pulled her close to him. They waited for several minutes, squatting behind the wall, not saying anything. Finally, Adrian stood up.

"We're okay now, let's go."

They walked back across the field, climbed over the wall and trotted down the road to Adrian's car, its lights still on.

Fiona was the first in, and with a shudder, locked the door behind her. At least in the car she felt a little safer.

Adrian reached for the ignition.

"Damn them, they've taken the keys!" he exploded. "My house keys as well, damn them!"

"Oh God, we're not going to have to walk are we?"

Adrian was feeling beneath the drivers seat, searching.

"I hope not, I think I have a spare, but they've got my bloody house key. That's what really ticks me off."

After a moment of searching, he produced a key and started the car, turned it around and drove off down the road in the opposite direction to which the two other vehicles had gone.

They drove for a mile or two before either of them spoke again, Adrian constantly peering into the rear-view mirror. Fiona was still shaken but feeling at least out of immediate danger.

"Do you want to take the long way home in case they follow us?" she asked.

"I don't think they're behind us, at least I don't see any lights. Anyway, it's not a bad idea. I don't want them to find out where you live," he replied. "You'll have to give me directions."

They drove on at high speed, with Fiona telling Adrian where to turn.

"Those were gun shots weren't they? He was shooting at us?" she asked rhetorically, finding it hard to believe what had happened. "He could have killed us."

"Yep, they were serious. But don't worry, it's all over, we've seen the last of them."

"Shouldn't we go to a police station and report them before we go home?" Fiona was still rattled and trying to make sense of the situation, but Adrian seemed unaffected; he seemed to be calm and indifferent to what had happened.

"No, there's no point, the local police don't have a chance of catching these kind of people."

"What kind of people are they for God's sake?"

"Who knows?" He paused. "I'll call the police in the morning and file a complaint."

"Thank God you were along, Adrian. I wouldn't have had a chance without you. Why do you think they picked on us?"

Again he didn't answer for a several moments.

"I suppose they just saw an expensive car. It wasn't just my driving that pissed them off," he chuckled. She could see in the faint light reflected on his face that he was amused by the thought.

They drove on without talking and arrived at her cottage just after midnight. Perhaps it was adversity that often brought people closer together, Fiona thought, but knew at that moment she liked Adrian very much.

"Are you okay? If you wish I could stay here tonight," he offered as they got out of the car. "But we weren't followed," he added sensing her uncertainty.

Fiona was filthy, her skirt ruined, her blouse had been ripped when she went over the wall, and her morale in tatters. All she could think about was soaking in a hot bath and going to bed.

"Thanks, but I'm alright." Then as an afterthought she added, "You can stay on the couch if you like, but it's not very comfortable."

"Thank you, but if you're okay, I'll just kick on." He walked her to the door, gave her hug, a peck on the cheek, and drove away.

Tired to the point of total exhaustion and emotionally drained, she undressed, slid into a steaming bath and soaked until she was almost asleep. With the last of her remaining strength, she dragged herself into a huge bath towel and into bed. Through a cloud of confusion, she fell asleep.

CHAPTER 5

Fiona slept until almost noon, and after making a light brunch, spent the remainder of the day reading and sunbathing in the garden. Still apprehensive, she was reluctant to phone Adrian but was nevertheless relieved when he finally called her in the early evening.

"I'm terribly sorry about last night," he said. "I feel awful about what happened and want to make it up to you."

"Adrian, don't worry, I'm okay, you don't have to apologize, it wasn't your fault. Did you call the police?"

"No."

"Will you?"

"Probably not"

"Why not? They may know who those men are."

"Mm, I doubt it."

Adrian seemed reluctant to discuss the matter any further and Fiona was happy to put it behind her. She declined the offer of lunch, or to do anything for a few days. She continued to feel emotionally drained; any degree of normalcy appealed to her at that moment and new adventures were entirely out of the question.

"Adrian, I just want to lay low for a couple of days. I'm not used to being shot at." She brightened, "I'm delighted you called, though."

"Well, just get some rest. I'll call you later in the week. 'bye." He rang off.

Other than riding work for a couple of her trainers over the next several mornings, she did very little. The thought of going to the police did seem futile, just as Adrian had said. If it were an

13263-RUSS

attempted robbery that had her running for her life, it was unsuccessful and behind her now; a dead issue. She was just relieved that it was not her that was dead, she reflected with sardonic amusement.

For the first time in her life she was glad that she was not riding in any races, at least for the next several days, although vaguely concerned that she had not heard from Timothy Rand. The association that had recently developed and the opportunity to ride Dantes had become important to her, even if the relationship with Adrian was a bit tenuous. While still debating as to whether she should call him or not, upon answering the phone, she was pleased to hear Rand's voice.

"Fiona, there's a race at Nottingham that Viscount Harrington wanted to run Dantes in, and he would like you to ride him," Rand said after exchanging pleasantries. "It's a relatively easy race, but frankly, it is a very small purse. We'd be passing up a much better race at Ascot the following week, but I'm afraid you couldn't ride him in that. Are you free to ride on Wednesday?"

"Yes, certainly, and I'd very much like to ride him," she replied. "But I would rather you ran the horse where you think it best, even if someone else were to ride him."

"Well it isn't that critical. To be perfectly honest, if he were to run at Ascot I would have to give Eddie Handley the call since that would be a very difficult race. If you can ride him at Nottingham, though, it would please Harrington."

Fiona, not offended by Rand relegating her to second fiddle behind Handley, understood the priorities that a trainer was obliged to consider. Handley was the stable rider, and she appreciated Rand's honesty. She was also well aware that decisions of where to run the horses was always difficult for any trainer, often torn between good business sense and surrendering to the compulsive wishes of an owner.

After a moment's thought, she said, "I appreciate your position, but if it would make it easier for you to deal with Viscount Harrington, I could decline the offer."

He laughed. "No, no, that's not necessary. Since you're free, then we shall go ahead and run at Nottingham. It'll make Harrington happy and you should be able to win another race, and that's fine with me."

She tried not to sound too relieved. "That's good of you and I do appreciate it. I'd certainly look forward to riding him again and I shall do my best."

"I know you will. Then it's decided. See you at Nottingham," and he rang off.

That evening, Fiona answered Adrian's phone call with some uncertainty. She suspected that he had requested Rand to put her up on Dantes more for her benefit than the benefit of the horse, and almost certainly to further their relationship rather than simply to win a race.

"Adrian, it was good of you to persuade Tim to give me the ride on Dantes, but honestly, I don't want to be indebted to either of you," she blurted out.

"Come on, Fiona," he protested. "Don't worry, I just thought it would be fun for both of us. Don't you want to ride him?"

"Yes, of course I do. But only if it makes good business sense," she said, immediately regretting her outburst. "Please don't be offended. It's very kind of you, but I don't want favors at the expense of the horse."

"Fiona, don't be silly, don't give it a second thought." His breezy nonchalance came through as he attempted to put her at ease. "This is just for fun, I think we could win a little bet at Nottingham, and I want you to be part of it. No strings attached, okay?"

There was a long pause.

"Okay?"

"I'm sorry, Adrian," she said at last. "I had no right to say that. Of course I'd like to ride for you. Forgive me?"

"There's nothing to forgive. Look, I don't want you to worry either. By the way, you probably won't hear from me before Wednesday. I have to be out of the country for a few days so I'll see you at Nottingham. Okay? Cheer up."

"You'll be back for the race, then. Are you going to America?"

"Yes, why?"

"Oh, I'd just like to hear more about it, particularly the racing. Do you go racing there?"

"Occasionally, but usually I don't have time. I'll take you there one day. Would you like that?"

"Yes, I'm sure I would, particularly if we can go racing."

"Well we'll talk about it when I get home."

"Have a safe trip Adrian, cheers."

The drive up to Nottingham was not the carefree ride that Fiona generally enjoyed while whipping along in her little car. She was concerned about the upcoming race, and although it was another beautiful summer day and she loved driving through the country roads, she was uneasy. Her confusion over why she felt as she did was even more perplexing. Not prepared to admit that her attraction to Adrian caused any special pressure over the race, she nevertheless was unusually tense. After all, she rationalized, she hardly knew the man, and what little she did know was that he was mysterious, cool and suave, with an underlying volatile temper.

She had trouble reconciling the fact that she was anxious to meet him again with a dread of perhaps disappointing him and not winning on his horse. Her customary self-confidence was giving way to self-doubt.

She drove into the jockeys' parking lot, retrieved her riding tack from the car, and with the bag slung over her shoulder, went into the changing room. The usual greetings were exchanged with other riders. The ribald good humor that was invariably the atmosphere in the jockeys' changing room, eased some of her anxiety. By the time that she had changed into the racing colors and walked out into the saddling paddock, a good deal of apprehension had begun to fade.

Adrian was standing in conversation with Timothy Rand when Fiona approached them. She gave them an uncertain smile as Adrian held out his hand, took hers, and bowing, kissed it. She assumed the formality was for the benefit of Rand, whom she noticed was faintly amused. The moment passed.

"Ahem," Rand cleared his throat. "Now, Fiona, the horse is in good form, how are you?"

"Very well, thank you sir." She turned to Adrian. "Did you have a good trip?"

"Frankly, it was bloody awful," he replied with a forced smile. "I just tried to cram too much travel into a few days. It's very good to be home."

"I don't know what you do on these trips but you always come home knackered," Rand admonished. "Why do you push yourself like that?"

"Governments have a way of making unusual demands," Adrian replied vaguely. He clearly had no intention of elaborating. "Can we take a flyer on Dantes today?"

"Well I should think so, what do you think Fiona?" Rand turned to her. "Have you had a chance to look over the race?"

"Yes, I think you've picked a good spot, but he's a pretty hot favorite" she replied, glancing toward the odds board. "It hardly looks like a race to win much of a bet."

"Oh, I don't care about the odds," Adrian grinned. "I'm going to take a flyer anyway."

That was all that Fiona needed to hear to renew her anxiety. She fidgeted with her goggles and helmet, and nervously tapped her boot with her whip, shifting from one foot to the other. She was yet to get used to people betting large amounts of money on horses that she rode.

Rand understood and appreciated all that was going through her mind. He put his arm around her, pulling her gently toward him.

"You'll be all right, don't worry," he said quietly. "Just ride him the same way as you did at Newmarket and you'll do just fine."

The field of horses was walking around the parade ring under the watchful scrutiny of Adrian and his trainer, both discussing the merits and shortcomings of several of the contenders. To Fiona they all appeared capable of winning, but a little confidence was restored by the way that Dantes looked. His dark brown coat glistened like a wet seal in the afternoon sun, and he walked with an energy that suggested an impatient anticipation of the upcoming race.

Finally the order came from the paddock judge. "Jockeys up!"

Rand lifted Fiona into the saddle and Dantes took a short jump forward, shaking his head, pulling hard against Fiona and the restraining groom. She knew that he was anxious to run, and that he would run well. Cantering down to the start gave her the usual thrill as Dantes surged beneath her. Finally, all the gremlins galloping around in her stomach began to settle, and she soon felt that she was on top of the world.

The race turned out to be another facile victory for Dantes. He cantered home with little urging carrying a rider whose profound sense of relief showed in every inch of her being. As they crossed the finish line she pumped a fist at imaginary demons, and leaned forward to give Dantes' sweating neck a hug.

Leaving the course, they were met by the groom that led them into the winner's enclosure. Timothy Rand was there to help Fiona unsaddle, but Adrian stood discreetly off to one side by himself. Fiona weighed in, and then joining Rand, was surrounded by newspaper correspondents and photographers. After Fiona answered all of their questions with patience, and directed queries about the future of Dantes to the trainer, the journalists turned their attention to the next race, gradually drifting away to write their stories.

Throughout the entire ceremony, Fiona was aware that Adrian stayed off in the background until the newspaper and television people had left. Fiona thought that his avoidance of the press was an unusual indifference to publicity and uncharacteristic of most victorious owners. She remembered that Adrian had also avoided publicity when they had won at Newmarket, but decided that it was nothing more than a reflection of his modesty and quiet reserve.

Eventually he came over to offer his congratulations.

"Well done," he said, beaming happily. "I'm very pleased, and insist that you join Tim and I for a victory celebration."

"Yes of course," Rand agreed, "Run along and get changed, we'll be in the champagne bar."

Half an hour later, Fiona found them sitting quietly in a corner with a bottle of champagne on ice. Drinks were poured all around and the conversation turned to the race. How had the horse felt? Did Fiona have any trouble in the race? Could he have gone on another quarter after he had run the mile?

She answered all of their questions in detail and with careful thought, but resisted the temptation to ask Adrian or the trainer about her prospects of riding Dantes again. She suspected that would depend to some extent upon her future relationship with Adrian. But ultimately, all other considerations aside, she knew Timothy Rand would decide who was going to ride Dantes in the future. She understood perfectly how those decisions were made.

When the champagne was finished and the bill paid, Rand excused himself with a promise to keep in touch and discuss what the upcoming program would be for Dantes. He hurried off to attend to necessary arrangements for his horses while Fiona and Adrian walked out to the parking lot together.

When they were alone, Adrian's attitude became less formal. Fiona appreciated his distinct reserve in the presence of his trainer and the warm familiarity when they were alone. He obviously wished to give the impression to Rand that his association with her was nothing more than a business relationship. She wondered if perhaps that was really the case anyway, and it was simply wishful thinking on her part to read any more into it than that.

"I cashed a substantial bet today, thanks to you, Fiona. How would you like to stay over at my place in London and do some shopping this weekend as a celebration? I could get some theatre tickets."

"Oh, that isn't necessary. I just appreciate the chance to ride the horse."

"No, really, I'd be very pleased if you would," he insisted.

"Well certainly that'd be fun, I'd like that very much," she replied. "Will you call me?"

He kissed her lightly on the cheek before she got into her car, and with a cheerful wave, she drove off.

The following day, after riding morning work and making another visit to Dantes in the stable of Timothy Rand, Fiona happily retreated to her little home, surrounded by the familiar and comfortable. The stone cottage was centuries old with a thatched roof and leaded windows opening onto a small lawn surrounded by a profusion of wildly growing flowers. Perched high above the Vale of Aylesbury, it reflected a part of England that seemed for ages to be frozen in time; a subject often found in the romantic paintings of 18th century artists. There were only three rooms: a combination dining and sitting room with an enormous stone fireplace, a detached kitchen, and a bedroom and bathroom en suite. French windows opened onto a flagstone patio and a rear garden shaded by overhanging ancient trees. Fiona had only lived in the cottage for a little over a year, but she had loved it from the first day. Despite it being rented and far less grand than her parents' home where she had grown up and now enjoyed occasional visits, she considered it as her own.

By early evening, with the terror from the life threatening attack having subsided, and with the excitement of another win on Dantes having worn off, Fiona was anxiously anticipating the phone call from Adrian. He repeated the invitation to stay with him in London.

"I'm riding down at Windsor on Saturday afternoon, I could stop in London after the races," she offered.

"Why not come into London in the morning and leave your car at my place?" he countered. "I could go to the races with you."

"Wouldn't you be bored hanging around there all day?"

"Don't be silly, I enjoy the races," he protested. "Anyway, you bring me luck. We could drive down to Windsor together and have lunch on the way. How does that sound?"

"That'd be lovely, but I'm warning you, this horse that I'm riding is no star."

"You don't think I should bet on him?" Adrian sounded unconvinced.

"I think he'll need a lot of luck to win and I'm not mad about you watching me bumping along at the back of the field."

He laughed. "Don't worry, I've ridden a few old dogs myself."

"You have?"

"In amateur races when I was in Singapore. I know what that's like."

"You rode in Singapore?"

"During the school holidays. They were amateur races for bad riders," he confessed. "So are we on for lunch?"

"Yes of course, I'd enjoy that, and you can tell me all about your riding career on the way."

He gave her instructions on how to find his house and hung up the phone.

CHAPTER 6

Saturday dawned bright and clear, with the early morning traffic sufficiently light that Fiona had no trouble getting into London and finding her way. She pulled up to Adrian's address, and taking her bags from the car, turned them and the keys over to Albert, the ever-present doorman. His portentous manner, and the ostentatious uniform and the grandeur of his silver whiskers amused her. She appreciated that his stiff formality was probably appropriate for the guardian of Adrian's front door, but was nevertheless always unimpressed by the condescending scraping of servants. She felt fortunate that her life had been spared from some of the suffocating pompous traditions of aristocracy.

"Mr. Adrian is expecting you, Miss," Albert said, stiffly touching his cap. "I shall take your bags up and have your car parked."

She was escorted up to Adrian's suite where he greeted her at the door, a moment after Albert knocked.

"Fiona, I'm delighted. You've arrived just in time." He instructed Albert to have his car brought around. "We'll leave your overnight case here but we must get going."

Fiona had time to appreciate the elegant luxury of the apartment, no less opulent than she had expected. She wondered vaguely if she would have the option of her own bedroom that evening, or if that situation was later to become an issue.

Adrian was, as usual, aggressive behind the wheel, a contrast to his otherwise calm demeanor. Fiona had become familiar with the speed at which he drove and appreciated the security of the high performance car. They drove southwest out of London along the M-4 motorway.

Upon being prompted, Adrian told of his days in Singapore,

and of how at the age of fifteen he had the thrill of riding his first amateur race. He told of how he had also played polo, and ridden jumpers in horse shows, but considered the speed and side-by-side competition of racing as the ultimate thrill.

"Are you ever afraid when riding a race?" he asked, momentarily taking his eyes from the road to watch Fiona's reaction.

She considered the question as if it had never occurred to her before; that she might be afraid when simply riding a horse was never a serious consideration.

"Yes I suppose I am, sometimes," she said eventually. "But I don't think of it in that sense. I suppose the distinction between fear and exhilaration is a very fine line, and perhaps I don't appreciate the difference. If that's the case, I suppose I find both stimulating."

Adrian reflected for a moment.

"I would imagine that in any dangerous sport," he offered, "when a competitor's too aware of fear, and recognizes too clearly the distinction between simple exhilaration and fear, then he becomes inhibited and looses some of the incentive to win."

"I think that's probably true. I don't think I'm there yet," she replied with a quick glance and smile in his direction. Then as an afterthought, "Do you think I'm there yet?"

He laughed. "No, I don't think so," and then added, "You could be afraid of me though."

"Should I be?"

"Probably," he replied, looking straight ahead. "How would I scare you the most?"

She shook her head and hesitated for some moments before answering. "By being indifferent toward me. By not being completely honest in thought, word and deed." She hesitated again and then corrected herself. "At least in word and deed."

"So you would forgive my thoughts?"

"I'd have to unless you told me what you're thinking. What are you thinking?"

He hesitated. "I think you'd be easy to love."

He was altogether too comfortable with himself, she thought; she wanted to shock him.

"Does that mean I'd be easy to get into bed?"

She was examining him closely while he drove. She was smiling while Adrian's expression had not changed, his face a mask, betraying nothing.

"Not necessarily. Would you be?" he asked.

"Would you ask me?"

"It would be ungallant of me not to, and if I have enough nerve, I am sure I will. Would you accept?"

"I don't know, probably not, but I'd be flattered if you did ask."

They stopped in Windsor at a small restaurant, ordering lunch from a veranda table overlooking the river Thames. Pleasure boats, barges and a variety of swans and waterfowl traveled to-and-fro upon the river, a bucolic scene reminiscent of a Constable oil painting that Fiona remembered from childhood. The setting was a welcome distraction, but when Adrian asked if she would join him with a glass of wine she declined, her mind returning to the upcoming race.

"I'd rather not if I'm riding. But please have something for yourself."

He smiled and ordered a tall gin and tonic. "You're very professional about you're riding. Is that the main focus in your life?" he asked.

"I suppose it is at the moment, but there are other things. I enjoyed going to school and loved university, and I'll probably go back at some point."

Fiona fiddled with her napkin as they sat without speaking for a while. She felt him staring at her, and avoided eye contact by gazing out upon the river.

Leaning back with hands upon the table, slowly turning his glass, he regarded her with quiet admiration. Her face was beautiful and sensual, but her eyes, cool both in color and by inflection, told of the underlying strength that he knew she possessed. He was fascinated by the quick, almost imperceptible smile that flirted with the corners of her mouth, and the way that the reflected light from the river played upon her face, illuminating her golden, flawless skin. He wished he knew what her thoughts were as she gazed out across the water.

After a short time, Fiona became uncomfortable with his attention. Taking the initiative, she turned to look directly at him. "Why do you travel so much?"

"I have to work for a living."

"What do you do when you go abroad? Do you work for the government?"

He shifted in his chair and took a sip from his drink, weighing his answer. "Not in the strictest sense," he said slowly. He paused before continuing.

"I negotiate contracts in Western Europe and South and North America which involves a lot of travel. You might say I'm a broker trying not to be broke," he offered with raised eyebrows, vaguely waving a hand in the air.

"What sort of contracts?"

"Any that need negotiation and . . . " his voice trailed off. "Persuasion," he said finally with a shrug.

He took another sip of his drink, then frowning as he lowered the glass to the table, looking into it and continuing to turn it slowly between his fingers.

Once again Fiona wondered why he became evasive whenever she pressed him upon the subject of what he did. A cold shadow hardened his otherwise handsome face. Her curiosity persisted.

"Are you a spy?" she asked in low tones, teasing and leaning toward him, conspiratorially.

He laughed, a mock look of horror upon his face. "I wouldn't be very good at it if everyone knew that I was, would I?"

She regarded him through half-close eyes. "I bet you are!"

"You're very inquisitive aren't you?" he retorted, still smiling. "Let's talk about you."

"You already know too much about me," she said with feeling.

"I'd like to know more."

She quickly changed the subject. "What are you going to bet on today?"

"You tell me. You should know which ones are going to win." He was laughing again, more at ease.

"The one I'm on today isn't going to be much help. I'm afraid you're on your own."

They finished lunch talking about the condition of the racecourse, the pedigrees of various horses and possible plans for Dantes that, Adrian insinuated, may include Fiona.

She was still sure that Timothy Rand would make the final decision on that situation. She doubted that he would be persuaded by Adrian to permit her to ride the horse in his future races since they would be increasingly challenging. To avoid being obligated to either her or Adrian, she was sure the trainer would not make any future concessions on that point unless it was in the best interest of the horse.

"Is Dantes the best horse that you have ever ridden?" he asked.

Fiona thought for a moment. "I think he could be," she replied slowly. "I don't know that much about him but I think he could be very good."

"Could he win a classic?"

Fiona hesitated again.

Adrian was insistent. "Would you like to ride him in a classic next year?"

Fiona shook her head, smiling broadly. "Adrian, that's not a fair question. You know I would but that is so improbable that you shouldn't ask."

"Why is it so improbable?" Adrian refused to let go. "Isn't he good enough?"

"He may be next year, I don't know." She was now serious and looked directly into his eyes. "But even if he was good enough, Tim would want to ride Eddie Handley in a race of that importance, so you shouldn't tease me."

"Suppose I insisted that you should ride him?"

"Then you would probably be making a big mistake. You'd have a big row with Tim and I would probably make a mess of it if I did ride him. Anyway, girls don't ride in the classics in this country."

"Well maybe I'll just take him where girls do ride in big races."

"Maybe I wouldn't want to ride for you even if you did," she said. She pursed her lips in an unconvincing sulk, her brows knitted together, but at the same time he could see her eyes were laughing.

They left the restaurant and drove the short distance to the racecourse. Fiona took her tack and went immediately to the jockeys' room to prepare for her upcoming race while Adrian disappeared into the Club Member's enclosure to spend the afternoon betting and rubbing elbows with other punters at the bar.

An hour later, Fiona came out to the paddock to meet the owners and the trainer of Sagittarius, the horse that she was going to ride. He came into the walking ring looking well, but in Fiona's opinion, he was a rather indifferent individual. The trainer was well known to Fiona; she had been riding work for him all summer. They both knew that this particular race was probably not going to produce a winner, although if he were not ridden excessively hard, it would provide the horse with valuable experience for the future. He was lazy in his work, so it was impossible for the trainer to know if he had any ability or not. A race or two might wake him up and put him on his toes, but at this point he had shown very little promise. Fiona also knew she was not as strong as the male jockeys, and she was often engaged to give horses relatively easy races. This appeared to be one of those occasions.

The owners, a pair of middle-aged ladies were similarly dressed in florally decorated wide brimmed hats and floral print summer dresses. One was a remorseless divorcee and the other a dedicated spinster, but both giggled with unconcealed excitement over the upcoming race. They chatted about their racing colors and how they had almost come to blows over their selection and the naming of their baby, Sagittarius. They fussed and hovered around Fiona like frenetic bees. Both of them were new to racing and were obviously enjoying their moment in the limelight. Listening with feigned interest to their incessant chatter, Fiona noticed Adrian standing at the rail of the walking ring. She gave him a quick glance and a smile, reading his lips as he silently wished her good luck.

After what Fiona considered an interminable five minutes, the jockeys were thrown up onto their horses to leave the paddock and canter down to the start. Fiona felt confident that Sagittarius would run well enough to beat at least half the field, but she doubted he had much chance of winning the race.

She placed him far back in the field of fifteen runners after the break, going easily but a good ten lengths behind the leaders. Around the bend into the straight, with a little over two furlongs to go, she sensed that she still had a strong horse beneath her and with only a little urging, moved him to within three lengths of the lead.

She began pushing him on in the final furlong to join the leaders, surprised that they were tiring and being hard ridden. Fiona tapped Sagittarius down the shoulder with the whip, and started pushing him with all her strength, pressuring him to try harder than he had ever done before.

Coming down the stretch for the last fifty yards, Sagittarius and two others were matching strides, heads apart. Flashing across the finish line, Fiona thought she might have won but it was too close to be certain.

"Photo! Photo!"

Fiona heard the announcement over the public address system. Blowing as hard as Sagittarius from the effort expended by the desperate finish, she turned him around and jogged back to the unsaddling enclosure. They were immediately engulfed by a wildly cheering group of owners, their trainer and groom. Infected by their excitement, her heart pounding, it was suddenly terribly important to Fiona that they should have won the race, as improbable as it may have seemed.

Minutes seemed to drag into an eternity as she dismounted, and undoing the girths, slid the saddle from the steaming horse.

As she stepped onto the scales to be weighed, the announcement came over the loudspeaker.

"First, number eight, Sagittarius . . . "

Cheers drowned out the remaining results; to Fiona's happy little group it hardly mattered. They were ecstatic, the jubilant owners almost overwhelming Sagittarius and Fiona with hugs and kisses. Fiona was invited to the bar for the traditional celebration and round of drinks. She accepted and headed off to the changing room, happy but relieved to get away for a shower and a chance to relax.

Rejoining the group half an hour later, she was once again the center of attention in the midst of the celebration. The champagne was poured and endless toasts were offered to Sagittarius, his jockey, trainer, breeder, owners, and anyone remotely connected with the horse. The party became increasingly boisterous, and Fiona, with thanks and an apology, eventually escaped to go in search of Adrian. She found him at the walking ring rail, studiously appraising the field of horses for the last race of the day.

"My God, that was clever! How did you do that?" he said shaking his head. "We could have made a fortune."

"I'm sorry, I'd no idea," she apologized. "Did I talk you out of betting on him?"

"You tried, but I didn't believe you." Grinning broadly, he hardly looked disappointed. "I made a good bet on him anyway. You're on a roll."

"I was just lucky."

He threw his arms around her, picking her up, dancing around in circles, and laughing all the time, his cool reserve having melted completely.

"So you bet although I told you he couldn't win? You're incorrigible!" Fiona was also laughing.

"I didn't need to wager much at odds of forty-five to one," he confessed, putting her down and taking her face in his hands and kissing her. "But I know you're better than you think you are, so I took a flyer anyway."

13263-RUSS

CHAPTER 7

Adrian insisted they return to the Member's bar where Fiona ordered lemonade and he a gin and tonic for himself. They sat unnoticed by the Sagittarius team that was still celebrating on the other side of the lounge. By the time the drinks had been brought to their table and paid for, Adrian's mood had changed. Fiona sensed the shift from elation to thoughtful.

"Adrian, is something wrong?"

"Look Fiona, I'm terribly sorry but I have a problem."

He paused, reached across the table and took her hand. "I received a call an hour ago," he continued, "and I have to leave this evening for the States. I'd like you to stay at my place, but I'm afraid I must leave on a six o'clock flight. Are you terribly disappointed?"

"Yes, a little, but I understand."

"How can I make it up to you?"

"You don't have to, it's okay, Adrian, I understand," she said, hardly understanding at all. "But I may as well go on home rather than stay in London by myself."

"Well there's something else. I have to ask you for a huge favor. I want you to do something for me that may sound a little odd, but it would help me out of a bit of a jam," he continued, still holding her hand and looking earnestly into her eyes.

"Yes, of course, if I can help."

"On the way back to London, I need you to drop me off at Heathrow Airport and take my car back to my place."

"Okay, I can do that," she said smiling to reassure him. "I'll drop the car off and then just trot on home. That's not a bit of trouble."

"Great, I do appreciate it."

Fiona sensed there was something else to come, but other than having lost her date for the evening, she thought with a mental shrug, it had been a fun day. She really did enjoy being with him, but now resigned herself to a long and lonely drive home.

They finished their drinks, picked up Fiona's tack at the jockeys' room and walked out to the parking lot. Adrian opened the trunk of the car, put in Fiona's bag and stood looking at a brief case that Fiona was sure had not been there when they arrived at the races. He slowly and deliberately bent down and opened the case, aware that Fiona was watching with curiosity. Holding the case open, Adrian made a point of permitting Fiona to see the contents.

Fiona gasped. "Phew, Adrian, what is that?" she asked incredulously, staring at the open case packed with bundles of hundred pound notes. "Where did that come from?"

"It's a lot of money," he said calmly.

"Where did it come from?"

He closed the briefcase and then the trunk of the car.

"Come on, let's go," he said and held the car door open for Fiona to get in.

"That wasn't in the car when we came here was it?" Fiona asked as they drove away.

There was a long silence, Adrian seeming to weigh an explanation. Finally he turned to her. "Would you believe that I won it on Sagittarius and the bookie placed it in the car after the race?"

"No I wouldn't, but if that's true, I'm delighted for you," she replied in a voice heavy with skepticism. "Surely that's a very odd way of paying you."

Adrian offered no other explanation. After a while he said, "Fiona, I want you to do another favor for me. I want you to take this briefcase and put it into my safe in the London apartment, and I want you to stay there tonight. Will you do that for me?"

She turned in her seat to study him. She thought that since he trusted her with a considerable responsibility it would be disingenuous to refuse. She was flattered, if not naïve, she admitted, but would probably do almost anything within reason that he asked. This didn't sound too unreasonable.

"If it's important to you I don't mind. You certainly don't want to leave all that cash in the car. But why do you want me to stay there tonight?"

"Because I want to call you from Miami when I get there in the morning and give you further instructions about the money."

Fiona took time to consider before answering. Bookmakers don't dump that sort of cash in someone's car without having them present to receive it and give a receipt for it. Whatever Adrian was up to, she really thought it none of her business, but if she were to hang around for more instructions, she would be involved in whatever was going on, like it or not. The bookmaker explanation was too implausible; she knew that. However, she would hardly be implicated as an agent mixed up in some international intrigue by merely tucking the loot away for him. She was more amused than alarmed by the thought. Nevertheless, she wished that he could be more forthright with her, although she realized that being involved in government affairs doubtless required a high degree of secrecy.

"Very well, I'll stay at your place. I really had looked forward to staying anyway, but you must promise that I won't get murdered in my bed if I do."

He laughed. "You're a star, Fiona. I love you. And I promise you'll be as safe as the realm. I'll call the housekeeper, and tell her that you'll be staying and to make you comfortable."

He picked up the car phone and dialed a number. When it was answered, he gave instructions that included notifying Albert to make arrangements to have the car taken down to the garage when Fiona arrived.

"There is a safe behind a bookcase in my apartment. It's open and you can just empty the briefcase into that and lock it up."

"How much money is in that case, anyway?" Fiona asked.

"Twenty thousand pounds sterling," Adrian replied, turning toward her, studying her reaction. "Would you like some?"

"What makes you think I won't take a runner with the whole lot?"

He laughed. "Because you won't."

"No I won't," she agreed with a sigh. "It had never occurred to me that money was important, but I suppose it is."

"It makes the world go around, you know. Don't you want to go around with it?"

They were now driving into the long, convoluted maze of roads leading into Heathrow Airport.

"What are you going to do for clothes while you're away?" Fiona asked, still not understanding how anyone could just take off halfway around the world on such short notice.

"Oh, I keep a kit in the car, and I have clothes at my place in the States," he replied as if it were routine. "I just keep them there for when I drop in."

"Do you just drop in often?"

"Too often. I'll take you there one day," he replied, and looked over at her with a conspiratorial wink.

They drove up to the British Airways International terminal where he leaned over to kiss her before getting out. Fiona went around to the driver's side as he pulled a small overnight bag from behind the driver's seat and turned to her.

"I'll call you in the morning," he said holding her for a kiss. She returned his kiss; she realized that she would regret not being with him that night.

Driving away from the airport, she suddenly felt very alone and vulnerable, burdened by the responsibility that she had accepted. She had grown up in relative comfort albeit not great wealth, and held a youthful indifference concerning money. But now, the thought of being the custodian of twenty thousand pounds in cash presented her with a different perspective. The possibility of being robbed, or even worse, began to dawn upon her. That little episode with Adrian when they were returning from York, dodging bullets and diving over walls, was all too vivid in her memory. The twenty thousand had appeared mysteriously and the possibility that it could easily be taken away became a reality. She had a dim view of people who coveted money so dearly; at that moment she despised it.

The traffic on the M-4 going into London was slow and heavy, making the driving tedious. Fiona was becoming irritable and frustrated. At any other time she would have relished being behind the wheel of a powerful luxury car. Thoughts raced through her mind in a kaleidoscope of confusion. She was attracted to Adrian. She wanted to be with him, but he seemed to take inexplicable incidents like the sudden appearance of twenty thousand pounds as a matter of course. Uncertainty about his mysterious occupation both intrigued and repelled her. His explanation about the money was implausible and she was beginning to wonder if the incident driving back from York was really an attempted robbery or something far more sinister. She then remembered, with growing alarm, Adrian's acrimonious encounter with the scarred stranger outside the pub in Yorkshire. She was certain that Adrian had been addressed by another name on that occasion, although for the moment she could not remember what it had been.

She also became curious as to why he had been present when she had won a race and on each occasion he had avoided any sort of public celebration, shunning the press of photographers and reporters, and hanging back almost in the shadows. That, of course, could be accounted for if he were in fact some sort of agent for British Intelligence as his father had been, she rationalized. With growing apprehension she wondered if she was now recruited into Adrian's clandestine world. Damn this money, she thought, it stirred the darkest depths of her imagination.

Albert was waiting for her, looking smart and authoritative in his navy blue uniform sporting enough gold braid to provoke envy in an admiral of the navy. His military presence guarding the front door should have given Fiona some sense of security, she thought; but it didn't.

"Good evening Miss, we have been expecting you," he greeted

her. "Just leave the keys with me and I'll have the car taken around to the garage."

"My bag is in the back, would you have it put into my car?"

"Yes, of course."

Fiona took the briefcase out of the car and clutching it to her breast with crushing fervor, sprinted across the lobby, relieved to find the elevator unoccupied. Arriving on the third floor, the door to Adrian's apartment was opened by a stout woman of middle age, wearing a blue apron over a floral-print dress. An unlined broad face with dark brown eyes matched her hair pulled severely into a bun at the back of her head. She was distinctly European but her age was hard to define.

"Welcome, Miss Fiona, it is nice to have you stay," she said in a strong French accent. "My name is Maria. I have a nice dinner for you, and I have put your things in Mr. Adrian's room."

"Thank you Maria, but I shall be staying in the guest room, and only for tonight."

"Oh no, Miss," the woman protested, wide eyed. "Mr. Adrian's guests never use the guest room, only the gentlemen do that."

"Oh? And how often do guests stay in Mr. Adrian's room?"

Maria became evasive and insisted that only the "very special" guests, and only upon Mr. Adrian's instructions.

"Ah, I see." Fiona smiled, feeling honored to fall into the category of a "very special" guest. She reassured the housekeeper that she indeed understood, but nevertheless preferred the guest room. She thought she might take up the question as to how "special" she was with Adrian at some future point.

"Would you show me the study?" she asked anxiously. "I have to put this briefcase away."

Maria waddled off down a hallway with Fiona in tow. She was shown into a room lined with mahogany bookcases and a large mahogany partners' desk. Behind the desk was a dark green, leather, wing back chair of the same heroic proportions, in front of a heavily draped bay window. An oriental rug covered most of an oak planked floor. The walls were a deep burgundy, giving the entire room a sumptuous but distinctly masculine appearance.

Maria turned and left the room while Fiona closed and locked the solidly paneled door behind her. Adrian had informed her that on the fifth shelf of the bookcase to the left of the window was a copy of Winston Churchill's Gathering Storm, the name of which, Fiona thought with foreboding, had an ominous ring to it. She removed the book as Adrian had instructed, and released a latch that it had concealed, permitting her to swing a large section of the bookcase that was hinged upon one side, into the room. Behind were shelves surrounding an open, empty wall safe.

Fiona opened the briefcase, noting that initials 'JMH' were on a small brass plate between the latches; she wondered to whom it might have belonged. She took the bundles of hundred pound notes and stuffed them all into the safe, closed the door and spun the dial. After closing the bookcase and replacing Churchill's tome, she stepped back to lean against the desk with a sense of profound relief, surveying the room. If robbers descended upon her now, they were out of luck. As far as she knew, Adrian was the only person that knew the combination to the safe.

The remainder of the evening passed quietly. After Maria had left to go home, Fiona enjoyed a glass of wine and a light meal that had been prepared for her. She retired to the guestroom and crawled into a large feather bed and turned on some light music. Unable to sleep, she returned to the library in search of a book to read.

She was casually scanning the bookshelves when suddenly the shrill of a telephone ringing on the desk behind her, jarred her almost to panic. She froze for a moment, then with heart beating wildly, decided to let it ring, knowing that Adrian was not going to phone until the morning. There were several rings before an answering machine intercepted the call. First there was the greeting in Adrian's voice, and then Fiona could hear a man's voice being recorded, sending more chills down her spine.

"Hansen, this is Max. When you get back from Brazil, give me a call." There was a click, and then silence.

Fiona assumed at first that the caller had dialed a wrong number, until it dawned upon her that she had previously heard Adrian referred to by a similar name. She was certain that she had not been mistaken, and wondered what new significance this latest revelation could be attached to the secret life of Adrian Harrington.

If he did have an alias, and it was Hanson or something like that, the briefcase almost certainly belonged to him since the last initial was an 'H'.

She returned to her room, and wide-awake, lay in bed musing at length over what the other initials 'JM' could stand for. 'Just Mysterious' would be appropriate, she thought. She also wondered why the caller expected Adrian to return from Brazil when, in fact, he had gone to the United States. Logic suggested that the caller had reached a wrong number but Fiona was unable to dispel the suspicion that there were just too many coincidences. With no more interest in the book that she had selected, a farce entitled 'The Demise of Friar John', and beginning to wonder about her own demise, she turned the light out. After what seemed an interminable length of time, she eventually fell asleep.

The horse refused to go into the starting gate. He was huge and powerful, and Fiona felt that he controlled her completely. Her efforts to force him into the gate were exhausting her, and the handler who was on the ground that was supposed to be assisting her, was laughing at her. The animal was too large to fit into such a small space and yet she knew that he had to go in. The man continued to laugh, mocking her, and when she looked down at him she was shocked to see a distinct resemblance to Adrian. She was crying, and could not understand why the man continued to laugh. She knew that she hated him because he continued to mock her, and she became aware that he really had no intention of helping her. She wanted to scream at him but was unable to make a sound. The man continued to hold the horse, which continued to just stand, refusing to move in spite of her urging. Finally the man

13263-RUSS

released the horse and began to back away, and through the blur of her tears she could see him slowly disappearing, grinning up at her, leering, ever scornful.

Then, slowly, either the horse moved forward or the starting gate moved back to it, but Fiona sensed more than saw that they were in a stall. She was desperate to break from the gate and leave all of this behind. And then, as if from a great distance, the starting bell began to ring but the gate in front of her remained closed. She saw that the gate had a dial upon it that appeared to require a combination of numbers before it would open, but she was unable to remember the sequence no matter how hard she tried. The bell continued to ring and ring. She wanted to scream. What were the numbers? Why didn't she know the numbers? The gate in front of her remained closed; she was trapped.

Fiona woke with a start, trembling and bathed in sweat. The telephone beside her bed was ringing; she had no idea for how long it had been, but it seemed an eternity. She felt the panic subsiding within her, draining away from her pounding heart as she slowly realized where she was. Reaching out with a shaking hand, she picked up the receiver.

CHAPTER 8

"I thought you'd never answer." It was Adrian. Even over the telephone Fiona could hear the relief in his voice. "I was afraid you'd left."

"No, I'm still here, but I wish I were home. You woke me from a bloody awful dream. Where are you?"

Adrian avoided the question. "I'm sorry, about the dream, I mean. Listen, I want you to do me a big favor. Are you up to it?"

Fiona hesitated. She looked at her watch and took a deep breath. "Adrian, it's only seven o'clock, I've had a miserable night, I've risked my life stashing that damned money for you, and I don't know if I'm up to anything at the moment. What do you have in mind?"

"This one's easy, Fi. I just need you to pick up a little more money for me. You don't even have to meet the person that has it. It's a piece of cake."

Fiona was wide-awake and her initial impulse was to refuse. Being a courier for what might well be large sums of contraband or money acquired by illicit means, or money that had simply gone missing, was not in the least appealing. She had a natural compunction about going missing herself because of it.

"Adrian, can't you do it when you come home?" she implored. "How much are you talking about, anyway?"

"About twenty grand."

"Oh, just another twenty grand, is that all?"

He ignored her sarcasm. "All you have to do is take my car to a drop off point, disappear while a briefcase is put in the back, and drive the car back to my place and stick the money in the safe."

"Why can't you do it when you get back?" she asked again.

3-RUSS

"The problem is that these people need to drop the money off in a hurry and I won't be back for a couple of days. The money is from out of the country, Fiona, and it can't be transferred through a British bank. There would be too many questions asked."

"Well I've got a few myself," she objected. "To begin with, who is Hanson?"

There was a silence for several seconds before Adrian forced a laugh. "That," he said, "is a business name that I use. I don't want undue influence drawn to me as a result of my real name. My name's too well known in social circles."

"That still doesn't explain why this money can't be transferred through normal channels," Fiona fired back.

"I'm sorry but I can explain better when I come home. Can't the inquisition wait?"

There was a long pause.

Adrian asked again, almost pleading. "Can I count on you Fiona? It's perfectly safe and you'd be doing me a great favor. I can trust you."

Another long pause. Fiona was tempted to simply refuse, but thought she was probably being paranoid about a perfectly legitimate matter. After all, it may be nothing more than some complicated government operation that had to be kept confidential. The more she thought about it, the less threatening simply picking up money seemed, particularly if she did not have to meet the people depositing it. It wasn't her money and she wouldn't be spending it, so there was nothing to implicate her anyway, she rationalized.

"What do I have to do?" she asked, still hesitant. "Give me the details."

"Fiona, you're a star," he said with relief, assuming that she had agreed. "Here's what you do. Take my car out to Heathrow. There is a multi-level parking structure across from British Airways International arrivals. Park the car in any spot on the top floor of the garage, but don't lock it. Go into the terminal and get a cup of tea, or whatever, but leave the car for at least an hour, even longer would be better. The courier will be coming in on a flight at 11:30 so you must be there by then. He knows the car and will leave a briefcase in the boot. Are you still with me?"

"Yes, I'm still here. What next?"

"It's easy. Just go on back to my place, let Albert park the car while you put the money in the safe."

"Adrian, I don't know the combination to the safe. I wish I did. I struggled with that for half the night."

"With the combination? Was it locked? Couldn't you put the other money away?"

Fiona sounded tired, sulky but indulgent. "Yes I put the other money away, don't worry. But now the safe's closed. I'll explain when you get back. What's the combination?"

"The combination is six right, twelve left, and twenty-four right. Can you remember that?"

She repeated the numbers. "Adrian, I'm scared to death trotting around with that sort of money. When are you coming home?"

"Do you miss me?" She could hear the amusement in his voice.

"Not nearly as much as you might think," she replied, barely humored. "You'll miss me if I trot off with this bloody money!"

"You won't. Anyway, I want you to come along with me the next time I go away."

She had no idea whether or not he meant that, but she decided at that moment that she would reconsider going anywhere with him ever again despite her fascination with him.

"Adrian, I'm furious with you for asking me to do this," she said with weak conviction. "I'll do it this time, but when you get home we've got an awful lot to talk about. You've got a lot of explaining to do."

"I love you. You are a good sport," he said with emphasis on the "are", and hung up.

It crossed Fiona's mind that if risking her neck and flirting with the law meant she was nothing more than a "good sport", she would much rather not play the game.

After taking a quick shower and dressing, she made herself a piece of toast and a cup of coffee before phoning downstairs to the

13263-RUSS

lobby. "Albert, would you have Viscount Harrington's car brought around, and give me a buzz when it gets here?"

"Yes of course Miss, it'll be here in five minutes, I'll call you as soon as it arrives," the voice replied.

Fiona packed her overnight bag, anxious to leave for home in her own car as soon as she had completed her errand, and poured herself another cup of coffee. Perhaps it was the caffeine, but she began to feel a lot braver about her assignment. She was even beginning to wonder why she should really worry even if she didn't have a clue as to what was going on.

Somewhere across town Fiona could hear the chilling wail of police sirens, at first in the distance but rapidly approaching. She wondered idly what could be happening to disturb the relative peace of a Sunday morning. As much as she enjoyed an occasional trip into London, she was glad that she lived in the country, far away from this sort of disturbance. The sirens continued to approach until they finally stopped, one after another, somewhere close by.

Fiona waited impatiently, ten and then fifteen minutes for Albert to call, becoming more anxious to leave by the minute. Finally, as she was about to pick it up, the telephone rang.

"Miss Kent, this is Albert, I'm afraid there has been a problem with bringing the car around. I'm sorry but you will have to wait for a while."

"What sort of problem?" She was becoming alarmed now that it was already past ten o'clock and she had to get to Heathrow before eleven thirty. "I need the car in a hurry."

"I'm afraid I'm not at liberty to tell you but an Inspector Barker of Scotland Yard would like to have a word with you. I'll send him up."

Before Fiona could protest, Albert rang off. She was bewildered. What could the police possibly want, she wondered, unless it was something to do with Adrian? What should she tell them? She considered trying to give them the slip but realized there was no back door to the apartment. Why, she thought with growing resentment, why the hell should she become a fugitive anyway?

By the time the doorbell rang, irritation was dissolving into dread. Fearfully, she opened the door to be confronted by two grim looking men, both ominously dressed in dark suits.

"Miss Kent?" one of the men inquired. "I'm Inspector Barker of Scotland Yard," he said, producing his credentials.

He was tall but stooped, and on the fading side of middle age, his suit hanging off a pitifully thin frame. With a drooping moustache and wispy gray hair, his overall demeanor was more mournful than threatening. Fiona thought that his appearance was more befitting of an undertaker than a guardian of law and order. Under almost any other circumstances she would have hardly been intimidated, but now she was petrified by the thought that she had just been caught on the threshold of committing a crime, and a good chance that she was inextricably involved with criminals. Her imagination was running wild.

"This is Inspector Andreas Mikolos, temporarily attached to our unit but a member of Interpol," Barker continued, closing the door behind them. "May we come in?"

Fiona backed away defensively, flight utmost in her mind. "Yes, yes of course," she stammered. "Please sit down."

The two men entered; Barker holding a battered fedora, preceded his associate. They both glanced around the room in a perfunctory manner and selected two armchairs on opposite sides of the sofa. Fiona dropped upon the sofa.

Inspector Mikolos did not offer a greeting, but even before hearing his name, Fiona would have guessed that he was at least Mediterranean. Judging by his name and his appearance, his dark complexion and dark, receding well-oiled hair combed straight back, Fiona presumed that he was Greek. He regarded her through heavily lidded eyes, giving the impression that he was half asleep. He was much shorter than his companion, and to add to the dissimilarity, thick set with a considerable paunch and a double chin.

"Miss Kent, I have some very unfortunate news," Barker began. "Perhaps you can throw some light on the matter. How well do you know Mr. Harrington?"

"Quite well, obviously," Fiona replied, trying desperately to gain her composure. "I am, after all, a guest in his apartment."

"Where is Mr. Harrington at the moment?"

"In the United States. He left last night."

Barker pulled out a notebook and began to write. "Do you have a phone number for him?"

Fiona hesitated, wondering if she should tell him that Adrian had called that morning. She wondered if she should tell him anything.

"No I'm afraid I don't," she said. "He calls me."

The fat man was not writing and had yet to say anything, but Fiona was aware that he was watching her intensely, adding further to her discomfort.

"When do you expect Mr. Harrington to return?" Barker asked.

"I have no idea. He doesn't divulge his business affairs to me, and I don't ask him," Fiona replied. "May I ask what all this is about?"

Barker ignored her question and continued the interrogation. "Where were you going to go in Mr. Harrington's car when you called for it to be brought around?"

"I . . . .I was simply going for a drive," she stammered.

She was resigned to answering some of the questions but decided to volunteer as little as possible, and certainly not mention the money in the safe. Stashing it, she was sure, implicated her to a degree in some sort of crime, and to make things worse, she had agreed to embark on another collection of what could be stolen cash. She had no intention of incriminating herself by volunteering information to these detectives. They would have to drag it out of her.

"For a drive?" Barker sounded unconvinced.

"I thought I would go out for lunch. You don't think I was going to steal the car do you?"

Again he ignored her question. "The doorman said that Mr. Harrington always picks up and drops off his car himself. Why would you have the valet service do it for you?"

Fiona's apprehension was subsiding into defensive indignation.

"I have no idea what Viscount Harrington does or doesn't do with his car," she responded testily. "And furthermore, I have no idea where the garage is, so I asked the doorman to have it brought around. I'm not trying to swipe it if that's what you're worried about."

"Do you know of anyone who might not like Mr. Harrington? Someone who might want to hurt him?"

Immediately the incident returning from York with Adrian flashed through her mind, but Fiona, now adamant about volunteering any information, shook her head.

"I don't know any of Viscount Harrington's friends, let alone his enemies," she huffed. "Would you mind telling me what this is all about?"

The thin man continued to write. There was a long silence. Mikolos sat motionless on the other side of Fiona, still watching and listening but not offering any comment or asking questions. Fiona wondered if he even spoke English. After much scribbling, Barker finally closed his notebook and tucked it into a hip pocket, put his pen into an inside pocket, and mournfully regarded Fiona.

"Miss Kent," he began slowly, measuring his words. "There has been, shall we say, an accident involving Mr. Harrington's car. When the valet went to start the car to bring it up from the garage around the corner, it exploded. The driver, we're assuming it was the valet, was killed and the car was almost totally destroyed. You do realize, Miss Kent, that if you had gone to get the car yourself, you would most likely have been killed."

Fiona turned pale, her hand covering her mouth. She was stunned. Speechless. Both men waited for her response, watching her closely.

"God, someone was killed? Why . . . . why did it explode?" she stammered. "Was it . . . was it a bomb or something?"

"Oh yes, we're certain about that. But what we would like to know is if it was intended for you, or for Mr. Harrington."

There was another long silence before Fiona could speak. Her mind was racing but one thing immediately struck her: Adrian was the only person that would have known she was going to drive his car so it was certainly not intended for her.

"I think it highly unlikely that it was intended for either of us," she said. "But if it was intended for me it would have been in my car, not his. It must be all a mistake."

"That is true, possibly," Mikolos finally spoke. "But I think not. This Harrington, he goes to America often, no?"

"I know he goes abroad quite a lot, but I'm not sure where. As I said before, that is really none of my business."

"Ah, yes, you have no business with Mr. Harrington," the fat man said, nodding his head, sagely, with pursed lips. "Your business with him is, shall we say, l'amour, yes?"

Fiona reddened. "No, but I don't think that is any of your business either."

Her annoyance had overcome her shock and anxiety. She decided that she was certainly not going to offer any information about the money in the safe now, or the money to be picked up, not even the alias that Adrian was using. She would not disclose the phone call on the answering machine, even knowing then that it had been intended for Adrian. She would protect him, at least until she knew what was going on. But she also resolved at that moment to remove herself from this entire affair as quickly and as far away as possible. When Adrian came back, he was on his own. He could handle this mess.

"Look," she said, heatedly, "I can't offer you any more than you already know. May I go home now?"

"Yes, Miss, we can't keep you, but we must know where to reach you if there are any more questions we need to ask," Barker said, pulling out his notebook once again.

She reluctantly gave them her address and telephone number, and with immense relief, ushered them both out the door. She leaned with her back against the door, eyes closed for some time after they were gone, trying to regain a semblance of composure. It was certainly some consolation that she no longer was able to go to the airport with Adrian's car and pick up a load of money. She was damned lucky, she thought, that she was not deeper into this mess than she might have been. After a while, she called Albert to bring her car around.

Upon reaching the lobby, she could see that Albert, although clearly shaken by the events, stiffly attempted to retain his professional demeanor.

"This is a terrible tragedy and I am so sorry that Mr. Adrian has lost his car," he clucked as she dropped her bags into her old Talbot. "But it is the Lord's blessing that he was not in it."

As she drove away she reflected that it was even more of a blessing that she had not been in it either, although Albert certainly seemed less appreciative of that point. She and Adrian had dodged a couple of bullets; she was not going to be around for the next one.

For the remainder of the day, Fiona pottered about her little garden trimming roses and raking a few fallen leaves that forecast the shortening days of summer. She spent half an hour on the telephone to her parents, promising to go and spend a couple of days with them as soon as the racing season slowed down in the fall. Her mother intuitively sensed some tightness in Fiona's voice, but upon inquiring, was reassured that all was well, that Fiona was a little tired from all the running around that she had been doing lately. She wanted desperately to talk to Adrian before she dared disclose to her parents that she had been shot at and almost become a victim in an attempted murder of a man about whom she knew almost nothing.

It was late afternoon when the call came from Adrian. Before he could say a word, Fiona took the offensive. "Adrian, you've got to get back here, there is one hell of a mess and nobody knows where you are!"

"Whoa, Fiona, cool down, what's going on?"

She took a deep breath. "Adrian, somebody blew up your car and some poor sod was in it. Do you understand? Somebody was killed!"

"Killed? Who?"

"I don't know, probably the garage attendant. But anyway, the police came and took me apart. They wanted to know where you were."

She explained what had happened and about the detectives from Scotland Yard interrogating her.

"Didn't you pick up the money then?" he asked.

"Bugger the money Adrian, a man was killed, don't you get it? And I'm sure that by now the police are looking for you all over the world," she said angrily. "Thanks to you, they seem to think I'm some sort of criminal. Am I?"

"Calm down Fi, I understand, but I need to know if you picked up the money and what you told the police."

"No I didn't pick up the lousy money. I couldn't because your car was not available," she retorted sarcastically. "I don't know what I told the police."

She described the entire interview. She reassured him that she had not mentioned anything about money, but when he returned there were a few other things that she would very much like to know, not the least of which was who was trying to kill him.

"I'm sorry all this happened but I can't talk about it now," he said, and then added, in an attempt to humor her, "You did miss me then?"

"Oh yes, I missed you, but I'm not sure I want to see you again," she replied. "If I hang around with you I'll probably go to jail or get myself killed!"

He laughed and reassured her that no one was after her, or him for that matter. The whole thing was undoubtedly the stupid, bloody Palestinian Liberation Organization blowing up the wrong car. They did it all the time.

"I'm leaving here tomorrow morning so I'll be back in London late tomorrow night," he added. "I'll call you in a couple of days."

"Do be careful, Adrian."

"I will, don't worry. I love you."

CHAPTER 9

Fiona was out on the gallops the following morning riding work once again. Being around horses always gave her a rational perspective whenever she was troubled. The bright chill of an invigorating morning and riding across the heath was the distraction that she needed to bring some familiar order into her life. She talked to no one about the events of the previous day. By morning's end she had come to the conclusion that, despite her affection for Adrian, she should avoid any further social contact with him until a lot of loose ends had been cleared up. She needed some honest explanations.

After work, she was thankful to find her old friend Eddie Handley still at Rand's racing stable, sitting alone in a tack room, reading a racing journal.

The close-knit fraternity of racing people, and particularly that of jockeys, was an informal association that Fiona particularly enjoyed; she was popular and had many friends, but her feeling toward Handley transcended this. She had developed an attachment to him as if he were an older brother, certainly her mentor. The events of the last few days were too personal, however, to specifically discuss them or Adrian Harrington, even with Handley. Concern over complicity in a crime that had taken someone's life hung heavily upon her and she had no wish to discuss it with anyone but Adrian; only he could exorcize the guilt, she thought, but she felt compelled to bounce her apprehension off of someone.

"Eddie, what would you do if you found out that a close friend had become involved in something that turned out to be a serious crime? How would you deal with them?"

"You mean like fixing a race?"

"No, worse than that?"

"Well, if it was fixing a race I'd want a piece of the action," Handley joked.

"Come on Eddie, I'm serious."

"Fiona, that's a loaded question. I don't know what I'd do," he protested. "I'd certainly help them deal with it, but I'd want to know how serious it was before I'd try and protect them. I'm not a lawyer you know,"

"I know, but I trust you and that's why I'm asking you."

"Are you in trouble?"

Fiona considered. "I don't know. I don't think so but I suppose I could be if I'm not careful."

"Is it family?"

"No. No, just a friend."

"Well if you're the friend in trouble, I want to help. Okay?"

"Thanks."

Neither of them spoke for a while. Fiona fiddled with some tack, adjusted the stirrups upon a saddle and then turned to face Handley.

"Eddie, thanks, I'll talk to you again but appreciate your not mentioning this to anyone."

The conversation shifted to horses and racing in general. Handley had heard about Fiona's win at Windsor on the longshot, Sagittarius.

"They must have bloody well shooed you in," he scoffed good-naturedly.

"Well if they did, I wish you would do the same for me once in a while," she retorted, laughing.

"You don't need my help, you're on a roll."

Fiona regretted Handley having to rush off to the races; she would have liked more time with him. As she drove toward home, the fleeting shadows cast by the sun as it dodged in and out of an increasing blanket of cloud, hinted at an approaching storm and did nothing to lighten her mood. When she arrived back at her cottage, the sight of two familiar visitors waiting in their car across the road, only added further to her dejection.

She pulled into the driveway, and while debating the possibility of turning around and making a quick getaway, gaunt Inspector Barker and rotund Inspector Mikolos quickly crossed the road and headed her off.

"Good day, Miss Kent, we'd like to have a word with you," the inspector said, removing his battered fedora. "May we come in?"

Fiona, inwardly cringing, led them into her front room. Without an invitation, nor a word from either of them, they seated themselves. Fiona propped herself up on the arm of an old, well-worn armchair.

"I'm afraid I can't enlighten you any further about yesterday's events, if that's what you're here for," she said, verging on outright hostility.

"I think you can, actually," the Inspector retorted. "Perhaps you can explain to me why you lied about the whereabouts of Mr. Harrington."

Fiona glanced from the mournful Barker to his silent companion. She felt as though Mikolos' somber gaze was penetrating her inner soul. He sat leaning expectantly forward, his pudgy hands resting upon his knees as if ready to launch his bulbous form in her direction. She had no idea why she should feel overwhelmed with guilt, but she sensed that his hooded stare was an implied accusation. She decided to take the offensive.

"I beg your pardon," she bristled, turning her attention to Barker. "I told you I was under the impression that he was going to the States. At least that is where he said he was going when I dropped him off at Heathrow."

"You said that was around six on Saturday evening. Is that correct?" Barker continued.

Fiona nodded. "Yes, about that time."

"Well we checked all the British Airways flights and all the other international flights to the United States departing from both Heathrow and Gatwick. Mr. Harrington was not listed on any of those flights between six on Saturday evening and the time that his car was blown up on Sunday morning. How do you account for that?"

"I don't, that's for you to do. I can only tell you that I dropped him off at the airport, and he had said that he was going to America," Fiona insisted heatedly.

"Well, you see, if Mr. Harrington was not out of the country, he could have put the bomb in his own car," Barker continued, glancing over at his partner. "That would be very interesting since he knew that you were going to be the next one to drive it, wouldn't it?"

Mikolos seemed to relish the thought. "Ah, so sad between two friends. Maybe he is not so big a friend, no?" he said rubbing his hands together, leaning back in his chair.

"That's absolutely preposterous, we barely know each other," Fiona flared. "And besides, I'm sure he was out of the country because he called me last night and said he would be returning to England this evening."

Barker raised his eyebrows but retained his mournful demeanor, unperturbed by Fiona's outburst. "Where did he call from?" he persisted.

"I don't know, I didn't ask him."

"Did he know about his car being blown up and a man being killed in it?"

"No, apparently he didn't, not until I told him."

Fiona got up and walked across the room to stare out of the window at the distant hills, shrouded by a mantle of cloud and gloom. She had her back to the two detectives, not wanting them to read any more into her thoughts. They waited.

"It came as quite a shock to him," she said at last. "He suggested the Palestinian Liberation Organization or somebody had picked the wrong target. Frankly, I'm inclined to agree with him, so why don't you trot off and arrest someone?"

"Well that's an interesting thought, Miss Kent," Barker stood up. "We'll leave you now but if you have any more ideas, you know how to get in touch with us. Good day," he said. He handed Fiona a calling card as he and Mikolos departed.

The two men drove away leaving Fiona in a state of even more confusion. Why had Adrian not gone to America? Where was he when he had called her? She wasn't even sure she wanted to know, but her resolve that she must avoid him became even more compelling. She was convinced now that to prolong a relationship with him was to invite more lies. But she also knew that she would never be content until she discovered the truth. She wondered if Max, the voice on the message machine, had blown up the car. Apparently he knew that Adrian had not gone to America, that he had gone to Brazil. Maybe when he requested a call back it was to ascertain whether or not his victim was still alive.

The following two days passed slowly with Fiona's anxiety increasing by the hour. A chill of apprehension ran through her every time the telephone rang. She dreaded confronting Adrian, but at the same time was frantic for answers. Finally, late in the evening, he called.

"Where are you?" she asked immediately.

"Back in town. How are you?"

"How do you think I am?" she flared. "You skip town leaving me in the middle of an assassination; I have to hide a fortune for you and now I'm being hounded by the police like a common criminal. They even came to my house."

"They did?"

"Yes, and they had more news for me. They said that I lied to them about where you were going when I dropped you off at the airport. Apparently you didn't go to America and they know that. And now you have the nerve to ask me how I am!"

"I'm sorry, Fi. I know it's been rough for you, but I never intended you to get involved. I simply wanted you to pick up a little money and put it away for me," he protested.

"Well that didn't happen, but all the same, the police have come to my house and accused me of telling them stories. Where did you go?"

"Honestly, I did call you from New York, but I couldn't get a direct flight from Heathrow. Listen," he continued brightly, "I'll pick you up for lunch tomorrow if you're free, and explain everything. What do you say?"

There was another long pause, more for Fiona to impress upon him that no matter how conciliatory he may attempt to be, she was still irritated by the whole affair. He was still being evasive, and although she expected some answers, she had no intention of becoming further involved in whatever it was that he was up to. He was not to assume that she would be available at the drop of a hat. But irrespective of how he behaved or what happened, she reluctantly admitted that she still wanted to see him. He was damnably attractive, and she had never known anyone like him. Nevertheless, the nagging question of what he did and what was going on, persisted. She had considered the possibility that he was an international narcotics dealer. She quickly dispelled that scenario, however, as being just too improbable; it was far more likely that he was running some clandestine operation for the government.

"Come on Fiona," he insisted. "When can I see you?"

"I have a couple of horses to get on for Tim tomorrow morning," she said at last. "Perhaps after that?"

"Great, I'll meet you over there."

"No, no, don't do that," she protested.

"Why not?"

"Well . . . " she hesitated. "I just don't want anyone there to get the impression that we are that . . . connected," she said, searching for words. "Anyway, I'll be home before eleven, so if you come by at noon, and are extremely nice to me, you can buy me a very expensive lunch."

He laughed. "Okay, you're on."

It was precisely twelve o'clock when he arrived at her door the following day.

"Adrian, what the hell is going on?" she asked as she opened the door to him.

"Look, there's absolutely nothing for you to worry about," he reassured her. "Let's go and have lunch."

Half an hour later they were seated at a table of a restaurant that he had carefully selected. Despite the cheerful ambience of an exquisite dining room, there was an obvious tension between them, with Fiona distant and unsure of Adrian, and he trying too hard to be congenial and reassuring.

Although she had little appetite, Fiona ordered a lobster salad and vintage champagne, deliberately holding him to the promise of an expensive lunch. By the time the check came, the conversation had skirted around the events of the last few days. Fiona expected him to volunteer explanations, and he wished to avoid them.

"Adrian, I have to know what you've got me involved in," Fiona finally insisted. "I don't know what's going on but I'd like to know what you've dragged me into."

"You're not involved in anything, it's just the bloody minded police that think you are."

"They're certainly bloody minded," she agreed.

"You can't be implicated in anything, don't worry."

"Don't worry? You could have had me blown up!"

Adrian made no response. He looked up from examining the check and gave her his most endearing smile.

"You know, you never did collect that money for me," he accused flippantly. "I don't know how I'm going to pay for lunch."

Fiona was not amused. "Don't you think you owe me some explanation, Adrian?"

"I suppose I do," he replied, now seriously. "I can tell you very little because for you to know too much might put you in danger," he continued, his level gaze searching her eyes. "And I must admit there is an element of danger in what I do."

"Oh yes, I know that, but what is that you do?"

"Fi, you've got to stop asking me questions that I'm unable to answer."

"Aren't I entitled to know? You've got me involved whether you like it or not," she argued. "I certainly don't like it."

"I admit that I was stupid for permitting you to get involved, as you put it."

"How else can I put it?"

"Okay, I'm sorry for what happened, but I promise that you're not in any danger now."

"So your justification for being evasive is for my protection?" she asked testily.

With a disarming smile, Adrian reached across the table and took her hand. "I hope you will accept that and consider it in that light. I have to do things that you'd never understand."

"Then I'll never understand you either."

Fiona held his gaze, searching for truth. Even in the absence of truth about his activities, she had to know how much he cared about her. Had she been nothing more than an intermediary for his operations? Was it really for her safety that he declined to answer her questions? After a moment she withdrew her hand, turning to look out of the window, not wanting him to read her distrust of him.

She folded her napkin deliberately and placed it upon the table. "Can we go?"

Without another word he paid the bill and they walked out to his car. He held the door open for her and received a chilly, "Thank you".

They drove for a few minutes before Fiona self-consciously attempted to resume a conversation. She felt compelled to restore some semblance of civility and was beginning to regret being ungracious at lunch.

"Is this your new car?" she asked without much real interest.

"Actually it's just a rental. What do you think I should buy?"

"I should think, judging by your recent history, you'd want to keep renting."

He smiled. "Hmn, that probably wouldn't be a bad idea."

They drove slowly back to Fiona's cottage, where Adrian, reluctant to leave her in her present frame of mind, invited himself in.

"Yes, do come in. Take off your coat and relax."

Fiona's cool demeanor was beginning to thaw. Although she wasn't sure why, she welcomed the intrusion; she was glad that under the circumstances she had not driven him off. She opened a bottle of champagne, not vintage, and led him out onto the patio.

The afternoon sun filtered through the surrounding beech trees, casting a warm, moving pattern of light and shade. The fragrance of honeysuckle and jasmine permeated the lazy, drifting air. Fiona, finally feeling completely relaxed and a little light headed from the effects of too much champagne, excused herself to go into her bedroom and change into nothing more than a pair of shorts and tee shirt. Barefoot, she reappeared and curled up on a stone bench, looking across the patio at Adrian.

Lounging in a deep, wicker lawn chair, without saying anything, Adrian waved her to come over to him. Obediently she went over and perched herself upon the arm of his chair where he put his arm around her slim waist.

"Feeling better?" he asked, topping up her glass.

"You know I can't stay peeved at you for very long."

"You tried."

"Why are you so bloody compelling?" She slid onto his knee. "Why do you take advantage of me?"

"I think it's the other way around," he said kissing her on the lips. "You take advantage of me."

He ran sensitive fingers across her long, slim thigh, becoming aroused by the touch of smooth, golden tanned skin. She was sensual and beautiful.

He kissed her again, putting his glass down and drawing her down into the chair with him. They kissed for a long time, both of them searching for each other. Finally, he picked her up and carried her through the open French-window into her bedroom, to lie on the bed beside her, both of them undressing each other between fervent and ever more urgent kisses, saying nothing, until they were both naked.

Kneeling beside him, her pulse throbbing in her temples, she let her eyes travel over his muscular body, now rigid with desire. She had a fleeting memory of the two youths that had loved her in college, but at that moment she was regarding a man so desirable that she could hardly breath. Her hands rested upon his chest and slowly, caressing, slid down to his hips.

Adrian's eyes fell upon the slim curve of her thighs as they arched into her pelvis below a flat belly and firm breasts that required no support. She was conscious of his gaze and was stimulated even further. She wondered at her lack of inhibition, but it didn't matter, she was consumed with desire and surrendered to his every move. He ran his fingers through her hair, down across her shoulders and onto her breast, gently stroking her protruding nipples. Slowly he pulled her down upon him where he entered her, unrestrained hunger consuming them both.

Later, as the afternoon faded into the twilight of evening, she dressed and left him asleep, going into the kitchen to make tea for them both. She sat and stared at the kettle, unaware of how long it took to come to a boil.

She reflected upon why she had become caught up with Adrian. Why had she offered herself to him without reservation? Would she have gone to bed with just any attractive man under the same circumstances? She hoped not, but then her failure to avoid him despite her earlier resolve must surely be significant. She wondered if she loved him. She really didn't know.

By the time the kettle had shrieked her back to the present, she swore never to compromise herself again. If she didn't love him, she was appalled to think that she had given herself to a man about whom she knew so little and had so many doubts. She agonized over what she should do. Perhaps she should break off their relationship entirely, just as she had intended. Everything told her that, before it was too late, she should never see him again; before she became totally and inextricably involved with him. But wasn't making love to him a total commitment? Until that moment she would have thought so. But now she was not certain that Adrian's passion had not been simply self-gratification on his part anyway; possibly even her consenting to his desire had been nothing more than her own self-indulgence.

Wearied by confusion, she took two cups of tea into the bedroom where he was now propped up on pillows, sleepy but awake.

"Adrian, you were beautiful," she smiled wistfully. She sat on the side of the bed and kissed him. "But this whole thing is a terrible mistake. This has all happened too soon, you know that."

He took the cup without saying a word, and sipped the tea. She could read nothing into his expression. He was gazing distantly out through the window.

Finally he spoke. "Fiona, we do need time," he said slowly. "We need time for me to get my life straightened out and for you to know that I have done so."

After a brief pause, he smiled weakly up at her. "But it isn't going to be easy," he continued. "At the moment I seem not to have control of my life, least of all where you're concerned."

"Well, in future I'll help you with that," she said with conviction. "This will not happen again."

He shook his head slowly, compressed his lips and said nothing.

Later they both dressed for dinner, Fiona having a quiche delivered from the local bakery in the village. She opened a bottle of Montrachet that they sipped with the meal, sitting at a small table by candlelight in the warm evening shadows of the patio. They talked quietly about everything but each other.

"Did you give Dantes his name?" Fiona asked.

"Yes, he was unnamed when I bought him as a yearling. Do you know who Dantes was?"

Fiona thought so, but for the sake of conversation, wanted him to tell her.

Adrian stared at his wine glass, slowly swirling the wine, as if recalling the past.

"Edmund Dantes was the real name of the Count of Monte Cristo," he began. "He had been wrongfully convicted by conspiring noblemen of France and was mistakenly presumed killed when trying to escape from a life sentence in prison. Many years later he returned after having amassed a great fortune. Masquerading as the Count of Monte Cristo, he planned to avenge the wrongs committed against him.

"It's a very complex story of unrequited love," he looked up at Fiona, "intrigue, murder, revenge and restitution, all taking place in Paris in the early eighteen hundreds."

"Why name a horse after a vengeful character?" Fiona asked. "Are you a vindictive person?"

"I prefer to think tolerant rather than vindictive," he smiled. "The name came from the stallion, Dumas, the sire of Dantes. Alexander Dumas wrote the novel and created Dantes the man; Dumas the stallion sired the horse."

"So you named his creation Dantes."

"Why not?"

"Does life imitate art?" Fiona mused rhetorically, shifting the topic.

"I suppose it does in many ways," she continued. "But unlike fictional characters that behave as the author wishes, to a large extent, we can control our destiny."

"I hope you're right." Adrian sounded doubtful.

"I don't believe the direction of our lives is ordained by a divine author. We have choices."

"So since you have a choice, where do you wish our relationship would go?" Adrian asked.

Fiona took almost a minute before answering. "Adrian, I also need time. The last few days have been really disturbing and I feel as though I am being swept up by events that I can't control. I have never experienced that before. I need to be removed from everything that has happened between us. I need to look at you and myself from a different perspective. Can you understand?"

Adrian reached over, placing his hand over hers. "I understand, but all I ask is that you give me a chance, Fi."

"Haven't we had our chances?"

"I know it's been difficult for you but I want us to stay in touch."

The evening drew on with little more said. Adrian got up to leave as the last of the light faded into darkness. A perfunctory kiss on the cheek was his departing goodbye.

CHAPTER 10

Adrian called Fiona the following day, asking her to join him for dinner; she declined. She declined again several days later when he extended another invitation.

She was not convinced that he would not, in future, use her again to advance some sort of illicit activity. She no longer regarded him as simply the charming, affable person that she had been so willing to accept when they had first met. Perhaps she did love him, she wasn't sure. He was undeniably handsome, and passionate when they made love, but she wavered at the thought of any further contact. She knew it would be too easy to sleep with him again, and too difficult to understand him.

Over the ensuing days, Fiona continued to struggle with her emotions. The comfortable and familiar routine of riding morning work and riding in the occasional race was overshadowed by the confusing distraction of Adrian. Time and again, without remedy, her rational mind resisted the thought of continuing their relationship. She recognized, that in the past, her almost total immersion into riding had been a substitute for companionship, but she doubted that a more active social life would replace the sense of isolation that she was now experiencing. Having one passionate interlude hardly justified continuing a relationship fraught with emotional risk and real danger, she rationalized. But she seemed incapable of filling the void that was a consequence of separation.

Adrian's phone calls became less frequent until eventually a week passed without a single call. Finally, late one evening, she answered the telephone intuitively knowing it was Adrian.

"Adrian?"

"Hello, Fiona, you knew it was me? How are you?"

"I'm okay, what about you?"

"In good form, but I've missed you."

There was a long pause, an uncomfortable silence.

"Fiona, look," he said finally as she was about to speak. "The reason I'm calling is because Tim has a couple of runners in Ireland, at the Curragh, the day after tomorrow. I'm going to pop over and have a day at the races and wondered if you'd like to come along."

Fiona hesitated, her mind and heart racing, her resolve to avoid him wavering. "I don't know Adrian," she paused, searching. "How long are you going to be over there?"

"Your call, as long as you'd like," he replied, encouraged by the uncertainty in her voice. He had been prepared for another abrupt refusal. "We could stay over if you wish."

Fiona faltered. "I couldn't stay over."

"That's okay, it doesn't matter. We can fly out of Luton, spend the day at the races and be home for dinner. What do you say?"

After more hesitation, as much to impress upon him a reluctance to take up where they had left off as to resolve her own self-doubt, Fiona consented.

"Very well, Adrian . . . "

"Great!"

" . . . but I can't go on with an intimate relationship, Adrian," she said. "I have no intention of repeating my little mistake with you."

"Little mistake?" he protested. "Little mistake? If you're referring to my making love to you I hope it was more than that."

"Well if it was, then it was a big mistake!" she shot back.

"Oh, well," there was resignation in his voice, no resentment. "I don't seem to be able to say the right thing, do I?"

There was another long silence. Fiona waited, again her mind racing, regretting that she had flared up.

"I'm sorry, Adrian, forgive me. It's just that I'm tired," she said in a warmer tone. "To be perfectly honest, I would like to see you."

"It's been too long. I know you'll enjoy Ireland. It'll be fun."

"I'm sure it will. I'm looking forward to it. Will you pick me up then?"

He agreed to be at her cottage at eight in the morning, and hung up.

She sat for a long time in a darkened room, staring into a dying fire, a book turned over at an open page on her lap. It was decided then, almost inevitably, she thought, she would see him again. She was determined, however, not to become further entangled in his odd business affairs. There was absolutely no reason why she should, she concluded.

Wednesday morning dawned with low scudding clouds and a light drizzle. Fiona, awake long before daylight, was up and into her first cup of coffee. The mornings were for remorse, she mused, and evenings seemed to be for rash decisions. Was last night one of them? Against all odds and her utmost resolve she had agreed to see Adrian again. He had caught her with her spirits at their lowest ebb; she was sure she would never have consented at any other time.

She had even more misgivings as she poked through her wardrobe, undecided for the first time in years as to what she should wear. What about makeup? Should she put on a little eyeliner, eye shadow; and what color lipstick? Why, she wondered, was it so important to worry about her appearance now? She never had before, not even for Adrian. She knew her lack of resolve was a symptom of her self-doubt and insecurity? It was a new and unwelcome feeling. Finally, with confidence slowly returning she was ready; minimal makeup, a cashmere turtleneck sweater in beige that complimented a twill skirt, a hounds-tooth tweed jacket and sensible walking shoes. She remembered having to run for her life, dodging bullets in those shoes. They were probably a good idea for this trip; the only wise choice she had made lately, she thought, her usual self-deprecating humor returning.

She examined herself in the mirror, drawing new courage from the face that stared back at her. She tried a smile. Was her mouth a little too large, she wondered? And then with amusement concluded that if so it was hardly surprising since she usually had her foot in it. Her jaw was strong with the hint of a dimple in her chin that she would prefer was not there. Her large eyes and flawless skin required no embellishment. Anyway, she thought, he'd just have to put up with her imperfections, like it or not, and besides, why the hell should she worry?

Adrian arrived as the rising sun forced insipid shafts of light through breaking clouds. Fiona watched him park the car from the kitchen window, appreciating the athletic grace with which he moved as he stepped carefully across puddles in the garden path. She made him wait for a few moments before opening the front door. Standing before him, studying his face, once again she was still unable to read beyond that engaging smile.

"Hello," he said. "Great to see you again."

"Good to see you too. Have you been traveling?"

"Of course. It hasn't been much fun though. What about you?"

"Nothing exciting. Ridden a few races but only one winner. Nothing for Tim."

They were still standing in the doorway, self-consciously exchanging trivia, when she realized she had not asked him in. "I'm sorry, would you like to come in for a cup of coffee or something?"

He declined the offer. "We'd better get going. We may get held up with the weather so we need to be on our way."

She left him standing at the open door while she turned to fetch a raincoat.

"Bring your passport," he reminded her.

As they drove away from the cottage, Fiona looked back, acutely aware that behind her was a safe haven and only uncertainty before her.

"Did you leave something behind?" Adrian asked.

"Not really. I don't think so. I hope not." She slid across the seat as near to him as possible. "I'm glad you're here."

The hour drive to Luton was through clearing skies, the sun

13263-RUSS

throwing shafts of light onto a patchwork of emerald pastures and sienna fields of wheat that sloped away from the gently rolling hills. By the time Adrian had parked the car and ushered Fiona through the airline terminal, the gloom with which she had started the day, faded with the clearing sky.

A short, distinguished looking gray-haired man in a navy blue uniform, approached and greeted Adrian. "Good morning, sir. The flight plan's filed and we're right on time," he said, taking their raincoats and Adrian's binoculars. "Would you like to fly it today?"

"No thanks, it's all yours, Miss Kent and I will sit in the back."

They walked out of the terminal to a twin-engine aircraft with engines idling, waiting on the ramp.

"Do you actually fly this thing yourself, Adrian?" Fiona shouted over the engine noise as they climbed aboard.

"Sometimes."

"Do you own it?"

"No. I just charter it occasionally when I'm on a tight schedule."

They took their seats onboard and the pilot closed the cabin door. Adrian reached over and buckled Fiona's seat belt, and hesitating as he leaned across, kissed her.

"I've been waiting to do that," he said.

She reached up, and with hands each side of his face, kissed him back. "So have I."

The flight to Dublin was uneventful, both Fiona and Adrian limiting their conversation to a few shouting exchanges above the engine noise. They landed after about an hour, disembarked, and entered the terminal to pass through customs with a brief exchange with the Irish officials.

"Nothing to declare, returning this evening, a short trip to go racing," Adrian explained.

Coming out of customs, they were immediately confronted by a stocky man dressed in a chauffeur's dark suite and cap.

"Top o' the mornin', sir, your car's waiting, this way please," he greeted Adrian in a strong Irish brogue.

Adrian looked skeptically at the chauffeur. "Ian is my regular driver, are you sure you are to meet me?"

"Oh, yes sir. Ian wasn't available so they sent me."

He was heavily bearded and wore sunglasses, which, Fiona thought, were unnecessary considering the anemic Irish sunshine, but then assumed they were standard equipment for chauffeurs. She and Adrian dutifully followed him out to the curb where they were ushered into a black limousine.

"You know the way to the Curragh?" Adrian asked. The driver responded by merely nodding. Adrian shrugged and settled back comfortably into his seat without further comment.

They drove for twenty minutes, ducking in and out of traffic through the busy streets of Dublin. This part of the city, aside from the many little bridges across the river Liffey, appeared tired and mostly lacked charm, Fiona thought.

Soon they were in open country, heading south, the signposts indicating that they were on the Naas road. The Curragh was about an hour's drive, Adrian explained, so they would stop in Naas for lunch before going on to the races.

As they drove out of Dublin and into the country, Fiona settled back and enjoyed the fleeting scenery with the blue-green Wicklow hills far off to the east. She was relaxed and happy to be with Adrian, grateful for the comfort of the limousine and the way in which he had organized their trip. He gave his inimitable style to everything that he did.

Twenty minutes later, the car slowed and turned off the highway onto a minor road. Adrian sat up with a start, opening the sliding glass behind the driver.

"Where are you going?" he asked, irritably. "This isn't the road to the Curragh."

The driver looked straight ahead. "We're just making a little stop, not to worry, sir."

Moments later, the limousine swung through the gate of a farmyard and pulled up beside a mud-splattered old jeep parked behind a haystack. Two men, one of them middle aged and the other much younger, extracted themselves from the vehicle.

Adrian leaned back with a sigh of resignation, and speaking to no one in particular, simply said, "Damn them!"

He turned to Fiona with an apologetic smile. "I'm sorry, we've got a little diversion I wasn't expecting."

The older of the two men was heavy set but walked briskly with a military bearing. He had a florid complexion half covered by a large reddish moustache below a hawk-like beak of a nose and bushy eyebrows. Dressed in a checked tweed jacket, battered brown tweed hat and green corduroy trousers tucked into high rubber boots, he gave every appearance of a typical Irish farmer. He stepped up and opened the door on Adrian's side of the car.

"Good mornin', Mick, I'm very glad to see you again. Have you been well?" he asked with a strong accent.

"Hello O'Neill, I didn't expect to bump into you today." Adrian got out of the car. "This is a bit of a surprise."

The two men shook hands, while O'Neill's companion, a youth who appeared to be in his late teens, leaned with an air of boredom against the jeep. He was wearing a long, shabby raincoat and a greasy checkered, tweed cap and muddy, broken down boots. Fiona noticed his hands were buried in pockets that either concealed something bulky beneath the coat, or covered an extraordinarily disproportionate body. With growing alarm, she realized that she could see the profile of a concealed gun of some sort under the raincoat.

Adrian turned to introduce Fiona. "Major, this is Fiona Kent. Fiona, Major O'Neill"

"Ah yes, for sure, I know of you." O'Neill removed his hat with the hint of a bow. Turning away, O'Neill took Adrian by the arm and guided him over to the jeep, beyond range of Fiona's hearing. She could see Adrian was shaking his head, frowning, and mildly protesting as the two men talked. Finally, with what appeared to be a shrug of resignation, Adrian returned to the car.

"Fiona, forgive me but we're going to have to go with Major O'Neill in the other car. I'm terribly sorry."

"Can't I just go on and meet you later?"

"I'm sorry, they want us both to go with them," Adrian replied. "Don't worry, you'll be alright, nothing is going to happen, but we don't really have a choice."

Reluctantly, Fiona slid out of the limousine and followed Adrian over to the other vehicle. O'Neill produced two large bandannas from his pocket. "Please turn around Miss Kent. I'm afraid you will have to put up with this for a little while."

"Adrian, why?" She protested with rising irritation.

"I'm sorry Fi, just do as he asks."

The weak apology did nothing to sooth Fiona's annoyance. Steaming, she permitted O'Neill to blindfold her.

"You too, Mick," he said.

After being blindfolded, they were assisted into the back of the waiting jeep. Fiona's annoyance was in no way abated by Adrian quietly consenting to the wishes of their captors, but her irritation was mixed with apprehension. She was well aware that the younger man, sitting in the front seat, did have a gun of some sort.

"Adrian, this is the bloody limit. I'd like to know what the hell is going on?"

Before Adrian could answer, O'Neill offered an apology. "I am really very sorry, Miss Kent, but we have to make a little trip into the country, and for our future safety it is better that neither of you see where we're going. 'Twill not take very long. We'll be there in no time at all."

"I understand," Adrian said. And then, in an attempt to placate Fiona, "I'll explain to you later, Fi."

"Damn later," Fiona fumed. "At least tell me who these people are."

The older man responded again. "Miss Kent, there are some political problems that have been going on for many years in Ireland and . . . "

"I know that," Fiona interrupted. "Why does that involve me?"

"My associates and I have tried in many ways to overcome the resistance the Protestant people of Nort'ern Ireland have toward rejoining the Irish Republic."

"Well you're doing a rotten job of it."

"Part of our solution for this problem, Miss Kent, is to negotiate with influential people such as your friend here," O'Neill continued. "Consequently, he has become a target for radicals . . . ."

"Like you?" Fiona interrupted again.

"I resent being called a radical, Miss Kent," O'Neill replied calmly. "I am working for the liberation of Nort'ern Ireland."

"I don't think the people in Northern Ireland appreciate your concern for their liberation. They continually vote to remain part of the British Commonwealth."

"They're misguided," O'Neill retorted. "Ireland must be united."

"United with people who have a violent agenda and are tearing lives apart?" Fiona argued. "The militants who demand unification are victimizing people who wish for peace and autonomy."

"Well there are a couple of chaps from up north who became aware that your friend is in Ireland today and would like to see him permanently planted here. They don't want peace; they want a piece of him. That's why, for his and your protection, we have decided to temporarily detain you both."

"How did they find out that I'd be going to the Curragh?" Adrian inquired.

"You have a leak in your organization, and so do they. There's not much we don't find out."

"Then why didn't you call me at home?"

"Because you and I need to have a little chat, and just so these boys won't be after you when you get home, we have arranged a little entertainment for them here. By the end of the day, they won't be botherin' you again."

O'Neill chuckled, seemingly enjoying the thought, and then added, "After we introduce ourselves to these lads, I shall make sure that you get safely back to your plane."

"Well that's a comfort," Adrian agreed. "I appreciate your concern."

"It is my pleasure, you're our best contact, you know."

Fiona was not satisfied. "What sort of entertainment do you have in mind for these people?"

"Let me just reiterate," O'Neill replied. "They will not be botherin' either of you again. Now I can't tell you more than that."

Fiona, still fuming inwardly, dropped any further objections and reaching across, searched for Adrian's hand. Although she assumed he was not entirely in agreement with what was happening, Adrian was apparently with friends. With no further conversation they drove on, the blindfold frustrating Fiona's efforts to keep track of the direction in which they were traveling. After fifteen minutes they turned onto a gravel road and, moments later, slowed and came to a stop.

CHAPTER 11

"Here we are. That wasn't so bad was it?" O'Neill announced jovially.

Fiona was not to be humored. "Thank God for small favors. Now, can I take this damn blindfold off?"

"Yes, of course."

For a moment the light dazzled Fiona's eyes before she could see that they had arrived at another farm. They had parked in front of a run-down, two-storied house: gray, stone, and uninviting. Across a gravel yard there was an old wooden barn that leaned at a dangerous angle, also in a state of disrepair. Its doors were wide open and hanging from their hinges, providing minimal shelter for a small delivery van, a tractor, and a collection of miscellaneous rusting agricultural implements. A long driveway, fenced by barbed wire on both sides and with a crookedly hanging gate, led to the road from the house. An assortment of cattle grazed in various fields surrounding the farm, but there was little to suggest that the place was much more than derelict.

As the group climbed down from the vehicle, a large heavy set, middle-aged woman with untidy graying hair, opened the farmhouse door. "Welcome back, Mick," she greeted Adrian with open arms.

"Good to see you looking so well, Agnes," Adrian turned to Fiona. "May I introduce Miss Kent?"

"Delighted I'm sure," the stout lady smiled.

"I wish I could say the same," Fiona retorted. "This has been quite an experience."

"We'll do everything we can to make you comfortable. I am

really very sorry for the inconvenience." The woman sounded genuinely apologetic.

Fiona and Adrian were led into a small living room, followed by O'Neill. Their younger, armed escort remained outside.

"Mick, I need you for moment in my office," O'Neill said heading off down a dark, narrow hall. "Agnes, please make Miss Kent comfortable."

Fiona was offered an overstuffed, threadbare armchair while Adrian disappeared with O'Neill, somewhere to the rear of the house. For the next half-hour she waited anxiously for Adrian's return. The stout woman flitted about and produced tea and unappetizing sandwiches from a paper bag, both of which Fiona politely refused.

"I'm sorry that you are being detained and we can't do better for you, Miss Kent. Perhaps one day you can come and visit us under better circumstances."

Unaccustomed to being rude to anyone, Fiona's petulance soon gave way to curiosity. The house appeared to be unoccupied and the food brought in. "Do you live here?" she asked.

"No, we just use this house occasionally. A neighbor runs the farm."

"Doesn't anyone stay here then?"

"I'm sorry I can't tell you that."

"You don't know?"

"I don't want to know. I couldn't tell you if I did."

Fiona got up and walked around the room pretending to examine a collection of old yellow prints of rural Ireland hanging in dusty frames upon the white-washed walls.

"Have you known Mick long?" the woman asked.

"Not long, in fact I didn't know his name was Mick."

"Ah, he's quite a boy is Mick," the woman said, fondly.

"Yes he certainly is," Fiona replied with feeling.

Fiona drifted around the room, continuing the charade of having an interest in the faded pictures. Glancing out of the single window, she saw that O'Neill's young companion was leaning against the wall just outside the front door, smoking a cigarette and presumably standing guard. The only other exit from the room was the hallway down which O'Neill and Adrian had departed. She realized with resignation that she had no chance of escaping and getting to a vehicle. Any further consideration of escape ended when Adrian and O'Neill returned.

"We're on our way, Fi," Adrian said brightly.

"Where to now?"

"To the races," O'Neill beamed. "You're off to the races and can enjoy the horses. It's a fine day for racing."

They returned to O'Neill's jeep where they were again blindfolded. With no further objections, they endured another fifteen minutes of bouncing around before arriving back at their waiting limousine. Adrian and Fiona climbed from the jeep and had their blindfolds removed. No sooner did they disembark, than two men who appeared to have been waiting for them slid into the back of the jeep. Adrian acknowledged both men with a nod but said nothing. The jeep, with its four occupants, followed Adrian and Fiona in the limousine out onto the main highway.

Safely inside the limousine, Fiona was much more relaxed, if still cool toward Adrian. As usual, Adrian was distant and evasive in answering her questions.

"I assume those were your friends?"

"Not really, just associates."

"Why do they call you Mick?"

"The Irish call everybody Mick. These people, for security reasons, don't use proper names."

"Do they also work in this mysterious British underground that you work for?"

"Not exactly. They do have a political connection, though."

"They're militants of the Irish Republican Army aren't they?"

Adrian turned to Fiona, looking her directly in the eyes. "Look Fiona, it would be dangerous for you to know who they are. After today, you'll never see them again. Just forget who they are."

"Is that place where they took us what you call a safe-house?"

"Fiona, forget that you were ever there."

"How the hell can I forget, I was bloody well abducted!" she flared, exasperated.

Adrian took a deep breath and exhaled slowly. "I am truly sorry about what happened. I didn't plan that excursion and in an hour it'll be all over."

"In an hour?"

"Yes, they're following us so that we have protection until we go home."

Fiona spun around in her seat, and saw through the rear window that the jeep was following them, some hundred yards behind.

"That is a great comfort!" she said sarcastically. "Protection from whom by whom?"

"Do you remember the attack by those two men when we were coming back from York?"

"How could I forget?"

"Could be the same chaps that are after me now."

"Adrian, if you weren't mixed up with these sort of people you wouldn't need protection. Whatever it is that you do, I hate it."

"I'm sure, you probably hate me too. I don't blame you if you do."

"At this moment, I don't know."

Fiona leaned back with a heavy sigh and closed her eyes. She was resigned to the fact that he would never explain why men from Northern Ireland would pose a threat to him. She supposed she would never know who might be dangerous or who might be harmless. She even wondered, at this point, which of the two Adrian might be. She concluded that if he worked for British Intelligence he would have no shortage of enemies on either side of the Irish border, or a lot of places around the world for that matter.

"Are we going to the races then?" she asked.

"Yes, sorry about lunch but we'll get something a little later."

It was noon when their limousine pulled up in front of the entrance to the racecourse; O'Neill and his companions close behind. Lines of people were entering through turnstiles, pushing and jostling, anxious for a day of racing. Adrian asked Fiona to stay in the car while he went to pick up their credentials.

Fiona watched from the car while Adrian crossed the narrow road and approached a small brick building off to one side of the grandstand entrance, a 'Credentials' sign above the door. Before he could enter the building, two uniformed police officers that appeared to be surveying the crowded entrance, suddenly stepped up to Adrian, one on each side. He stopped, and looking quickly from one officer to the other as if weighing his chances of escape, turned and started back toward the car. The police officers each grabbed an arm before Adrian had a chance to take two steps. With Adrian only offering token resistance, attempting to pull free, the three men started back across the road. Several people in close proximity, who saw what was happening, stopped and turned to stare. The scene that they were observing was evidently not too unusual, but nevertheless, elicited the inevitable curiosity. Adrian was obviously being arrested.

Fiona watched in mute fascination, witnessing from within the car what looked like a silent film unfolding before her; animation in slow motion. Undoubtedly the police officers had made an error, she thought. It seemed improbable that they should mistake someone as distinguished in appearance as Adrian for a pickpocket, terrorist, or whatever they were looking for, but there was no question about him being arrested. This bizarre event was the final straw, she thought; the culmination of all the events in which Adrian had become involved.

Onlookers, mute spectators all, continued to stare. Perhaps even then, Fiona hoped, there was a mistake; surely the police in Ireland wouldn't arrest Adrian for events that had taken place in England. They must have mistaken him for someone else.

The officers and their quarry crossed the street, passed the limousine, and were almost past O'Neill's jeep when he and his three colleagues stepped out from behind it, blocking their path. In an instant, Adrian's captors released him, turned and started to run, heading off through the parking lot, dodging in and out of the cars. Within seconds, half a dozen men dressed in civilian clothes suddenly appeared and surrounded them. There was no escape. In desperation the uniformed men attempted to break through the cordon, kicking and swinging wild punches, but badly outnumbered, they were wrestled to the ground. The entire incident took less than a minute. The small crowd of onlookers who had bothered to watch the entire episode, cheered when the police officers went down.

Watching the scene through the rear window in disbelief, Fiona was startled when the car door opened. Adrian slid in beside her.

"That worked out like a charm," he said matter-of-factly. "Are you ready for the races?"

Fiona was momentarily speechless.

"Well, what do you say?" Adrian prompted.

"What do I say?" she started. "What do I say? I say we get out of here and out of Ireland as quickly as we can. That was like a scene from some movie, but it wasn't very entertaining. I don't think I want to go racing. Can we go home?"

"Okay, that's not such a bad idea." Adrian agreed, now smiling. He reached forward, opened the dividing glass, and tapped the driver on the shoulder. "Let's go. Take us back to the general aviation terminal at Dublin airport where you picked us up."

Their car threaded its way through traffic and hurrying racegoers, and then gradually passed out of the racecourse and onto the main road. Fiona sat back in her seat as it gathered speed. What had transpired back there, she thought, seemed to have affected everyone but Adrian. A small mob attacking uniformed police officers still deserved comment.

"At the risk of sounding stupid, may I ask if you knew if that was going to happen?" she inquired.

"Well I'm sure you realize those were not policemen," he replied with hesitation.

"Oh, really, I never would have guessed."

He ignored the sarcasm. "O'Neill had information that I was

to be picked up at the racecourse," he explained. "He suspected they would look like officials of some kind, and he was right. They must have thought they could pull it off in a crowd if they looked like police."

"You knew they weren't police then?"

"I had a good idea they weren't, but when they high-tailed it, I knew then for sure."

"Were they from Northern Ireland?"

"I'm pretty sure they were the men from Belfast who tried to get us in England."

"What'll happen to them?"

"Oh, they'll probably be charged with impersonating police officers and even if the Irish authorities can't find anything else to pin on them, they'll still be put away for a while. They take a very dim view about Northern Irish Protestants breaking the law in this country."

"Well the IRA seem to have no compunction about being violent in Northern Ireland," Fiona retorted. "And I'm sure O'Neill and his crew would have no compunction about abducting people from the north if it served their purpose, either."

"Unfortunately, it works both ways," he agreed.

"Violent behavior seems to require little justification with any of your acquaintances."

"I don't blame you for that, but before you get too critical of my friends here," Adrian retorted, "remember O'Neill's boys did what they did for us both."

Fiona found little comfort in that. "I must say it is interesting to be used as bait for a trap," she reflected aloud.

Adrian just smiled. He suggested that they stop just outside the airport for lunch before taking the flight back to England. Fiona, although in better humor, said she would rather not, that she was unable to relax as long as they were in Ireland.

"I can't help feeling that at any moment someone will appear to either attack us or drag us off somewhere," she remarked. "And speaking of uncertain fates, I wonder if the two bogus police officers will ever see the inside of a courtroom."

The flight back to England was uneventful. By early afternoon she was delivered back to the comfort and security of her little cottage. Adrian came to the front door, apologizing again for the day's events but declining her half-hearted invitation to come in.

"Thanks, Fi, but I'll just push off. I'm sure you've seen enough of me for today."

She offered no objections, and standing in the door of her cottage, watched as he drove away.

CHAPTER 12

Several days had passed since the trip to Ireland, when Fiona, returning home from a day's racing, was surprised to see a familiar car parked at the end of her driveway. Any hope that it was a friendly visitor quickly evaporated as the persistent gumshoes, Barker and Mikolos, once again descended upon her.

"May we come in?" inquired Barker.

"I suppose so, but I can't give you any more information than I already have," Fiona replied.

Barker removed his hat and smoothed his remaining wisps of hair as the two men entered the sitting room. Without any invitation, both men took up their previous positions where they could watch Fiona and avoid her being able to simultaneously see them. She assumed this was their modus operandi for interrogations, so she elected not to be seated and moved around the room pretending to tidy up, avoiding eye contact with either of them.

"Miss Kent," Barker began as he pulled a set of photographs from an inside coat pocket and handed them to her. "I would like you to look at these pictures and tell me if you know this man."

Fiona stopped stalking about the room, and with one glance at the first picture, froze. Staring back at her from the photograph, obviously taken by police for identification purposes, was the man with the scar across his nose with whom Adrian had had the furious argument outside the pub in Yorkshire. The head-on shot was unmistakable, and the side view of the right side of the man's face distinctly showed the ugly scar running across the bridge of his nose, disappearing into his beard and ending just below his ear.

Fiona's reaction to seeing the photo was not lost on Barker or Mikolos, both of whom were watching her closely.

"You do know him then?" asked Barker

"No I don't," Fiona denied, offering nothing more.

"But you have seen him?"

Her mind was racing in an attempt to keep control. Answering any questions about the people she knew Adrian had met might in some way incriminate him; she was not prepared to do that. She was not going to volunteer information about the events or the people that they had met in Ireland either.

Before she could answer, Barker persisted. "When did you see this man?"

"I don't remember exactly," she replied after some hesitation. It was futile to deny that she had seen him. "It was some time ago."

She handed the photographs back to the inspector and in an attempt to appear casual and indifferent, accepting the inevitable confrontation, propped herself up on the arm of her favorite chair, facing the two detectives.

"He was a friend of Mr. Harrington's, no?" Mikolos asked.

"I don't know. I've told you before, I don't know who his friends are."

The two investigators glanced across at each other, and Barker leaned forward threateningly.

"Miss Kent, we can take you down to Scotland Yard for questioning if you don't cooperate," he cautioned.

"I don't know what this is all about," Fiona protested. "If you would tell me something about this man I may be able to help you. I have only seen him once with Viscount Harrington and certainly don't know if he is a friend."

Barker leaned back in his chair, glanced again at Mikolos and took a deep breath.

"His name is Carlo Tiriach," he began, "a Yugoslavian national granted temporary residence in the U.K., but then convicted of possession of stolen weapons from our military."

Fiona raised her eyebrows and shrugged.

"He was released from prison a year ago and deported, but we think that he illegally re-entered Britain, perhaps within months of his expulsion. Does any of that help your recollection?"

Both men were looking for some reaction from Fiona who merely shook her head. "Why should it? This is all news to me."

"Maybe you know why this Mr. Harrington knows this man, yes?" Mikolos suggested, his eyebrows climbing toward his hairline.

Fiona shook her head. "I have no idea."

"Let me go on," Barker continued, ignoring Mikolos' interruption. "At the time that Mr. Harrington's car was blown up, a security camera recorded everyone who came and went through the entrance to the garage. Our investigation after the explosion identified the explosive material to be that which is used almost exclusively by the military and we presume it to be stolen. When we reviewed the security videotape recording from the garage, we identified Tiriach as having gone into the garage with a backpack at about four in the morning of that day. He left about fifteen minutes later without the backpack."

Barker paused for effect, again hoping for some response from Fiona.

"Well that's easy then," she said looking expectantly from one man to the other. "Why don't you arrest him if he blew the car up?"

"Because he is dead," Barker replied. "Murdered."

Again there was a long awkward moment. Fiona was more deflated than alarmed. She had hoped that with Tiriach's arrest, the case would be solved and closed. Now the obvious question was why had he been murdered, and by whom? She was too well aware that Adrian was hardly a friend of the victim.

"He had been shot through the back of the head in an execution style killing, with his arms tied behind him," Barker continued. "The time of the murder was approximately twenty-four hours after he had left the parking garage, according to the coroner's report."

Fiona, reaching back in her memory, realized that Adrian had not returned from America for two days after the car had been blown up. He must have been out of the country at the time of Tiriach's death.

"Your friend, Harrington, he knew this man, no?" Mikolos insisted. "This man knew your friend, I think."

"He may have known him, but if you think Adrian killed him you're wrong." Fiona was defiant. "Viscount Harrington was abroad for several days during the time that you said this man was killed."

Barker nodded in agreement. "We have checked Mr. Harrington's departure and return dates and you're absolutely correct, he had gone to Brazil," he said in a conciliatory tone. "But we wondered if you could shed some light on the relationship between Mr. Harrington and the deceased."

"I'm sorry, you're barking up the wrong tree," Fiona replied, looking directly at Barker. "Why don't you ask him?"

"We have," the inspector replied with no change of expression. "And contrary to what you have just told us, he denies knowing the man."

Fiona flushed. "I told you that I had seen them together, that's all."

"Ah, yes you did say that, didn't you," Barker agreed as if it were a slip of his memory. "Do you have anything that might bring more light to the situation?"

Fiona shook her head without a comment.

"I thank you for your assistance in this matter," Barker continued, "but may I give you a word of advice? Your involvement with these people puts you in a very dangerous position. I would suggest that you be very careful."

"You are very close to the fire," Mikolos admonished, nodding wisely and shaking a pudgy finger in Fiona's direction. "Do not play with it."

Both men got up to leave. Fiona did not hesitate to escort them out of the door. As they drove away she watched from a window, wondering what new developments might be revealed next. It was impossible for Adrian to have killed Tiriach, but nevertheless, Fiona realized that she must separate herself from him as far as possible, and forever. She had visions of him being the next person with a bullet in his head. Almost in tears, she went to the telephone and called her parents.

"Dad?" she struggled for control. "Are you going to be home? I need to talk to you."

"Yes, we're not going anywhere, Fiona, what's wrong?"

"Nothing, I just want to see you. I miss you both terribly."

She promised to go down to stay with them soon; she could not remember ever feeling so alone.

Fiona was barely awake the following morning when the telephone froze her with apprehension. She waited for the answering machine to take the call and listened for the voice on the other end of the line.

"Fiona, this is Eddie Handley, sorry I missed you but I was . . . ."

Fiona picked up the phone.

"Eddie, I'm here."

"Listen Fiona, I'm going down to Newbury this afternoon and I noticed in the entries that you have a ride for Roger Markham, is that right?"

"Yes, the three o'clock," she agreed. "What've you got going?"

"Actually I'm on four and my first is at one. I thought you might join me and we could drive down together."

Handley frequently shared a ride with other jockeys to go to the races, and since he lived in Dunstable, only half an hour from Fiona, he gave her a lift or rode with her at every opportunity. She always appreciated his company and shared the driving even though they invariably took his car.

"Yes of course, that'd be great. Do you want to take the Talbot?"

Handley laughed. "No thanks. One of these days that bloody old thing'll fall off the road. We'll go in my car. You can drive on the way home if you don't go too damn fast."

"Will you pick me up on the way then?"

"Nine thirty sharp." Handley rang off.

Fiona was ready, tack bag packed and breakfast out of the way when Handley pulled into her driveway.

"Great to see you Eddie," she greeted him, sliding into the passenger seat. "Are you sure you don't want me to drive?"

"You can on the way home. I've got a busy afternoon and I'd appreciate it if you would drive on the way back."

Fiona settled back to enjoy the ride. "How many are you going to win today?"

Handley looked over at her and grinned. "I'm in the three o'clock with you, that's one I know I can win!"

"You think so? Well I might give you a chance if you're nice to me."

Fiona enjoyed the friendly rivalry that was not unusual between riders, but she was well aware that Handley had given her a break in a race on more than one occasion, although only when he knew he was unable to win on his own horse. If he did have a chance of winning, he gave no quarter to anyone; reason enough for his enormous success, she thought.

"Do you ride anything for Timothy Rand today?" Fiona asked.

"Two."

"Either of them owned by Adrian Harrington?"

"No not today. I think you're his number one jock since you did so well on Dantes," Handley said without a trace of resentment. He had plenty of business without Harrington and was pleased to see Fiona have a chance on a quality horse.

"You've bumped me off of that one," he added.

Fiona fell silent for a while. She watched the countryside slide by but was preoccupied with thoughts of Adrian. She had little need to reassure Handley that he was still the first rider for Dantes; she was sure that he knew that anyway, but was simply being generous and in a subtle way he was reassuring her that she was riding well.

"How well do you know Adrian Harrington?" she asked.

"Quite well. Why?"

"Do you know him from just riding for him or have you socialized with him?"

Handley glanced over with a quizzical expression. "I went shooting with him as a guest at his family estate in Yorkshire, and I've played a couple of rounds of golf with him. But I don't hobknob with him if that's what you mean."

"Did you stay with him?"

"No I just went up for a day of shooting. By the way, he's a damn good shot, so you'd better not screw up when you ride for him."

They drove on for a while before Fiona continued.

"Seriously Eddie, what do you know about his business?" she asked.

"Harrington's?"

"Yes, what does he do? He's always traveling abroad but it seems very mysterious as to what he does?"

Handley thought for a moment. "Well I know he works as some sort of agent for British Intelligence," he replied.

"Is it dangerous work?"

"Yes I think it is. But you know these chaps are pretty secretive, and if you ask me, they do a lot of things that we wouldn't want to know about."

"Like what? Do you think they kill people?"

"Good God, Fiona," Handley protested. "How would I know? Do you want him to kill somebody for you?"

Fiona laughed. "Yes, you if you don't let me win the three o'clock!"

"Then I'm a dead duck, you've got no chance."

Fiona fell quiet, reflective for some time before it was Handley who wanted to know about Fiona's relationship with Adrian.

"Why all the questions about Harrington?" he asked.

"I just wanted to know what you thought of him," Fiona hedged. "Do you like him?"

Handley nodded slowly, measuring his answer.

"I like the man," he said at length. "He's been good to me,

generous with his money whenever I've won a race on one of his horses. He's bright and I've enjoyed being around him. He's a good friend; what more can I say."

They arrived at the racecourse shortly after noon and immediately checked into the jockeys' room. By the time the three o'clock race came around, Handley had already won a race and finished third in another, but this was to be Fiona's only race of the day. Walking out to the paddock together, Fiona was challenged once more by her friend.

"You want to make a side bet, Fiona?" Handley asked.

"You're on the favorite, you have to give me odds."

"Two to one?"

"For ten quid?" she asked.

"Your on!"

Neither one of them won the race but Handley finished second with Fiona no better than fourth. Pulling up their horses after the finish, Handley called over to Fiona, "You owe me a tenner!"

"You didn't win!" Fiona shouted back.

"It was horse for horse. I beat you!"

Fiona laughed and shook her head. A few minutes later, after they had dismounted, she ran to catch up with Handley on the way back to the jockeys' room.

"You took advantage of me," she said.

"Fiona my love, you've got to get tough or everyone will take advantage of you," Handley replied. "I'll let you off this time."

"No you don't," she protested, laughing again. "I'm going to pay you."

But Handley was right, Fiona thought; it was time that she made positive decisions about her life.

Fiona took a long shower, then changed into street clothes and packed her tack. With almost an hour to kill because Handley had another race to ride before they could leave to go home, she left the jockeys' room and went in search of something to eat at the champagne bar. After buying a small sandwich and a mineral water, she then turned to see Timothy Rand sitting alone at a table in a corner.

"May I join you?"

Rand jumped to his feet. "Yes of course, please do Fiona; delighted to see you."

They were both seated.

"Congratulations, you won a nice race today," Fiona said.

"We were a bit lucky," Rand admitted. "Eddie rode a magnificent race."

"Yes I watched it, he certainly did."

"You're riding well Fiona."

"Thanks, I've actually learned a lot from Eddie, he's a great help and a good friend," she smiled appreciatively.

Rand thought about that for a minute before asking, "How are you getting along with Harrington."

Fiona was taken by surprise. "Fine," she said eventually, swallowing a mouthful of sandwich. "He's very interesting."

"I understand you've been seeing him. He said he was taking you to Ireland when I had a runner there, but I didn't see you."

Fiona gulped down some mineral water before answering. "Oh, yes. Well actually we didn't get to the races. There was a change of plans at the last minute."

"Well that's too bad, we had a good winner. What do you think of Harrington?"

Uneasy that the conversation was getting too personal, Fiona took her time before answering. "I think he's very nice," was all she could think to say.

"You're getting along with him then?"

"Yes, I suppose so, but I admit he's very hard to get to know really," she replied. "What did he tell you about me?"

"Oh, he thinks your brilliant and I must admit I'm very pleased about that." He paused for a sip of a soda that he had been nursing. "I warned you some time ago to be careful about him, but I'm pleased you're getting along well together."

"Then you approve?" Fiona smiled.

"Oh, yes, I think he's a fine chap, very upstanding from my experience with him. He's very bright you know, and I think he has a good career ahead of him."

"He travels an awful lot, so I've only seen him a couple of times since I rode Dantes." Fiona wanted Rand to get the impression that Adrian was nothing more than a friend.

"Yes, so I gather. But I must say he's in a business that seems a little dangerous from what I've read. No matter, I'm sure he knows what he's doing."

I wish I did, Fiona thought.

"He's a fine fellow," Rand went on. "I hope you can find occasion to ride for him, and I hope you'll forgive me if you don't ride Dantes all the time, I think that's what he'd like."

"There's nothing to forgive," Fiona protested. "I appreciate the chances that I've had."

Rand looked concerned. "I know you do, and I know you understand. But I'm not sure Harrington does."

"Oh, don't worry about him, and certainly don't worry on my account, just do what you think is best."

"I appreciate that, Fiona, and I just wanted you to know Harrington thinks a lot of you. He's a fine chap." Rand got to his feet. "Now I've got to run, take care of yourself."

Handley finished third once more in the final race of the day, and Fiona returned to the jockeys' room to wait for him. After he was changed they left the racecourse and started home with Fiona driving his car.

"Lousy day," he groused once they were comfortably on their way. "I should have won three races today."

"Oh quit grizzling, you're never satisfied," Fiona retorted good-naturedly. "You beat me out of a tenner."

"Yeah, I know, but you're an easy mark."

"I must be if you can beat me," she laughed.

They drove on for a while before Handley resumed the conversation in a more serious tone.

"Fiona, you never seem to have any friends, socially I mean. Don't you take riding a bit too seriously?"

"I don't think so," she protested. "I just want to be good at whatever I do."

"I understand that, but you don't seem the same lately," he continued. "You seem unhappy about something and yet you're riding well. I don't get it."

"Eddie, you're my best friend and that's enough for now. I don't have time for anything outside of racing. What do you suggest?"

"Get yourself a boy-friend in racing then. I may be your best friend but I'm almost twice your age. What about Adrian Harrington? Don't you like him?"

"He's okay, I suppose," she replied. "I know so little about him but everybody else seems to think the world of him."

"Well he's a good man, not as good looking as me of course," Handley joked. "But then you can't get me. Anyway, Harrington's got money and he thinks you're pretty hot stuff."

"How do you know?"

"He told me when I told him you're a pain in the arse."

"You know Eddie," Fiona said, pretending to be outraged. "Sometimes you're a pain in the arse!"

Handley laughed and slid down in his seat. "I'm going to sleep, pay attention to the road."

Fiona drove on, wondering why she was the only person that had any reservations about Adrian. She wondered if everyone else knew more about him than she did. Why, she thought, when all her friends brushed off the concerns about his occupation should she be so sensitive. Surely it was not because of the risks that he took; she took plenty of those in her own occupation and should be able to understand and live with that. If Adrian worked for a secret British intelligence agency, perhaps dealing with counter-terrorism, it was probable that people would get killed. She just didn't want to be involved nor perhaps become attached to someone who may himself disappear.

CHAPTER 13

The two investigators, Barker and Mikolos, would not let matters rest. Whenever Adrian returned to London from his trips abroad, and especially subsequent to the bombing of his car, he was aware of the continuous surveillance. A black sedan was constantly parked within sight of his home. Wherever he drove in his rented car, it followed. He took pleasure in shaking it off, which he did without difficulty on several occasions, but it always returned to park at what may have been regarded by its occupants as a discreet distance on the street outside his residence. The fact that Barker and Mikolos' original suspicion that he had blown up his own car, amused him immensely. Now that that theory had been exploded, he was not so naïve to believe that the perpetual surveillance might be there for his own protection. When Barker informed him that Tiriach's body had been found, he was not surprised, but drew comfort from the knowledge that the detectives were aware that Adrian was out of the country at the time of the assassination. Both investigators had interrogated him at great length about his movements, with little satisfaction.

"Did you know this man?" Barker had asked producing the photograph.

"Does he look like someone that I would be friends with?"

"I didn't ask if he was a friend. I asked if you knew him. Contrary to what you had told us earlier, Miss Kent seems to think you had met him at some time," Barker had insisted.

"She may be right; I may have met him. But I can't possibly remember all the people I have met in my travels. Did Miss Kent say when I had met him?"

"She couldn't remember. I realize you were out of the country at the time he was shot, but have you any idea why?"

"Why I was out of the country, or why he was shot?" Adrian had countered airily.

"You know what I mean."

"Well I can tell you that I didn't shoot him. I'm sure I would remember him if I had."

Barker had glanced over at Mikolos; neither man showed any trace of amusement.

"He was probably shot because he was a thoroughly unsavory character by all accounts," Adrian suggested. "He did blow up my bloody car, didn't he?"

"That is precisely what we had thought," Barker countered. "Although I must admit, blowing up your car is an unlikely motive for murder. There are other issues involved here."

The Inspector had also interrogated Adrian about all of his foreign business associates. Barker had been aware of the trip he and Fiona had taken to Ireland but Adrian also knew that what had transpired there was unknown to the detective, at least for the moment, and that was in itself reassuring. His connection with the IRA was no business of Scotland Yard, at least at that time, and that was how it should remain.

Barker and Inspector Mikolos were curious about his other activities abroad, particularly about why he had arrived in Rio de Janeiro instead of the United States as they had been led to believe. But Adrian was sure that neither of the investigators would bother to check him out with British Intelligence due to the fact that both detectives knew that this organization guarded the identity of their agents and their activities, and would reveal nothing about him. Adrian had insinuated that his activities would be closely guarded and that the detectives would gain nothing by pointing their investigation in that direction.

But Barker was not easily put off. "Why did you tell Miss Kent you were going to America when she dropped you off at the airport?"

"Miss Kent obviously was mistaken when she thought that I had caught a flight to America. I had told her I was going to South America," Adrian countered, shrugging it off as having no consequence. "A simple mistake that anyone could have made, you can't blame Miss Kent for that."

"We don't."

They questioned him about the attempt on his life, which he continued to claim was a case of mistaken identity, that some unknown terrorist organization had screwed up and put a bomb in the wrong car.

"How should I know who blew my bloody car up?" he protested. "I was out of the country."

He suggested that the PLO were the culprits simply because it was a foreign organization with which he had no contact, but he also knew that the investigators were far from convinced.

Without elaborating, Mikolos claimed he had information to the contrary, that the assassin knew whom he was after when he planted the bomb. Mikolos refused to disclose the source of this intelligence.

"I think this man knows what he is doing," Mikolos had said punching a stubby finger at the photograph of Tiriach. "I think this man is after you, Mr. Harrington, and I think you know him," Mikolos continued using the present tense as if Tiriach were still alive.

"Well I don't know him now, do I?" Adrian had laughed arrogantly.

"No you do not, but I think you are happy about that, no?"

"I'm certainly not going into mourning if that's what you mean."

Mikolos expressed his belief that the attempt on Adrian's life was only unsuccessful due to divine intervention, although he personally could see no justification for intervention of any kind under the circumstances. He warned, with little real concern for Adrian's welfare, that he had dangerous enemies.

"You are very lucky, Mr. Harrington."

"I'm always lucky. Aren't you lucky Inspector Mikolos?"

At least, Adrian thought, Mikolos no longer intended to credit Adrian with an attempt to murder Fiona.

"You have no quarrel over this love, yes?" Mikolos had asked.

"Which love? I have many."

"Miss Kent, no?"

"No."

Adrian was confident that the case against him was going nowhere. The investigation dragged on with no conclusive evidence as to why the car had been bombed, and he believed even Barker eventually concluded that it may indeed have been a misplaced bomb of the PLO, or some other disgruntled organization. However, both he and Mikolos admitted to Adrian, that even if Tiriach was acting on behalf of one of these organizations, his assassination had yet to be explained. It seemed unlikely that he had been killed in retaliation for the bombing. Adrian countered by suggesting that Tiriach might have been shot because he had been identified in the bombing, and his organization could not take the chance of him revealing who they were.

But it was obvious to Adrian that after interrogating both he and Fiona, the investigators were unable to confirm a positive link between either of them and Tiriach.

Adrian was uncertain at first as to whether or not Fiona had identified Tiriach. He was reassured when he realized that if she recalled seeing Tiriach, she apparently had not disclosed to the detectives the fact that they had met in the pub in Yorkshire, or that there was any significant connection between him and the dead man.

Adrian was confident that Fiona was divulging very little information about him to the authorities. He certainly owed her a debt of gratitude. He hoped that at some time in the not too distant future, he could enlist her upon his team. If that never transpired, at least he was making the best of the attempt; he could easily love her.

He attended the races on several occasions as the season wound down. The days became shorter, and so did Fiona's response when he insisted she join him for dinner, a theatre, or even have a drink with him on the racecourse. She was cool but polite when they talked by telephone and even offered a friendly smile when they bumped into each other on one occasion at the races, but she continued to resist any further social contact.

Dantes ran several times, winning two more races with Eddie Handley in the saddle before the season ended and winter set in. Adrian attempted to persuade Timothy Rand to give Fiona the mount, but the trainer, although not aware of the events that had led Fiona into distancing herself from Adrian, nevertheless sensed her reluctance to ride Dantes and never gave her the call.

Adrian was feeling increased pressure from his activities both abroad and, to a greater degree, at home. He knew why the attempts upon his life had been made and took extreme measures to insure his own protection.

He continued to rent when he was in England rather than buy a replacement for the bombed car, and never kept the same one for more than two days. It seemed unlikely that this precaution would throw off a determined assassin, but as a precaution, or if there were any doubt in his mind, he would take a taxi and leave the car to be picked up by an unsuspecting rental agency.

Despite strict British gun control laws prohibiting the possession of handguns, he was never without a light weight snub-nosed .38 revolver concealed in an underarm holster when wearing a coat, or strapped to his lower leg as an alternative.

Eventually he found that he was spending more of his time traveling, in part due to his connections overseas giving him more latitude to conduct his operations than had been granted him in England. He welcomed the liberal American gun control laws, knowing that if he were to be detained by authorities with a firearm in his possession, it was unlikely that he would be asked too many embarrassing questions. The Americans, he concluded, were pretty cavalier about their right to carry firearms, but he never carried one when boarding an aircraft. He always left his weapon in an airport locker when he traveled and retrieved it upon his return. It was a safe and simple procedure.

Over the winter, he spent most of his time in Miami, enjoying the warm weather and occasionally attending the races. He had considered bringing Dantes to Florida so at least he would have the pleasure of watching him race.

With this still a consideration by early spring, Adrian went to the trouble of discussing such a possibility with an American acquaintance that was familiar with racing.

By then, although no longer in contact with Fiona, he occasionally entertained a passing dream of how things might have turned out if they had continued their relationship.

CHAPTER 14

Before the winter rains had come and the leaves had fallen, the English countryside had turned to a blaze of red, orange, and yellow foliage. No matter how inspiring the colors of the season had become, something for which she always had an appreciation, Fiona began dreading the approach of the cold winter days. Since her dislocated friendship with Adrian, she had committed so much of herself to racing and her work with horses that once again her social life had become almost non-existent. As the gold of autumn turned to the gray of winter, the end of racing diminished the focus of her life. The shadows became longer, and the pervasive sense of gloom that began to settle over her became deeper. At the end of each day, returning to her once sun filled cottage of summer, this refuge was being transformed into a retreat of shadows.

The telephone calls and visits to her parents' home in the south of England became longer and more frequent. After the last of the races were run and Fiona had only an occasional horse to ride during morning training hours, she welcomed the opportunity to drive down to the old Georgian house not far from the battlements of Arundel Castle.

Her father, Peter Kent, was on the latter side of middle age, slightly stooped from long hours at the desks of the academic world. His shock of white hair was always a little too long and invariably untidy, suggesting no concession to vanity in his personality. His slim frame and chiseled handsome face was well creased with lines emanating from the corners of gentle brown eyes behind wire-rimmed glasses. Semi-retired, he spent much of his time hiking through Arundel Park and neighboring woods, while Jenny, his wife of twenty odd years, was constantly occupied with charity work for museums and wildlife conservation. She was still beautiful with slightly gray streaked, fair hair, and so much like Fiona, her only daughter, that when they were together they were often mistaken for sisters despite more than twenty years between them. She had married Peter after he had earned a doctorate in paleontology. Twelve years separated them, but regardless, they decided to have children only after his professional career had been established in teaching. Their only other child, Robert, was six years junior to Fiona.

The agrarian life-style that absorbed most of their time complimented their devotion to sailing. On many occasions when they would take their little yacht out off the south coast of England, Fiona would take the opportunity to join them.

"Going down to the boat in the morning. Why don't you come and join me, Fi?" her father telephoned one early December evening. "Your mother says it's too cold to be out on the water, but if you come on down we could either go out for a short sail or motor up the river. All the tourists have gone and the weather has been fine. What about it?"

"Dad, you should have taken the boat out of the water last month," she scolded. "You're mad, but if you're game, I am."

She drove down to Little Hampton the next morning, meeting her father at the Yacht Club for lunch. By the time they had taken a quick bite to eat and gone out to the mooring, the wind had kicked up to become a minor gale.

"You know, I'm getting a bit too old for this stuff after all," her father confessed. "Shall we just motor up the river and have your mother meet us for a cup of tea?"

This sensible alternative to a stormy afternoon's sail only whetted Fiona's appetite to spend more time on the water, particularly with Peter and Jenny. She loved the sea and from earliest childhood some of her fondest memories were of sailing on the Solent with her parents and her brother, Robert. The cold winters of England and their advancing age, however, were now limiting the amount of time that her parents would enjoy their boat. The prospect of having to give up sailing before many more seasons passed by was beginning to be a reality that they were reluctant to face.

It was late afternoon by the time the three of them sat at the window of a dockside tea shop, looking out at the wind blown waves of the river and their little boat tugging at its mooring. Fiona, regretting the lost summer on the water, became suddenly inspired.

"I've got a great idea," she declared. "I'm going to take all of you cruising in the Caribbean as a Christmas present. Robert gets out of school for three weeks at Christmas, doesn't he, so we can all leave as soon as he gets home. What do you think of that?"

Her parents both laughed, protesting that it would be far too expensive. They couldn't possibly do that.

"I made a little money this summer riding, and have no one to spend it on," she insisted. "So that's it, you have no excuse, you can't back out!"

They spent the rest of the afternoon discussing the idea.

"Oh, you'd get so bored with us along, dear," her mother objected. "Why don't you go with some of your friends?"

"Mother, I've been too wrapped up all summer with racing. There's absolutely no one that I'd rather be with than you."

She made no mention of Adrian, but nevertheless, wondered fleetingly what it would be like to spend time with him on an extended vacation, far from his dangerous occupation and crazy way of life.

By the time Fiona and her father left to sail back to the boat slip in the marina, they had all agreed that it would be a wonderful holiday, and since Fiona insisted, they would all do it together. Her mother, sensing the gloom that had descended upon Fiona over the last several weeks, was relieved to see her animated with enthusiasm for an adventure.

"Where do you think you want to go?" her father asked.

"Oh I don't know exactly, but I'll work it out. We can spend a couple of weeks sailing in the sun."

Two days after Christmas, the Kent family was deplaning in St. Thomas, the U.S. Virgin Islands. The warm, gentle breeze from the Caribbean Sea was an agreeable contrast to the bitter winter winds of England. The slow pace of passport inspection and customs examination set the tone for the unhurried two weeks the family was to enjoy. After checking into their marina hotel, they spent the late afternoon strolling among the many shops of Charlotte Amalie, amazed at the variety of baubles available to bargain hunting tourists.

The ancient port had been, until late in the 19th century, a market place for slaves imported from Africa. The products of their servitude had been rum, spices, and sugar that were traded between merchants and mercenaries of the Americas and Europe. The value of these staples and luxuries had been partially responsible for war between countries from both continents.

The most notorious pirates in history sailed the Caribbean seas, conducting systematic murder and mayhem in the name of their countries, but more often plundering for their personal enrichment. Eventually, a lasting peace had come to the islands as a result of the abolition of slavery enforced by the British, and the expulsion of many sugar plantation owners in a subsequent black uprising.

With the exception of a few modern hotels and luxurious homes of the affluent winter visitors from frigid parts of North America and Europe, not much had changed over the last hundred and fifty years in terms of architectural development. The narrow cobblestone streets and ancient brick and native stone buildings remained as testimony of a far different era.

After an overnight stay in their hotel, the Kents boarded the forty-foot yacht that they were to charter. Provisioning, and a briefing by the charter company on navigation and the operating systems of the yacht, took up most of the morning. By noon they were on their way under a cloudless cerulean sky, the sails full and drawing to the warm, winter trade winds from the southeast. By late afternoon, they had dropped anchor for the night off a virginal beach, its sand turning to gold, bathed by the descending sun. Within minutes, Fiona and Robert were in the water snorkeling over a coral reef, while Peter and Jenny stowed gear before relaxing in the cockpit with tall tropical drinks.

For two days the family lazily occupied their time by sailing, beach combing upon pristine beaches and swimming in warm, crystalline water. They occasionally stopped at some outpost of civilization for an eclectic meal, a change from those that were prepared on board the yacht. By the third day they were ready to welcome some other human contact and invited two young men that had anchored next to them to come aboard for evening cocktails. This particularly pleased Jenny, although when Peter initially struck up a conversation with the two youths, Fiona suspected his invitation was more for her benefit than any other reason.

One of that evening's guests was Mark McLennan, an American veterinarian in his late twenties whose sailing companion was Tony Simpson, a friend from their college days. Both accepted with pleasure the Kent's invitation to come aboard.

Mark had an infectious, booming laugh that displayed perfect teeth below a slightly deviated broad nose, a trophy from his days of playing varsity ice hockey. His wide brown eyes displayed squint lines around the corners, and his mass of dark hair, streaked blond in part by the sun, topped a muscular, athletic frame of medium height.

His friend was tall, very blonde, introverted and scrawny, presenting a profound contrast in both appearance and personality. They had also been cruising around the islands and were both obviously happy to enjoy a drink with strangers.

"We're going ashore this evening, would you guys like to join us?" Mark asked, stirring his drink with his finger. "The bar on the beach has a reggae band coming in tonight."

"Fiona and Robert I'm sure would enjoy that but you must

stay with us for dinner," Jenny replied, with a sideward glance at Fiona.

Fiona, who never appreciated anyone speaking for her, colored noticeably. "Oh, you don't have to do that," she protested. "We're only having some old lamb-kabobs, that are probably goat anyway. I've been delegated to cremate them over the barbecue."

"That'd be great! If it's a choice between goat or Tony's chicken, I'll speak for us both," Mark boomed. "We'll stay!"

The setting sun slowly sank below the horizon with a glorious crimson blaze. Before the light had faded entirely, the Kents and their newfound friends beached their two dinghies in front of a collection of palm-thatched huts. The bar which was the focal point of the settlement, was nothing more than a driftwood shack with a palm thatched roof covering a sand floor, but the steel band was as inspiring as the exotic rum concoctions that were served. Several yachts were anchored just off shore with their crews, mostly young, gyrating to the steel band while crowding onto what passed for a dance floor.

Halfway through the evening, Peter and Jenny excused themselves and took their dinghy back to the yacht. The two Americans kept Fiona on the dance floor, monopolizing her attentions to the envy of the locals and visitors alike. Robert found an abundance of young women from every boat in the harbor and of all nationalities to dance with and exchange shouted conversation above the din. The natural reserve of people in a conventional social setting evaporated quickly on the beaches of the Caribbean, particularly when lubricated with the island drinks and native music.

Shortly after midnight, under bright stars that slid between wisps of drifting cloud, Fiona and Robert were dropped off at their boat amid boisterous singing, laughter, and a promise for the two yachts to raft up at the next anchorage. As the dinghy pulled away toward his yacht, Mark, in a good imitation of the native dialect, could be heard above the noise of the outboard motor. "Mon," he sang, "she is boooootiful!"

Fiona missed Tony's reply, but Robert grinned and whispered, "Who the hell is he talking about?"

The next few days passed quickly as the Kents and the young Americans raced each other from island to island, rafting up and generally spending their time together. Fiona, Robert and the two Americans spent hours snorkeling and wind surfing in the clear, tepid sea. Peter and Jenny often walked upon secluded beaches and occasionally went farther ashore to investigate the ruins of ancient derelict sugar mills, overgrown with tropical vegetation among long deserted plantations.

The natural ease with which Mark and Fiona were drawn to each other was evident to her parents. They knew nothing of her relationship with Adrian but had sensed a melancholy over several weeks that was out of character with her usual cheerful disposition. Not wanting to pry into her private affairs, they had avoided any inquiry.

They discovered that Mark, although having grown up in the mid-west, was a veterinarian with an equine practice in New York. Only four years out of university, he now worked exclusively with Thoroughbred racehorses. However it was clear that horses were not the sole reason for Fiona and Mark's interest in each other. By the end of ten days they were frequently seen to be wandering off, often out of sight around the bend of some remote beach.

It was on one of these occasions, while both of them were resting upon a large beach towel, warming in the sun, that Mark rolled over onto his back, his hands behind his head.

"You know, Fiona," he said, "this has been the most wonderful few days that I can remember."

"Why, because you didn't have to eat Tony's cooking all the time?" She refused to get into a serious conversation with him, unable to remove Adrian very far from her thoughts.

Mark handed her a tube of sunscreen and rolled over onto his stomach. "Yep, that and because you're so good at rubbing sunscreen on my back," he said. "Would you mind doing it again?"

She straddled the back of his thighs and started to rub lotion into his back, running her fingers over firm muscles. He groaned aloud and reached back to run his hand up her thigh.

"Enough of that, you horny sap," she laughed, jumping up, throwing the tube of lotion at him. "You need to cool off. The last one in's a horse's butt!"

She took off sprinting down the beach, Mark trailing behind. She had no trouble reaching the water first, but he was a step behind as they both dived into the sea. They came up laughing and throwing water at each other until he caught her and shoved her under. When she came up spluttering and flailing at him, he grabbed her arms and pulled her into an embrace, kissing her hard on the lips. After a moment of resisting, half-heartedly trying to push him away, she slid her hand behind his head and holding him tenaciously, returned the kiss.

After a while, they parted and still holding each other, searched within each other's eyes.

"What happens when this trip is over, Fiona?" he asked as they waded ashore, holding hands.

"I don't know. I don't want to think about it," she replied, frowning and shaking her head.

"Would you like to come and see me in America?"

She was slow to answer. "I don't know Mark, I have a lot to sort out at home. Things are complicated at the moment and you don't make it any easier."

"Is it someone back there?"

He was persistent if not subtle, she thought. But she knew that to be fair to him, she had to be blunt.

"Mark, I have a friend," she began as they both flopped upon the beach towel, "who I care about a lot. I don't understand him or even what he does, but I must admit that I have become emotionally involved with him."

Mark said nothing, but propping himself on one elbow, turned to look at her. She avoided his eyes and lying on her stomach, appeared to be examining the sand, drawing patterns in it with a finger as she spoke.

"I think he's serious about me," she continued, "but there have been some things that have happened that have put a big dent in our relationship."

"Then come to America with me. Ditch the guy."

"Mark, I can't. I can't tell you more than that, but when I get home and spend a little time away from both of you, I'm sure I'll know then what I should do."

He offered no further argument. Rolling over onto his back, he put his hands behind his head and gazed up into an empty sky. Neither of them said anything for a long time. Fiona continued to draw in the sand until she drew a face with a mouth turned down at the corners.

"Is this you?" she asked, quietly.

He rolled over and looked at it. "Yep, that's me," he replied with a weak smile. "Let's go back to the boat and join the others. I need a tall, strong drink."

Days of perfect sailing often ended with dancing in the late hours to native bands on remote island beaches, fringed with palm trees and coral reefs. The blazing sun was tempered by cooling trade winds and occasional warm, winter squalls that refreshingly drenched everyone and everything for the few minutes that they lasted. Friendly natives sold the sailors mangos, bananas, and other fresh tropical fruit. Spectacular sun-splashed beaches washed by crystalline, warm water under almost cloudless skies, presented images that were happily absorbed by the visitors from cold northern shores. The magic of the Caribbean worked its spell as crews of both boats were drawn to each other, many inhibitions vanishing as easily as their winter pallor.

The English family and the two Americans sailed their yachts with skill, covering ocean miles during the day and anchoring in friendly harbors at night. Fiona and Robert handled the running rigging while Peter spent much of his time at the helm of their boat, and Jenny read charts and provided the necessary navigation to avoid any threatening reefs. Mark and Tony occasionally shanghaied Robert or Fiona to crew for them, but shared most of the sailing duties between each other.

After several days of sailing, the entire group chartered a scuba diving boat and took a side trip to Anagada, an island known for thousands of wrecks on its barrier reefs. The waters were shallow, making no special demands upon the inexperienced divers although Mark and Tony were certified experts. Both, as part of their university studies, had spent a summer at the Scripps Institute of Oceanography in La Jolla, California, learning much of the fauna, fish and mammals of the sea.

Guided by native scuba divers, the group began to explore several of Anagada's ancient wrecks. Fiona, holding Mark's hand for most of the dive, was not entirely comfortable when confronted by anything larger than a small angelfish. Trailing behind the others, she reached out to him, pulling his powerful frame into her at the slightest provocation. In Fiona's mind, thousands of pounds of horseflesh traveling at forty miles an hour presented nothing like the danger that slippery sea-life could offer as it slowly slithered past. Besides, she enjoyed the close contact with Mark that the opportunity provided.

He responded by holding onto her, until they gradually fell behind the underwater guided tour. They eventually circled back to the deserted boat where they climbed aboard. Pulling off his gear first, he turned to Fiona to help extract her from the heavy compressed air-tank.

He slid the harness from over her shoulders, and by accident, pulled her bikini top down off her breasts. Searching his face for any sign, she slowly started to retrieve the top, but before she could, he pulled her into an embrace, kissing her, letting the diving gear slide to the deck, feeling for her naked breasts. After a few moments he gently pushed her away to stand there gazing down at her perfect form, with Fiona's head thrown back, her eyes closed.

Fiona slowly took his hand from her breast and kissed it, before replacing her bikini top. He was completely aroused and became embarrassed when she reached down and touched him.

"How do you do that?" she asked, smiling, gently stroking him and inflaming him even further.

"I don't, you do," he retorted, laughing quietly, pulling her hand away and parting from their embrace.

Only the threat of returning family members prevented their hunger for each other from consuming them entirely. They both turned away from each other to remove the remainder of their gear.

"I'm sorry, Mark. That was taking advantage of you, I'll never do that again." She was now serious, sitting across from him on the railing of the boat.

He ran his fingers through his hair and looked up into the sky, avoiding her eyes. "Don't apologize," he said quietly. "I shall remember that moment forever."

"Do you really mean it?"

"Absolutely."

"I hope so because it was something that I wanted to happen," she admitted. "But I don't want to hurt you."

The returning divers, snorting and burbling through the water, interrupted them. Mark, now fully composed, helped them aboard.

"You missed an incredible wreck," panted Robert as he climbed up on deck. "Where were you?"

"I just became nervous and didn't want to go any further," Fiona lied.

Robert made a face. "Gawd Fiona, you're such a wimp!"

On the last day of their charters, the crews returned their yachts to their respective home bases. Before they separated, they promised to keep in touch, not admitting that in the real world, the world of constant change from which they had been so insulated over the last two weeks, the probability was that they would never meet again. Peter and Jenny philosophically accepted the time they had all spent together as a blessing that, even if it were never to be repeated, they would cherish for the rest of their lives. Tony and Robert shook hands with a slap on the back, admonishing each other to "stay cool" and "hang loose", their optimism for the future far outweighing any nostalgic reminiscences of the past weeks.

For Fiona and Mark it was different. They both hoped that their meeting would result in a lasting friendship for the future, a friendship they intended to sustain, nevertheless fearful that they might drift apart.

"Will you write?" Fiona asked as she and Mark sat quietly away from the others on the bow of the family's boat.

"About what?"

"About nothing, you oaf!"

"Should I?" He knew the answer.

"You'd better!"

They spent much of their last hours together, saying very little, but communicating through more than words in a way that is a consequence of a strong bond and deep affection.

CHAPTER 15

Far from the sun-drenched Caribbean, at the crest of Warren Hill on Newmarket Heath, two men formed a faint silhouette against the pale yellow light of dawn. A crisp frost from the previous night whitened the expanse of the gently rolling hills. As the drifting morning mist unveiled a string of horses cantering up toward them, Timothy Rand turned to speak to the man beside him. Dressed in a tweed jacket, cavalry twill slacks and highly polished tan jodhpur boots, the military bearing of Rand could not have been more dissimilar to his companion Donald DeWitt, a diminutive figure huddled against the chill of early spring in an old faded windbreaker, well worn designer jeans and scuffed loafers.

Those who knew DeWitt uncharitably referred to him with more insight than affection as "Droopy", due to his stooped shoulders and shuffling gait. He had a sallow complexion with a narrow face prominently displaying a predatory nose and dark intense eyes behind horn-rimmed glasses. His stooped posture and long untidy hair gave him the appearance of a man with much worry upon his shoulders, which had aged him beyond his fifty odd years. He had established himself as an astute dealer in the racing world, and a little over twenty years prior, had graduated from law school with honors. An honor bestowed upon him of any kind seemed gratuitous in the judgment of many acquaintances that regarded the sharp featured and shrewd little man's integrity as being on the devious side of questionable.

The two men watched intently as the twenty or so horses galloped towards them, their nostrils flaring from heavy breathing induced by exertion, and their hooves thudding on the half frozen ground.

13263-RUSS

"The chap leading is Dantes. He won four races last year as a two-year-old," Rand advised. "He's the one you want."

DeWitt shrugged the collar of his windbreaker higher up around his ears and squinted at the approaching horses.

"He won't win a classic for us over here this spring," Rand continued, "but he's a lovely horse and a good mover. He'll certainly have enough speed for America."

"He moves okay," DeWitt agreed.

"He's wintered well," Rand went on, "and if he could stay sound on the hard ground we had last summer, and he certainly did that, he'll do very well for you in America. Quite honestly, I can't understand why the owner wants to sell him."

"He looks pretty sound, so I think he'll have a chance," the American grudgingly admitted. "But you're asking too much for him."

"That's rubbish and you know it. He'll win a good race for you. And anyway," Rand turned to DeWitt with a wry smile, "two hundred thousand dollars is nothing to an American breeder. You chaps pay twice that much just for a stud fee!"

DeWitt secretly agreed, but he felt compelled to make a token effort to beat the price down. He was not going to make a fat commission on this one, although Rand was not aware that DeWitt was not buying the horse for himself. It went against the grain and out of character for DeWitt not to quibble over the price.

After going through a contentious divorce settlement two years previously, DeWitt had discontinued his law practice and concentrated upon operating his small farm, accommodating a few of his own moderate horses and a handful of boarders. Earnings from this enterprise were more difficult to document than those that would be derived from closely regulated legal work, giving DeWitt the excuse to deny much of his income from the insatiable appetite of his covetous ex-wife.

The dozen or so horses had now cantered past, and the two men turned to walk back across the heath to Rand's car.

"What about Monte Cristo, the horse I looked at yesterday?" DeWitt asked. "What about throwing him in to sweeten the pot?"

Rand looked sideways at the little man shuffling along beside him. "He isn't much good to us here," he said at length, "and I would think the same of him over there, but he's safe and quiet and useful for me to train the apprentice riders on. I can't let you have him for nothing."

DeWitt was not put off. He had no doubt that he would buy the horse for his client but was also careful not to press the point at that moment. A short time later, as they drove back to Rand's stables, he broached the subject again.

"I'd like you to reconsider," he insisted. "I really do need to pick up the pair together."

"I'll tell you what I can do," Rand was becoming exasperated; this was the second day of bargaining. "If you take Dantes for two hundred thousand, I'll throw in Monte Cristo for ten thousand dollars, but why you would want such a cheap horse over there at any price is beyond me."

DeWitt shrugged. "I want him for a traveling companion for Dantes, that's all."

"He's only won one little race in the south of Ireland," Rand warned. "I know they look alike and are by the same sire, and even owned by the same chap, but they're two different animals altogether."

DeWitt, unaffected by Rand's increasing irritability, made what he hoped sounded like his final bid although he was quite prepared to pay full price. "Alright, make it ten thousand for Monte Cristo and you pay his shipping to New York and it's a deal. I'll just take a chance on him. What do you say?"

Rand swung the Bentley into his yard with undisguised annoyance. Unaccustomed to quibbling over a few pounds, he was anxious to get rid of this irritating little sod.

"You drive a hard bargain DeWitt, but if we can wrap this up this morning, and get you on your way, it's a deal."

Several days later, Dantes was shipped to the United States without his "traveling companion", Monte Cristo, the latter being taken instead to another stable in England. Timothy Rand, aware of the misrepresentation made by DeWitt of the two horses traveling together, was nevertheless disinclined to challenge him on the matter, putting it down to a ruse by the American to reduce the price of a cheap horse. Rand was reluctant to pay the shipping fee on Monte Cristo to New York, but did so in keeping up his end of the bargain. "Bloody American crook!" he grumbled.

It was on a later flight, and several days after Dantes had landed in New York, that Monte Cristo arrived at Kennedy Airport with a different shipment of horses. DeWitt had not made a commission on the purchase of either horse; he had an unusual arrangement with his client. But he had persuaded Rand to pay the shipping on Monte Cristo without the purchaser's knowledge. DeWitt would bill his client for the shipping and stick at least that amount in his own pocket.

Monte Cristo was checked through quarantine with the usual formalities, including being identified for the Jockey Club. The same arrival procedures had been imposed upon Dantes, but a week earlier: customs clearance, identification papers examined, blood samples taken for testing, and forty-eight hours of quarantine in the Department Of Agriculture facility. Eventually both horses were once again stabled within the same barn, at DeWitt's farm on Long Island. Only two other people knew that DeWitt, through clever manipulation of almost identical registration papers, had switched the identity of both horses.

Within weeks of their arrival, Jockey Club registration certificates were issued, with a description of each respective horse. A serial number was issued to each, printed upon the papers and later tattooed on the inside of their upper lips, indelibly marking them for life. The certificates also named the sires and dams of each horse, this information being catalogued in the British and American Stud Books. In addition, on the back of the registration certificates were the racing records of each respective horse, showing how many and what class of races each animal had won. The authorities were unaware that the dubious record of Monte Cristo, his name and his identity, was now credited to Dantes, and vice-versa.

Donald DeWitt counted upon the fact that the internationally accepted but archaic system of identifying racehorses had occasionally led to mistakes. Because the methodology was not an exact science, it had also, on rare occasions, opened the door to mistakes and even devious practices. This was one of those occasions.

Both horses went into light training on DeWitt's farm some thirty miles east of Gateway Park. The period of time for acclimation to their new home was not difficult since the climatic conditions of New York and England were similar during the month of March. Both horses started to shed their winter coats as they progressed in their training. They were subjected to mile after mile of steady gallops before they eventually progressed into faster work that then required them to be moved to the racetrack. By April, the arrival of the warmer spring weather coincided with the progression of their training; they were ready to go into the racetrack at Gateway Park.

Vincent Cinotti was a shrewd businessman, and generally regarded with profound respect by the handful of people that knew him. A few of his associates had died prematurely, the result of, as he put it, "the pressures of business". His official residence seemed to be his car, a mobile and elusive address that neither the sheriff nor even the mailman could easily locate. He occasionally stayed at cheap hotels, but never for more than a single night, not unusual with the clientele of hostels of this type. Under a fictitious name, he also rented a small apartment that was used for any business that could not be conducted on the street. He had one telephone, a cellular, of which only the privileged or the recently departed would have the number. Cinotti considered Donald DeWitt, for the moment at least, a fortunate member of the former category: privileged.

It was on a cheerless spring morning at the tail end of a gray winter that the two men sat huddled in a corner booth of a seedy diner along Jericho Turnpike, a mile or so from Gateway Park. It was crowded with mostly blue-collar workers fortifying themselves for another day of labor. Between the clatter of dishes and loud conversation, it seemed unnecessary for Cinotti and DeWitt to speak in furtive tones, but they clearly had no wish to be overheard.

"Where'd you take this horse, Droopy?" inquired Cinotti.

"DeWitt please," the older man snapped testily. "Don if you like."

"I want to take a look at him. I like to see the horses train," explained Cinotti, undeterred.

"Look, you've got to stay away. You can't be seen anywhere near the horse. The question of ownership could come up and I don't need that."

"Don't make no mistake about who owns him." Cinotti was threatening.

"Don't worry, I know that. Anyway, we're going to make a big buck so just be patient. We're in good shape."

"Good shape? You telling me to be patient? If you don't show me somethin' soon, you ain't goin' to be in no good shape. I can easily find another partner."

"Damn it Vince, there's no problem, just relax," Dewitt protested pushing an omelet around his plate with almost no interest in eating. Unlike his companion, he had little appetite.

Cinotti was enjoying watching DeWitt squirm, and anticipated with relish the day when their relationship might become more "intimate". He liked that word, and used it frequently when he would describe how he would impose his will upon an unfortunate associate. The perpetual grin and easygoing manner belied the fact that Cinotti had a reputation for being brutally efficient in his business dealings.

Youth and Mediterranean good looks gave little hint of his accomplishments. He was tall and slim with well-oiled, curly black hair above dark eyes, a straight, narrow nose and a congenial smile. His dark suit was expensive and severely cut, hanging fashionably loose and concealing his muscular frame. He was of the opinion that he was irresistible to women, and liberally dispensed his affections among them.

"The best I can do is give you a copy of the insurance policy on the horse," DeWitt continued, leaning even closer. "You're the co-beneficiary on the policy, so you're covered. You'll make a score on this, I give you my word."

"Your word?" Cinotti said grinning through a mouthful of bacon and eggs.

DeWitt winced and shifted uncomfortably in his seat. "Look, we've only had the horse here for a couple of months, and if anything happened to him immediately after being insured, it would stink up the whole deal. You've got to be cool."

"You'll be more than cool, you'll be on ice if nothin' don't happen soon."

Cinotti chased his mouthful with a gulp of hot coffee, came up for air, and sat back in his seat.

"Okay, I'll cool it for now, but I want to see that insurance stuff," he continued, belching and wiping his mouth on the back of a manicured hand.

"I'll get a copy to you in the mail."

Cinotti slowly shook his head. "Uh, huh, nothin' through the mail."

"Okay, okay," DeWitt protested as he got up. "I can meet you here tomorrow with it." He was drooping more than usual as he paid the bill and headed out the door.

"Tomorrow, same time." Cinotti had enjoyed his meal, particularly since he had stuck DeWitt with the check. "Bill me for breakfast," he laughed.

CHAPTER 16

The sublime warmth of the Caribbean had fortified Fiona with new energy and a fresh outlook by the time that she had returned to England. Riding work for her several racing stables was yet to begin in earnest, so she had ample time to spend with her family. However, thoughts of both Adrian and Mark were never far from her mind.

Adrian had called on several occasions during his periodic trips back to England, and although they had talked at length, Fiona had resisted the temptation of seeing him. She could not deny that she missed him, but nevertheless continued to vacillate between distrust and infatuation.

Mark phoned within days of his return to New York, dispelling any remaining doubts concerning how he felt about her.

"I miss you terribly," he said. "I love you and want you to come to New York."

"Oh yes, just drop everything and trot off to New York. Mark, you're mad, I couldn't do that," she protested without certainty.

"If you don't, I'll come to England and kidnap you."

"Well I'd agree to half of that."

"Which half? The kidnap half?"

"No, that's negotiable" she replied. "Come to England first and we'll talk about it."

Several days later, it was Adrian that phoned, once more insisting that they get together.

"Why don't you come up to London for dinner and a show?" he asked. "It's time we got together. I don't expect you'd want to stay over, but it would be lovely if you would."

Fiona was at a point where she felt that her independence had returned; she was beginning to feel less threatened than curious about their relationship.

"Adrian, you've not made it easy for me, you know that. I care too much about you, but I don't understand you," she said. "I would like to see you without any emotional ties, but you must accept that."

"Well that's up to you Fi."

"I know, but you have to avoid the sort of event that has come between us in the past, and I'm certainly not going to jump into any compromising situations again."

"I promise that I am getting things worked out, Fiona. We can see each other and nothing will happen, I promise."

"Nothing? That's a bit ambiguous."

"Well, you're not going to get murdered and, as I said, the rest is up to you."

There was a long silence. Adrian's insistence was a red flag, yet Fiona was still reluctant to turn him down.

"Come on Fi," he continued. "Trust me, what has happened with us is history."

"I can't believe that you're mixed up in all that political nonsense. You can't just shrug that off, and honestly Adrian, I just don't want to continue feeling involved."

Adrian took a deep breath, he sounded exasperated. "You don't need to worry about that, you just happened to be in the wrong place when a couple of things happened that were beyond my control. Give me another chance."

Another long silence. Fiona was unable to deny her attraction to Adrian, but was now resolute about not continuing a deeply personal relationship. She had made love to him in a lighter moment, and realized how much that had meant to her. But she was determined not to let that happen again; she would resist any intimacy that he might show toward her.

"Very well Adrian, but if you'd like to meet for dinner then you can come down here."

"Great," he replied without hesitation.

"I'm staying with my parents, though."

"That's okay, Fi, whatever you wish. What about tomorrow evening?"

Fiona gave instructions how to find the house. They rang off, and immediately she had misgivings for not putting him off, reproachful of herself for being easily manipulated again.

Adrian arrived the following evening, exuding his usual charm. After introductions were dispensed with, he politely declined an invitation to join Peter and Jenny for a cocktail, and proceeded to usher Fiona out to his car.

As they drove away, Fiona wondered if her reservations about seeing Adrian were unfounded. She knew it would be easy to make love to him again that night, but she also knew that the events of the past would continue to haunt her.

The evening passed pleasantly with them dining and dancing to romantic music. The conversation was cordial if not intimate, but a sense of finality to their relationship began to creep in upon Fiona. Driving home about midnight, she reflected upon the time that she had spent with Mark in the Virgin Islands. Different settings and vastly different people; the gregarious Mark so dissimilar to the calm, sophisticated Adrian. She hesitated to commit to either of them, and even wondered if she could ever really love either of them?

"You seem a little distant, Fiona. Is it something that I have said?" Adrian asked as they drove through the dark country roads.

She took his arm and moved toward him to lay her head upon his shoulder. "I'm sorry, Adrian, it's not you. I've enjoyed the evening. Thank you."

"When can we do it again?" he asked very quietly as if sensing the answer.

She did not reply immediately. "I don't know, Adrian. I don't even know how I feel. At this moment I never want to let you go, but I honestly don't know where I'm going."

They drove on for a short time before he spoke again. "I love you, Fiona. I don't want to take you home. Why don't you come up to London and stay with me?"

Again there was a long pause. She squeezed his arm and pulled closer to him, but did not answer.

"Fiona, let me take you away. Now. I want you to come with me. Will you?"

Again she wavered before answering, but at last said, "You know I can't. Not now, and perhaps never."

She wanted to love him, but the shadow of suspicion constantly gnawed at her faith in him. She loved his touch, and the sensation of touching him. She loved his strength and impeccable manners; his beautiful dark eyes when he looked into hers, and the touch of his sensitive hands when he caressed her. But was he always surrounded by violence, or even innately cruel himself, or were the circumstances of his profession distorting her view of him? Whatever, the specter of doubt was constant.

"How do I know I could always love you knowing so little about what you do?" she said after a long silence. "I can't commit to you, not now, Adrian. I'm sorry."

He fell silent. They drove the rest of the way without talking, until he pulled up in front of her parents' house. He walked her to the door where she kissed him, then gently but firmly, pushed him away.

"Thank you, Adrian," she said, and slipped through the door, wondering if she would ever kiss him again.

She leaned against the door within the refuge of the house, and stood with eyes closed, an ache in her chest far bigger than her heart. She held her breath, listening to the sound of his car as it crunched upon the gravel driveway, fading into the distance.

Spring was slowly replacing the gray mantle of winter in England, bringing with it the rebirth of life and a renewal of the joy of riding that Fiona had let slide into a melancholy indifference. Trainers were calling her with requests for her to ride work in preparation for the new racing season. Although she was answering the phone more frequently, a message from Adrian on her answering machine had gone unanswered. After wavering with uncertainty, she decided not to return his call. She did, however, talk to Mark by the hour, pleased by his attention and the distraction from thoughts of Adrian. Then, in the middle of April, Mark called to say he was on his way to England.

"I leave tonight and I'll be coming into Heathrow in the morning. What are you doing tomorrow evening?" he asked.

"Oh, I don't know. I'll have to check my social calendar and see how many dates I have," she replied. "I might be able to cancel some. Are you coming just to see me?"

"Of course, just to see you. I may take a few minutes to look at some horses one of my clients is paying me to examine though."

"So you're not coming just to see me at all, you're going to be looking at horses."

"Well sort of," he confessed, "but I want to spend most of my time looking at you."

"How long are you going to be here?"

"Four days."

"Where are you going to stay?"

"Don't know. What do you suggest?"

"You can't stay with me, I have only one bedroom."

"Oh, I see," he said, sounding disappointed.

Fiona met him at Heathrow shortly after noon the following day, and drove him up to Newmarket, checking him into the Bradford Arms. It was a small hotel, as comfortable as anything in the town of Newmarket, but his disappointment at not staying with her had not been lost on Fiona.

Later that evening she joined him at a cocktail party at the home of a local trainer, Roger Markham. She and the trainer were well acquainted, so for the sake of appearances if nothing else, she informed her host that she would drop Mark off at his hotel on the way back to her cottage.

"I can't stay too long, it's a long drive home," she apologized as an excuse for leaving early.

"You can stay over here if you would care to," Markham offered.

"Thanks, Roger, I must get home."

Fiona and Mark left the party in mid-swing, making the appropriate apologies to the other guests, and returning to his hotel. They stopped in the hotel bar for a nightcap where they found a quiet corner by the fireplace. They talked quietly, intimately reminiscing over the Caribbean holiday. Fiona recalled how much Mark had meant to her, and expressed how much she appreciated him at a time that had been so difficult for her.

"I knew you were having a tough time of it when I first met you," Mark said. "You seemed to change by the time you came home."

"Very perceptive. I have to admit I was not at my best," she admitted. "I needed a change. You came along at the right time."

"I'm back again, how's the timing?"

Fiona reached across the table and took his hand to her lips. "I don't know. It is great to see you though, I missed you."

It was very late, when by mutual yet unstated consent, they left the bar and went to his room, her arm linked through his and her head resting upon his shoulder. They kissed for a long time once they were inside the room. His hands slipped down to her waist, pulling her closer to him. She could feel him firm against her through the sheer silk of her clothes. She offered no resistance as he slowly unbuttoned her dress. They held each other for several minutes, kissing with increasing fervor, until eventually they moved across the room to lie upon the bed. Slowly they undressed each other, taking pleasure in the experience, exploring and caressing each other's inflamed bodies. Eventually they were naked, totally submissive to each other's wishes, desire overcoming any remaining discretion.

Fiona stayed until almost dawn, making love to him, and completely immersed in an unqualified commitment.

"I love you, Fiona. I love you and want you to marry me," Mark whispered as she lay beside him.

She knew in that instant that she could love Mark without reservation, forever. "Yes, oh yes," she whispered as if it were a secret only they would ever know. She kissed him again and again, fervently. She never wanted to release him.

With the break of dawn, when deep shadows were retreating into a brilliant morning, Fiona drove slowly home. She knew that it was the dawning of a new life, her heart lifted by unrestrained love for Mark and with hope for the future. The greening of the countryside under a warming spring sun orchestrated her irrepressible joy.

That afternoon, after Mark had examined horses in Roger's stable, Fiona returned to Newmarket to join him for a late lunch before checking him out of the hotel and driving with him back to her cottage.

"Am I on the couch tonight?" he asked when she reminded him that, indeed, there was only one bedroom.

"No you're not," she laughed. "There isn't room for both of us there."

When they arrived, she lit a roaring fire and opened a bottle of wine. They sat on the floor, propped up against the sofa, gazing into the crackling flames, talking quietly. Warmed by the influence of the wine and the fire that was dwindling to a mound of glowing embers, yet appearing ever brighter with the fading light of evening, they retreated to the bedroom.

The following morning, Mark rose early and telephoned his client in New York concerning the purchase of the horses that he had vetted. Fiona rode her old bicycle a mile into the village to shop while Mark took care of his reports. She returned and produced a few scrambled eggs, a rasher of country bacon, and fresh baked bread from the village bakery with farm butter and marmalade. Soon they were sitting outside on the patio under a warming sun, enjoying a late breakfast.

"I've already called my parents. They want us to come down and stay with them. Do you mind?" she asked Mark uncertainly.

"No of course not, they're good fun. I'd love to see them again. Did you tell them I've asked you to marry me?"

"No not yet, I wanted to spring that on them when we get

there. They certainly don't know we're sleeping together. We'll have to take separate rooms tonight." Looking apologetic, she smiled at him, and reached for his knee under the table.

"Oh no!" he moaned, making a face of mock horror. "But I suppose I must at least give the appearance of being respectable."

"That's something your going to have to work on," she teased. "They're pretty straight laced you know."

"No, they're a pair of pussy-cats. I know them better than you."

By nine, they were on their way in Fiona's little car, Mark's luggage and her overnight bag stuffed in behind them. Before noon they had stopped in London, where he insisted upon buying an engagement ring.

"I want to formalize our engagement," he said. "So this is your last chance to back out."

"Mmn," she pretended to consider. "Let me see the ring first, then I'll tell you."

By evening they had arrived at her parents' house where Peter and Jenny expressed delight at their visit. Later, when Mark asked if they would accept him as a son-in-law, neither Peter nor Jenny was in the least surprised.

"I knew from the first day," said Jenny, tears of joy welling up in her eyes. "Mothers always know these things."

Her father was not so intuitive. "Isn't it a bit soon?" he asked Fiona later when they were alone together. "I mean you've actually only known him a little over two weeks?"

"He's asked me to come to New York and spend a couple of months with him."

"Before you're married?"

"Yes, but Dad," she protested, "I know him and I love him. At least in New York we'll have time together before we're married, don't worry."

"We'd like you to be married here if you've made up your mind. We want you to take you're time but your mother would be shattered if you were not to be married here."

"We'll do that, I promise." She kissed him and hugged him. She held him for longer than she could ever remember.

Mark and Fiona left for Newmarket early the following morning so that the veterinary examinations could be completed on behalf of Mark's clients. Later, in a quiet moment, she asked Mark, "Do you think I would be able to do some riding in New York?"

It was still early in the year so if she decided not to stay in America, she knew that she would be able to return to England and pick up where she had left off. But the prospect of giving up riding was a possibility that she had, until then, refused to consider. She had no illusions about starting over again in a strange country; she knew it would be difficult if not impossible.

"I'm sure you'll have no trouble at all. There are just as many women jockeys in America as there are in England. Probably more. I'm sure you'll do well," Mark reassured her. He was aware that she would be giving up an important part of her life if she were unable to ride in races.

"You don't know if I'm any good or not. You've never seen me ride."

"With your looks baby, you'll knock 'em dead." He made eyes at her and warded off a playful punch.

"That's not the way I want it, and you know it!" she objected. "Anyway, some of the most successful women are as plain as peeling paint."

"I can't argue with that. But racing people like fast horses and fast women," he retorted. "Are you a fast woman?"

"You're incorrigible, you're never serious!"

The following day, Mark left for New York with plans for Fiona to follow as soon as she could wrap things up. The arrangements were for her to stay in New York in a bungalow out on Long Island that one of Mark's friends had for lease. The wedding date was to be set for late summer.

Between finishing her riding engagements, closing up her cottage and finalizing many other arrangements, Fiona had little time to dwell upon thoughts of Adrian. At least, she hoped, there would be a lasting friendship but no further emotional involvement. However, there was one piece of her life that she would leave behind with more poignant regrets. It was her old but beloved car.

"Robert, you can have Tally," she told her brother. "You'd bloody well better take care of her though."

"Well you drive the poor old thing like a lunatic," he protested. "I couldn't do worse than that. But I love you Fi; it's the nicest present you've ever given to me. I promise I'll be good to her."

CHAPTER 17

Mark, disoriented and through a hazy fog believed for a moment that he was still in England. He rolled over, pulled the bed covers and pillow over his head, wondering who could be phoning at such an hour, before even a hint of dawn. He knew with an intuitive dread that anytime after midnight phone calls to veterinarians invariably meant something terrible was happening to a horse.

The phone was persistent; the ringing continued with increasing urgency. Mark groaned and reached out in the dark to pick up the receiver.

"Hello. Doctor McLennan."

"Mark, this is Donald DeWitt." He sounded agitated. "You've got to get out here right away."

"Where are you?"

"Out at my farm."

"Damn it, Don, it's raining like hell and that's an hour's drive at best."

"Mark, this is an emergency."

"Oh God, Don, it's past midnight and I just got in from an emergency. Can't it wait until the morning?"

There was a pause before DeWitt answered.

"Look Mark, it's a bit tricky. It's the horse that I imported, Dantes. He's insured for over two hundred thousand, and he just stuck his hind leg through a door and bust it all to hell. We're going to have to put him down."

Mark groaned and propped himself up on one elbow, wide-awake, realizing that he was confronted with every veterinarian's nightmare. The prospect of driving for an hour out on Long Island in the middle of a cold, wet night in April was hardly appealing, but to administer the last rights to a dying horse made the exercise even less attractive.

"Is there any chance I can save him?"

"Not a chance Mark, it's a multiple compound fracture. Too many pieces and too much ligament and tendon damage, we could never stabilize it."

"Well, what's the point in me coming out?" Mark protested. "Why don't you get your local vet to put him down?"

"You're the insurance company's vet and I need to notify you before I do that." DeWitt was hoping for the instruction to go ahead.

Mark hesitated, weighing his options. Dewitt was hardly a favorite client but he had helped settle the estate of Mark's father shortly after Mark had first come to the racetrack. That had not been an entirely satisfactory situation, since he suspected that DeWitt had grossly overcharged him, but Mark nonetheless felt a debt of gratitude. DeWitt had also put in a strong recommendation on behalf of Mark that was largely responsible for him now being associated with the insurance company, an important part of Mark's growing business. It was time to return the favor.

"Look, Don, if there's any chance we can save him, I'll be out there in an hour."

"There's no chance, Mark."

"Okay, since you're sure I can't do anything for him go ahead and have your local vet put him down. I'll come out in the morning after I make my calls at the track and fill out the report. This is a little irregular, so keep it under your hat."

"Thanks Mark, thanks a lot. There's no use in letting the horse suffer because of a little technicality."

Mark could hear the relief in DeWitt's voice before he hung up. Although uneasy for not going by the book and examining the horse prior to a lethal injection being administered, Mark was even more relieved that he didn't have to spend the rest of the night on a mission to euthanize a suffering animal. The destruction of any horse, no matter how inevitable, was an unpleasant aspect of his profession. He rolled over, unable to get back to sleep.

What rotten luck, he thought, for old DeWitt. He really had no affection for the man, but owning and being responsible for a horse, particularly a valuable horse that had to be destroyed, was a soul wrenching experience that he would not wish upon anyone. Horses were always vulnerable to injury, but fortunately it was not often that catastrophic injuries occurred, even upon the racetrack. He always watched races with a sense of anxiety, particularly if he was familiar with either the horses or acquainted with their riders.

His mind drifted to Fiona, just down the road in their friend's bungalow. He wondered if she was asleep at that moment. He could imagine her alone in bed, the thought reducing him to a comfortable, sleepy euphoria. He thought back to last winter when they had met in the Caribbean. He still wondered at the extraordinary coincidence of two people, their lives involved in the improbable business of Thoroughbred racing, dropping anchor that afternoon in the same isolated cove. Two people involved in the same business, developing an intimate relationship, each from countries an ocean apart, meeting thousands of miles from their respective homes. It is enough to make one believe in divine providence, he mused.

Memories were still vivid of how they swam and snorkeled together, and how that first afternoon, at her parents' invitation, they had enjoyed a drink and twilight dinner before going ashore to an evening of dancing. He remembered how he had been fascinated by her beautiful, lithe body in shorts and tee shirt, moving in rhythm to reggae music at Foxy's bar, a captivating, joyful smile fixed upon a perfect face, so quick to laugh, as she danced barefoot in the sand. He would never forget that occasion after scuba diving when he had accidentally brushed her bikini top aside and exposed her incredibly beautiful breasts. That image of perfection had been imprinted upon his mind forever.

He reflected upon the trip that took him to England to vet a few horses for one of his clients. He wondered if that had not happened, if he would have ever seen her again. Perhaps another coincidence, but he knew on that first night at the little hotel in Newmarket that he loved her without reservation.

Now, weeks later, lying alone in his bed, he finally fell asleep, the fate of Dantes and the uncertainties of mortal life drifting slowly from his mind into peaceful obscurity.

The promise of summer in New York coincided with the promise of a new life for Fiona; she embraced them both. Skeletal trees, too long bleak from the icy cold of winter, were filling with foliage and new growth. Dogwoods, and masses of rhododendrons and azaleas were spreading magnificent color in banks along the country lanes of Long Island. Much as Fiona loved the rolling countryside of England, she appreciated the beauty and the pastoral setting of her new home. She wondered if everything in America, including nature, indulged in spectacular excesses of wealth.

She had rented a fisherman's bungalow, built in the Cape Cod style in the late 19th century. Typically white with green shutters, it looked out over Long Island Sound from Oyster Bay Cove. Small but comfortably restored by a friend of Mark's who had been transferred by his company to Hong Kong, it was leased to Fiona on a monthly basis.

She had wanted to live alone, at least for a few months, wishing to find some solitude and space between herself and Mark. She was very sure of how much she loved him but felt the total commitment should be by degrees. Her parents were particularly pleased with this arrangement, still wary of the fact that her engagement to Mark had been so unexpected, but during the recent weeks that Fiona had been in New York, the numerous phone calls back to her family had erased much of their apprehension.

She spent the mornings riding work for several of Mark's clients, and the afternoons with him as he treated horses and performed surgeries at his clinic. She found the intensity and excitement of American racing exhilarating, and although Gateway Park was geographically thousands of miles and esthetically a world

13263-RUSS

apart from the English countryside, she loved every inch of it. Between two and three thousand horses and almost as many people from all walks of life were compressed into the equivalent of a small village, teeming with frenetic activity. She had not for one moment regretted coming to New York, although Mark was concerned as to how she would adjust to leaving her relatively tranquil home in England. Giving up the comfortable familiarity of her previous home was compensated for to a large degree when she had been granted a few mounts in races, impressing both owners and trainers who quickly appreciated her ability.

She soon believed that she had the best of all worlds, Mark and riding races. Despite the concern of her parents, she was determined to make America, racing, and Mark, her future. Their lives had come together in a whirlwind of joyful events that pushed aside her feelings for Adrian, shifting oppressive uncertainty to the absolute knowledge that she was now safe with a man she could trust.

They spent evenings together whenever he was not out treating horses for some emergency. On ever increasing occasions she would stay over at his house, but it was one evening when she was alone that she rushed to answer the telephone, anticipating a call from Mark.

"Hello Fiona."

She caught her breath, her heart skipping a beat. "Adrian . . . " she stammered. "Adrian, where are you?"

"Here in New York, in the city. How are you?"

"I'm fine, how are you? What are you doing here?"

"Here on business but really looking for you," he replied. "You left England in a hurry."

Fiona paused, an unreasonable twinge of guilt rising.

"I'm sorry Adrian, I should have written. How did you find me?"

"I called your parents. They seemed happy to give me your number."

Fiona hesitated again. "Did they tell you I'm engaged?"

"They did, and I must say it came as a bit of a surprise to me, and I gather to them as well. Who is he?"

"Oh, he's someone I met some time ago," she hedged defensively. The last thing she wanted to do was have a discussion with Adrian about her relationship with Mark.

"What does he do?" Adrian persisted.

"He's a veterinarian here at Gateway Park." Fiona wanted to change the subject. "How long will you be here?"

"Only a couple of days, but I must see you. I really want to see you," he urged. "Can I pick you up for dinner tomorrow evening?"

Again there was a momentary pause, the old dilemma returning. Adrian was ever persuasive, but despite her affection for him, she was reluctant to be manipulated by him again.

"Adrian, you know my situation," she finally said with difficulty. "I can't do that, you must understand."

"Frankly, I don't. Am I not going to see you then?"

"Well that depends."

"On what?"

"Adrian, I am not going to start all over again with you, but if you insist, I could come into the city and meet you for lunch." She immediately regretted making even this concession.

"I do insist," he replied without hesitation. "What about tomorrow?"

"Very well, I'm sure I could arrange that." The tension was eased. "Where shall I meet you?"

"The Congressional Club, at noon?"

"How do I find it?"

He gave instructions and rang off.

Fiona sat for a long minute before slowly replacing the phone upon its receiver. She wondered what it was going to be like to meet Adrian again. Would she be as indifferent toward him when they met face to face as she felt at that moment, or would that all change and she once again fall under the influence of his personality as she had so easily done before? Damn him, she thought, why had she ever agreed to meet him? He always had his way.

She picked up the phone again and dialed Mark's number. "Mark, do you mind if I go into town tomorrow and meet an old friend for lunch?" She sounded apologetic. "He's visiting here from England."

"No, of course not. Why would you even ask?"

"I suppose I really don't want to go and hoped you'd say you do mind."

"Don't go if you don't want to, Fiona. You have to make up your own mind about that sort of thing ol' girl."

"Yes, of course. I shouldn't have thrown that in your lap. Wouldn't you like to come along?"

"I can't possibly tomorrow, Fi, but don't go if you don't want to."

"Well, I said I would go and meet him for lunch," she said with a sigh of resignation. "We were friends not long ago but it's all over now. I'd just as soon not see him, but it would be rotten to stand him up, so I'll go anyway."

"You don't have to explain to me, dear heart," he said, and then with a chuckle, "The wages of sin. Serves you right!"

Driving into Manhattan the following day, Fiona's apprehension over the impending meeting with Adrian intensified. Mark had been flippant about the "wages of sin" and although Fiona was faintly amused by his remark, she now worried that her next encounter with Adrian would again have a profound influence upon her life. The 'original sin' was the only offense that she had ever committed with Adrian, she thought; or was it?

Leaving the Northern Parkway and entering the gaping mouth of the Mid-Town Tunnel just heightened her anxiety. The descent into the lower depths of the earth seemed symbolic of the descent into the lower depths of her psyche. She felt guilty over terminating her affair with Adrian in the way that she had, but she was afraid that to confront him and reject him would be impossible. She thought that his constant, calm, self-assurance was probably the source of the control he had over her, and suspecting that that was true, she should have resented it. All of those feelings, her emotional attachment to him, his sexual attraction, and even an unfathomable sense that she had been somehow inadequate, were coming back to her as she entered the concrete canyons of Manhattan.

Fighting back the urge to turn around and go home, she mentally prepared herself to deal with his persuasive personality. While admitting to herself that she was always being too dramatic, she envisioned her involvement with Adrian as a two-edged sword: on one side the passion to which she had once been vulnerable, and the other, the risk that came with it. Either edge could cut her, and she was not prepared to bleed for him again. God, she thought, what a unbearably morbid idea.

A few minutes after leaving the tunnel she drove up to the Congressional Club, turned her car over to a valet parking attendant, and entered the lobby.

"Hello Fiona, good to see you." Adrian was waiting for her by the entrance to the restaurant, leaning casually against a stone pillar, arms folded. As usual he was impeccably dressed in a dark-gray suite, and Fiona was once again struck by his appearance as he came toward her.

"Hello Adrian," she said offering her hand. "Have you been waiting long?"

"A couple of months, actually," he replied with an engaging smile. "You look marvelous."

He was struck by the transformation of this self-assured beautiful young woman, who was no longer the diffident child of their first meeting almost a year earlier.

Fiona turned her head almost imperceptibly so that he kissed her gently upon the cheek. He hesitated for an awkward moment, and smiled again.

They were ushered into the restaurant and were seated at the secluded window table that Adrian had reserved. The room was elegant with copious floral arrangements, and although busy with the crowd of business people, it was an intimate setting and relatively private. Adrian ordered a bottle of Montrachet, not too cold.

13263-RUSS

The wine was poured while Fiona sat fiddling with her silverware, vaguely smiling, her inner turmoil well disguised, but intentionally avoiding Adrian's eyes. She was aware that he was watching her intently.

Finally, he raised his glass. "To us."

"Cheers."

He returned his glass to the table and placed his hand upon hers, fingering the engagement ring that she subconsciously had left exposed. "Why have you been avoiding me? You could at least have called before you left."

Fiona was ready for the frontal attack.

"Adrian, we live in two different worlds and to be honest, I didn't like being dragged into yours. I am sorry that I didn't call you or write, but I needed a clean break."

"Well you certainly did that."

"I was afraid to give you any encouragement, that would have been unfair to you. Besides, I had to get away before I became so involved with you that I would never escape."

"Escape, escape from what? You know I could protect you."

"Oh I know you could protect me from other people," she said earnestly. "But not from yourself. I thought that I loved you but I never knew you. I still don't."

"Suddenly I sound pretty ominous," he said, eyebrows raised, a quizzical smile flickering around his mouth. "I thought it was just the people that were after me that you were worried about. I didn't know I was so threatening."

"It was all of you. Particularly your friends, they scared me to death. And I was sure I would never really know you."

He released her hand and leaned back in his chair. Fiona searched his eyes, hoping to find some truth about him, but his usual cool gaze gave nothing away, no emotion, no anger, and no sympathy. Just the calm, imperturbable Adrian she would never understand.

After a few moments, he asked, "Shall I order for you?"

"Please do." Fiona attempted a smile and failing that, took a long sip of her wine.

Adrian ordered lobster salad for both of them. She appreciated the fact that he remembered it was a favorite of hers.

Anxious to relieve the growing tension, Fiona attempted to change the subject. "Have you been racing?"

"A little."

"What about Dantes, has he run yet?" she asked, now with genuine interest.

"I sold him, I needed the money. Anyway, he wasn't any fun, you didn't want to ride him any more." He sounded indifferent about the horse; she didn't know if he was sincere or not.

They talked in general terms about racing, Fiona deciding to avoid any further reference to Dantes. Although she was curious about the horse, she wanted to keep the conversation as impersonal as possible. An hour passed with only trivia discussed; how well Eddie Handley was riding; the growing deterioration of service on the airlines; the abysmal exchange rate of the British pound compared to the dollar; and the upcoming vote of confidence that the prime-minister had called for. Finally it was late afternoon and Fiona made excuses to leave to avoid the rush-hour traffic.

"Fiona, I wish you'd spend the day with me," Adrian said as the waiter brought the check. "There's a wonderful French impressionist exhibition in town."

"I'm sorry Adrian, I can't, that's impossible."

She was unyielding and hardly apologetic. By the time they had walked out to where the car was being delivered, he tried again. "You know there are great shows in town. I'm on my own, I wish you'd stay."

"Please don't Adrian. It has been a lovely lunch, thank you." She climbed into the car, smiling up at him, not wanting to refuse him again.

Resigned, he leaned through the open window, where again she turned her head, only to permit him to kiss her lightly on the cheek.

"When shall I see you again?" he asked stepping back.

"I can't make any promises Adrian, but I hope it's not too long. I would like us to remain friends."

He shook his head slowly, as much in resignation as in disagreement. She expected some comment but he made no other response. She waited a moment longer, managed a weak smile, and drove slowly away. She looked into the rear view mirror and saw him once more, the elegant figure, standing expressionless with his hands in his pockets. "Some closure," she thought, but there were no tears.

CHAPTER 18

The bustling, informal activity within the stable area of Gateway Park, on the surface, appears to be a paradox to the business that is conducted there. Transactions frequently involving hundreds of thousands of dollars are negotiated by casually dressed people in a setting that is a striking contrast to the offices of Wall Street. The old wooden barns, patched and repaired so many times, bare no resemblance to the modern glass, concrete and steel buildings of the conventional business world.

Beneath ancient sycamores, and tucked away on the bend of one of the many winding horse paths, is a tiny coffee shop known as Louie's Kitchen, where both the lowly and the mighty crowd around a few tables under the mist of steaming coffee and frying bacon.

In one corner, trainer Tommy Carrow, a short thick set figure with an old tweed cap and an Irish brogue, tilted his chair back, drew a deep breath on his ever-present cigarette, and addressed the owner of one of his horses, Donald DeWitt.

"We can run Monte Cristo in a race on Saturday, at a mile on the turf if it's to yer liking," he said through a cloud of escaping smoke. "But I do have another fella in there. He's just won one race and isn't a bad sort of mutt for a non-winner of two. The Trapper's his name, but he would be the only one in the race to give your hoss a run for it."

Carrow had been a jockey in his native country, but after an abbreviated and insignificant career, had moved to America where he had found almost immediate success as a trainer, and was now in much demand for his services. His wit and general good humor

13263-RUSS

was reflected in his blue eyes, with deep crow's feet slanting from the corners, lines that carved his weathered features.

Knowing well that he should defer to Carrow's advice, DeWitt, nevertheless, hesitated. "You're sure Monte Cristo can beat him?"

"Sure, Trapper wouldn't beat your hoss. Maybe after this, we might have to run Trapper in a wee bit cheaper race anyway, but in this one, he would be the only hoss to give Monte even a bit of a run. But not to worry, Monte has always worked better than this little fella."

That was all DeWitt needed to hear, after all, it wasn't Monte Cristo that would be running, he was dead, and DeWitt's end of the money collected on the insurance was going to finance a substantial wager. Young McLennan had not hesitated in filling out the death certificate for the insurance carrier when he had seen the extent of injury to the hind leg. DeWitt was relieved that McLennan had not been too inquisitive, and also that Carrow was in the dark.

It was now a month since the insurance had been paid and everything was falling into place nicely. DeWitt regretted having to deal with Vincent Cinotti, but a substantial profit on the insurance and the prospect of betting on Dantes when he ran, had eased the pressure from that quarter. Much as he'd like to, he dared not have the horse win without his cohort being in on the action; Carrow was no problem but Cinotti was.

"Okay Tommy," DeWitt said, "let's go for it, we'll run him on Saturday."

Carrow got up from the table. "On paper, Monte Cristo has terrible form you know Don, and he'll be fierce long odds in this race, but he's training awful well. Would you be wanting to make a little wager?"

DeWitt looked startled. "No, Tommy, that's not my style," he lied. "What about you?"

"Ah no, Don, not me, I've got a few hours of me time invested in him, that'll be enough for me," Carrow replied with a smile. "But if I were a gamblin' man, I'd certainly have a touch."

Even better, DeWitt thought to himself. As far as he was concerned, the higher the odds at race time, the better. Carrow would not be betting and only uninformed gamblers would make insignificant wagers on a horse with the form of Monte Cristo. The big punters would bet against him.

On Friday afternoon, DeWitt's car pulled up alongside a shuffling, derelict figure that was slowly making its way between the barns in the stable area of Gateway Park.

"I've got something for you Hap, get in," DeWitt ordered.

Harry 'Hap' Hazard turned and looked quizzically at the ex-lawyer, hesitated a moment, then climbed into the car. He knew of DeWitt's less than pristine reputation. He had even tried to hit the lawyer up for a fix a couple of times since DeWitt had defended him on a marijuana possession charge several years before. Now Hazard was hard pressed, not only by tightening security on the racetrack, but also by the fact that he had just been fired from his last job, one of several that he was unable to hold for any length of time.

DeWitt knew all of this; Hazard was just the man he was looking for. He was capable of doing anything, but was also cunning, secretive, and tight lipped to the extent that he had survived for many years with only a couple of minor raps against him despite almost constant scrutiny by the authorities.

"I've got a job for you Hap," DeWitt said, handing him two small sponges. "Do you know what these are?"

Hazard knew exactly what they were; sponges that could not be detected by casual observation after being inserted into a horse's nostrils. Once inserted, the sponges would have no effect when the horse was at rest, but when stressed during a race, breathing would be restricted and make it impossible for the animal to perform anywhere near its potential. Hazard was not going to admit to knowledge of anything that might be construed as an illegal activity, however, not even to DeWitt.

"I know they're too small to wash a horse with," he said. "What are they?"

"Well, they can be stuffed about six inches up a horses nostrils. Do you think you could do that?"

Hazard squinted sideways at DeWitt, and scratched his filthy beard.

"Now, if you can't do it yourself, Boss, it must be pretty sticky," he said, shaking his head as he spoke. "An' you know I've got a reputation to protect. I aint goin' to take no chances. No, sir, that kind of work is just too tricky."

Hazard started as if to get out of the car.

"Too bad, Hap, I just thought you could use five hundred," DeWitt said with a sigh. "I must have been wrong."

Hazard hesitated. "Well now, Boss, you know I wouldn't do it for no one but you. But you know me, I aint for hire for no peanuts, and besides, what about my reputation?"

"Your reputation's precisely why I'm talking to you, Hap."

"Reputation's worth somethin', aint it? Maybe a thousand?"

"Okay, a thousand it is."

"You know a good man when you see one," Hazard grinned through rotten teeth, getting back into the car. "When do I start?"

"Tonight, after about ten o'clock. I'll give you a thousand cash tomorrow. Now listen carefully," DeWitt continued, "I'll stop at the end of barn twenty two, around ten o'clock. I'll stay in my car and call the night watchman to the end of the barn and ask if everything is okay. I do this occasionally, and Jimmy's always looking for someone to chat with for a few minutes."

"Yeah, I know the sonofabitch."

"At the other end of the barn is a horse called The Trapper, in stall thirty-four, the end stall. Do you know him?"

Hazard shook his head. "No, but if he's in the end stall, I'll find him."

"Good. I want you to slide these sponges into his nostrils. You'll have about four or five minutes while Jimmy and I talk."

"Nothin' to it, Boss," Hazard was grinning. "I know that barn. I used to work for that fuckin' Carrow."

"I know you did," DeWitt smiled. "You're my man."

CHAPTER 19

It was as the early morning light filtered through the trees of Gateway Park that Fiona rode a steaming horse from the track back to its barn. Donald DeWitt trotted alongside, perspiring from exertion and the heat of the summer morning while struggling to keep up.

"How did he go? Was he sharp?" he asked, breathing hard.

"Well we only jogged a little this morning but he went really well," Fiona replied. "He's seems just as sharp as when I rode him at Newmarket."

"What?" DeWitt was startled. "You rode this horse in England?"

"Yes, I know it's an odd coincidence that we should get together all the way over here, but Dantes and I are old friends," Fiona declared, patting him affectionately upon the neck. "I won two races on him. I'd love to ride him here when he runs."

"What did you say? You know this horse?"

"I rode him in England. We're old friends."

"You must be mistaken, you've never ridden this horse," DeWitt contradicted. He looked puzzled, then alarmed as the reality sank in.

Mopping his face with a handkerchief, he attempted a smile, shaking his head. "You're mistaken, young lady. This is a horse called Monte Cristo."

"I don't think so, I'd know Dantes anywhere."

DeWitt's mood changed to anger. "You are mistaken, there are a lot of horses that look alike."

"I know but I can't mistake this one. He's special," Fiona insisted, trying to muster a reassuring smile.

13263-RUSS

"You're dreaming!"

Fiona was shaken by DeWitt's sudden vehemence.

"I'm sorry, but I think you should know that unless you've changed his name, this is Dantes," she insisted meekly.

"Nobody has changed his name and he was never named Dantes. His name is Monte Cristo. You're completely mistaken!" DeWitt was almost apoplectic, his voice rising. "Don't meddle with things you know nothing about!" he warned. "I don't want to hear any more about it, his name is none of your damn business, anyway!"

The horse was ridden back to his stable where Fiona unsaddled him and departed without another word, confused and embarrassed. Tommy Carrow was neither there to defend her nor to clarify the matter. DeWitt hovered nearby watching her as she left, mopping his face with a trembling hand. He was on his cell phone before Fiona was out of sight.

"Vince, this is DeWitt."

"What'd I tell you about names on this phone?" Cinotti replied in a low voice. There was a pause for effect. "What you want?"

"We've got a problem Vince. I'm going to have to scratch the horse. We can't run him this afternoon."

"Scratch him? Why?"

"There's a girl that rode him in a race in England, and the little bitch got on him here this morning."

"So?"

"She knows who it is."

"So tell her to fuck off."

"If she finds out we're running him under a different name she may blow the whistle, and if she does that, I've had it."

There was a pause as Cinotti absorbed the information.

"Man, that's your problem," he finally said. "But you better run the horse 'cause we're not goin' to wait no longer."

"Damn it, Vince. I just can't take the chance."

"You gonna take a bigger chance if you don't run him. Who's the girl? What's her name anyway?"

"It's that new jock, Fiona Kent."

There was another long silence. "Well now, ain't that interesting?" he finally said, slowly. "I'll meet you at the diner in half an hour."

The encounter with DeWitt had unsettled Fiona. Unable to let it rest, she dropped into Mark's office at the end of the morning for a cup of coffee. She sat on the corner of his desk and waited for him to get off the telephone. The distraction pleased him as he admired her slim figure, beautifully defined in a hot pink polo shirt, blue jeans and riding boots. He cut his phone conversation short with an apology and a promise to call back.

"What's up?"

"Mark, I just had the most extraordinary run in with one of Tommy Carrow's owners this morning," she said.

"Oh no, who was it?"

"A man called DeWitt, I think. He was an absolute swine."

"Oh DeWitt?" Mark was relieved. "Did he oink at you?"

Fiona flushed with anger. "Damn it Mark, it's not funny. I'm serious, he was an absolute bastard!"

Mark, surprised, pulled her over onto his lap and kissed her, regretting his flippant remark.

"I'm sorry," he said, gently. "Tell me about it."

"I was on a colt he owns called Dantes that I had won a couple of races on last year in England. When I mentioned it to him, he flew off the handle," she fumed. "He said the horse was Monte Cristo, or something like that. I don't give a toss if he changed its name, but why would he get so upset and attack me?"

Mark was sympathetic. "Don't worry, Fi, he's only upset because Dantes had a terrible accident and had to be destroyed."

"Destroyed?"

"Yes, he had an accident in his stall and was put down."

"No he didn't," she protested.

"This horse, Mont Cristo, the one that you were on is just a cheap horse, not half as good as Dantes," Mark went on. "It's easy for you to have made a mistake, I know both horses and there is a strong resemblance."

"Mark, I know this horse too," Fiona insisted shaking her head. "This is Dantes. I'm not mistaken, even if everyone else is."

She thought for a moment, and then continued.

"Mark, I know it's him because he has a habit of hanging his tongue out of the right side of his mouth. No other horse does that. I admit that I only got on him this morning for the first time over here, and we only jogged a little. But I know it's him."

Mark frowned. Fiona seemed convinced of the horse's identity. Could it possibly be a mix up and DeWitt had lost the wrong horse, or the right horse, depending upon the point of view? If this were the case, DeWitt should be told. But since Mark had signed the death certificate himself, it dawned upon him that he had some culpability if in fact a mistake had been made and a considerable insurance claim had been paid on a live horse. If Fiona was correct, it was obviously going to be an embarrassing situation. Surely, he thought, there was a chance that Fiona was mistaken.

"Well, Fi, if it will put your mind at rest, I'll look into it."

He picked up the phone and dialed a number for Alan Brady, the track's official horse identifier. Brady's duties were to identify each horse for registration with the Jockey Club, the governing body of American racing, and the authorization of which was required before any horse was permitted to race in America.

"Alan, this is Mark McLennan here. I have a question for you. Do you remember identifying a horse called Monte Cristo for Donald DeWitt?"

"Yes, of course, it was a couple of months ago. Why?"

"Well I just wondered if there were any marking discrepancies with his papers when you examined him."

Mark needed an excuse for his inquiry. "I think I have a billing problem. Perhaps I am billing for the wrong horse," he said, vaguely.

There was a slight hesitation before the official replied.

"Now that you mention it," he said slowly, "I recall there had to be a correction made on the papers. He had a cowlick under his mane that was not listed on the original papers. He had no other markings."

"Does that sort of discrepancy happen very often?"

"No, not often, but occasionally small inconsistencies like that occur, and we simply send in to the Jockey Club for a corrected certificate."

"And you did that on this one?"

"Yes, of course, the horse couldn't run until then. This horse's papers were corrected. It's funny that you should call, he's actually entered to run this afternoon."

"Thanks Alan, I'm sure I'll get it worked out. Thanks for your help." Mark hung up the phone and turned to Fiona.

"The horse runs today as Monte Cristo," he said. "The horse identification guy said that a corrected certificate was issued on him, which means they possibly could have been issued in error. There could have been a mistake."

"I'm sure that was the case then, Mark." Fiona was even more insistent.

"If you're absolutely sure you're right, Fi, then we should report it."

"Who to? DeWitt won't believe me."

"To the stewards."

"What will they do?"

Mark shrugged. "They may very well scratch him and not let him race until it gets sorted out. That could take a month or two, so you have to be absolutely positive that you know what you're talking about. You certainly don't want to rattle DeWitt anymore."

"Mark, I do know what horse that is." Fiona said with conviction; she was more composed. "But you're right, I don't want to have another scene with DeWitt like I had this morning."

The realization that he could have been partially responsible for an insurance claim on a horse that was probably still alive put Mark in an awkward position, and that was a considerable concern. In deference to DeWitt, he had not followed strictly established procedures in signing a mortality certificate. But if he were to get restitution for the insurance company that had paid out over two hundred thousand dollars because of an error, it would of course be a monetary loss to DeWitt, although the owner would no doubt be pleased to find out that the better of his two horses was still alive.

The worst consequence of the confusion would be to Mark's reputation. He could not be held accountable for the misidentification, if in fact there was such a problem, but it seemed inevitable that an investigation would reveal the fact that he had examined the horse after and not before its destruction. In his defense, Mark rationalized, the damage to the hind leg was so extensive that it was inevitable that the animal should be humanely destroyed in any event. Damn DeWitt, he thought, through stupidity or carelessness, he has put me in a hell of a position. With some hesitation he explained his concern and possible liability.

"There's something else you should know, Fiona. If this is Dantes, and I'm beginning to believe it is, I may be in a bit of a jam," he said thoughtfully, full realization sinking in. "I issued a mortality certificate on him and helped DeWitt with one hell of a big insurance claim."

"It wasn't your fault, you didn't misidentify the horse," Fiona protested. "How could you know which horse it was?"

"No, but I should have examined the injury before he was put down, and as a favor to DeWitt, I didn't do that."

"Oh Mark, it would be a terrible spot to put you in if I reported this then. What shall I do?"

Mark considered the implications and the sequence of events leading up to his predicament.

"It is possible," he said, thinking aloud, "that DeWitt had intentionally switched the identity of the two horses, you know."

"Well, intentionally or not, somebody has, and it wasn't you."

"But to give the devil his due," Mark went on slowly, "it seems highly unlikely that even he would mutilate a living horse's leg just to collect an insurance claim."

He continued after a moment's pause. "But of course, if this were true, it is possible that the horse was not alive at the time the leg was mutilated. I only saw the injury the morning after the horse had been euthanized."

He picked up the phone, searched his directory and dialed a number.

"Doctor Richardson?" he asked.

"Yes?"

"This is Mark McLennan. Do you remember putting a horse down in the middle of the night about a month or so ago for Donald DeWitt?"

Fiona watched intently as Mark discussed the event with the other veterinarian. After several minutes, he rang off.

"Well that's interesting," he said, turning to Fiona. "Richardson said that when he went to DeWitt's, he was a little surprised that the horse was relatively calm, didn't seem distressed, but there was a hell of a lot of blood all over the place. When he offered to examine the wound, DeWitt told him not to bother, that it was only a cheap horse and he wasn't going to pay any more vet bills on him. DeWitt told him to just go ahead and put the horse down."

"Didn't he see the leg, then?"

"Richardson said the leg was bandaged and the horse was standing, but with only a flashlight he really couldn't have seen very much anyway; just a lot of blood. There was no light in the barn."

Fiona shook her head. "That's incredible, didn't he know the horse was insured?"

"He said he assumed it wasn't since DeWitt had told him it was just a cheap horse. He didn't even know its name. He's not a track vet, he just does farm animals out there on the island."

"But I still don't understand," Fiona frowned, "Didn't you see the injury?"

"Yes, the next morning, after the horse was dead."

"If it was bad enough to put the horse down, surely he wouldn't have been calm when the vet got there?"

Mark paused before answering.

"That's the point," he said at length. "There may have been

nothing wrong with the horse. Richardson said that he was reluctant to put him down but DeWitt insisted, saying he would do it himself and save the vet bill if Richardson didn't."

"So Richardson did it?"

"Yep." Mark thought for a moment. "When I saw it, the leg was badly fractured and irreparable, but DeWitt could have smashed it up after the horse was euthanized."

"What about all the blood? He wouldn't have bled if he was already dead when the leg was smashed, would he?"

"DeWitt could easily have nicked an artery or two while the horse was alive and before the vet got there without causing him any real distress. I saw the blood the next day, it was as Richardson said, all over the place."

Fiona slid off the desk and walked over to the window. Looking out upon the peaceful stable area with her back to Mark, she asked, "Do you really believe that anyone could do such a thing?"

Mark was thoughtful before answering. "It sounds unlikely, but it's possible. What worries me is the way that you say DeWitt acted when you told him it was Dantes."

"He was furious."

"He shouldn't have been, he should have been delighted," Mark said shaking his head. "There's no telling what people will do for money and there is a lot at stake here. But even if DeWitt made a legitimate mistake, I screwed up. I should have gone out and examined the horse before he was destroyed."

"What shall we do, Mark? Shall we report it?"

"We don't know for sure that any of this did happen. It's speculation on my part, but you think this horse is Dantes, right?"

"I'm positive," she said with emphasis, turning to look at him.

"Well, think it over, and don't worry. If it is as you say, you'll have to make the report, but whatever you decide, I'm with you. I suspect the stewards probably wouldn't scratch him before the race without positive evidence anyway, so there's really no need to panic."

He got up, walked over to her, gave her a kiss and slapped her on the rump. "Let's go and get some breakfast. I'm starving and I've got a lot of work this afternoon. What about dinner at the club tonight?"

"Okay," she said with a smile, "I'll look forward to that."

CHAPTER 20

It was not far from Gateway Park to the cottage in Oyster Bay where Fiona lived, a drive that she always took with pleasure but fretted for every mile that morning. The incident with DeWitt had upset her more than Mark had imagined, and she was anxious to get home and call her parents in England. She was hesitant about her roll as an informer, and wanted desperately to talk to her father. Her respect and affection for him transcended all other considerations, and whatever advice he would offer, she would follow. It was always to him that she turned in time of trouble or doubt. If Mark was to be held accountable to the insurance company for not following protocol, she certainly didn't wish to bring it to their attention unless her father advised her to do so.

She reflected over the fact that here again, without ever intending to, she might be shielding another man for another indiscretion. Was that devious, dishonest, or through association, even the conduct of a criminal? She didn't feel any remorse. Maybe it was pretty easy to be a crook after all. It was disconcerting, nevertheless, to think that she was becoming indifferent about matters of integrity; her father would be appalled at the thought. Why, she wondered, should all this fall upon her shoulders anyway? She certainly didn't go looking for complicated situations and least of all, complicated men.

Going out to the Yacht Club for a sail on Mark's little sailboat, catch some sun and relax, she thought, would be a good distraction. She was almost resigned to call Mark and tell him to forget the whole affair unless her father advised to the contrary. Irrespective of what her father advised though, and he couldn't possibly know the truth, if there had been an insurance fraud, she would be an accomplice by omission if she neglected to report it. Voluntarily omitting to divulge the facts, something at which she was unhappily becoming quite adept, was more of a moral obligation than a legal consideration that just wouldn't go away.

Turning into her driveway, she noticed without any real interest, a car stopped on the lane in front of her cottage. Parking her car, she was only vaguely aware of a man that got out of the vehicle and opened the hood. Before she had reached the front door of the cottage, the stranger stepped up to the gate at the end of her lawn and called to her.

"Excuse me Miss, I got car trouble. I think I'm outa gas. Can I borrow your phone?"

He was smiling, and although not her type, she thought, he was quite good looking. He seemed friendly.

"There's a small petrol station about a mile away," she called back, "but I doubt if they will deliver. Would you like me to drive you over there?"

"Yeah, if you don't mind," he said with a wide grin. Then as an afterthought, "I'll get my wallet."

He turned and crossed the road to retrieve his coat from out of his car, and waited with it draped over his arm.

He was a little too smooth, showing more teeth than was necessary for merely a friendly smile, Fiona thought, but he was obviously trying to impress her. It would be a long walk on a hot day to get a can of petrol, so under the circumstances, he was in a bit of a bind. Anyone would be happy to help her out if she were in the same situation.

She backed her car out of the driveway. "Hop in."

He slid into the passenger's side, closed the door and turned toward her.

"You're very kind," he said, still grinning. "But now you gotta do what I tell you."

Fiona turned and looked into the barrel of a gun. She was stunned for a moment, her eyes wide.

"What the bloody hell are you doing? Get out of my car!" her voice rising.

The smile was gone. "No baby, just do what I say and you'll be all right. Now drive."

"Get out, damn you!" Fiona was screaming. "Get Out!"

Cinotti grabbed her by the hair with his free hand and jerked her face within an inch of his.

"Drive," he hissed through clenched teeth, and pushed her away.

She had no choice. Trembling violently as much from anger as fear and with tears blurring her vision, she started to drive.

"Where are we going?"

"I'll tell you where. Just do what I say, baby, an' you won't get hurt," he replied grinning again, obviously enjoying his control over the girl.

Other than him giving directions, they drove without talking. After a few miles, Fiona returned from the verge of hysteria and began to consider her predicament. She considered her chances of either crashing the car or jumping out, but realized both options were too dangerous. The probability of being shot, injured in a crash, or both, were too high to justify any sort of drastic action. The man was probably a psychopath who would have no compunction about killing her. She had no choice but to stick it out and humor him as much as possible.

"You know you don't have to do this," she said. "You can have the car."

"And you too if I want, I know that, baby," he sneered. "Just drive!"

"I don't know who you are or what you want. If you let me out now, nothing will happen to you," she urged.

His chuckle was devoid of humor. "Nothin's going to happen to me anyway, an' if you don't give me no crap, you'll be okay too. We might even get to be friends."

He directed her to turn north off the Long Island Expressway, and within minutes, Fiona noticed the sign identifying Port Washington. They drove through a residential district for several miles, and eventually into a small marina. Fiona, looking for any avenue of escape, was aware that they were somewhere on the extreme northern shore of Long Island.

She was told to park in front of a row of large cabin cruisers and yachts tied up to what she assumed were probably private rather than public wharves. Some fifty yards away, there were a couple of men that were working on boats, seemingly unaware of the arrival of Cinotti and Fiona. Other than these preoccupied deck hands, the area was deserted, remote, and away from any significant activity. It was obvious to Fiona that there was no chance of escape and little hope of anyone intervening on her behalf.

"Now get out on my side of the car and don't yell or try to run. Don't screw up," Cinotti warned as he backed out of the car.

He shoved the gun, concealed by his coat, into her ribs and roughly pushed her across the dock over to a large power yacht. She estimated that it was about sixty feet in length with two decks, an elevated pilothouse, and conspicuously luxurious. They stepped onto the deck and proceeded down a dozen steps of a gangway leading into a large and richly appointed main cabin.

"Miss Kent, nice to see you again," greeted Donald DeWitt, rising from an overstuffed couch. "I see you've met Vincent. Won't you sit down? We have a lot to talk about, and not much time."

Fiona flushed with anger. So this obnoxious little sod was the reason for her being abducted, she thought. Cinotti pushed her unceremoniously down into an armchair, crossed over to a bar, poured himself a whiskey and lit a cigarette.

"Perhaps you should offer Miss Kent a drink, Vince," DeWitt suggested with an ingratiating smile that conveyed no warmth.

Fiona ignored the offer. "Why have you brought me here?" she fumed. She knew at least part of the answer.

"Miss Kent," DeWitt began, returning to the couch. "You seem to be confused over the identity of the horse you were on this morning. He runs this afternoon, and whether there is some doubt as to what his name is or not, it has nothing to do with you."

13263-RUSS

"I don't give a toss about his name, or what ever it is that you're up to," Fiona protested.

"My friend and I," DeWitt waved a hand in the general direction of Cinotti, "have quite a lot invested in this horse, and this morning you seemed to think you should clear up the matter of his name."

"I only thought that you should know his correct name," Fiona said angrily. "I frankly don't care what you call him, but I'm sure you wouldn't have gone to all this trouble if it weren't bloody important to you. What do you want?"

DeWitt's attitude had changed appreciably from that which Fiona had seen that morning. He feigned amusement at Fiona's outburst, although she noticed that he kept glancing nervously over at Cinotti as if searching for his approval. The younger man had his elbows hooked into the bar while leaning against it, silently watching Fiona. He had put the gun back into his coat, which had been thrown over a chair, but Fiona realized that it was easily within his reach. She accepted the fact that she had no chance of making a run for it.

"I'll make you an offer," DeWitt continued. "I'll give you five thousand dollars, payable in two installments, to stop you from meddling into the identity of the horse.

"I want you to talk to no one about this matter," he went on, leaning forward and thumping his fist on the arm of his chair to emphasize the point. "And I want to be able to run the horse when and where I please. In addition, after today's race, I shall permit you to ride the horse in his next race if you so wish. What do you think of that?"

Fiona sat motionless, her mind racing. She looked back and forth at the two men and slowly shook her head.

"In other words," she said, finally, "You want to pay me to be your accomplice."

"Not exactly, that's your choice of words, but I simply want you to mind your own business, and get well paid for it."

Fiona hesitated. Even though her heart was no longer pounding, her mind continued to race. She hoped that she at least gave the appearance of being in control.

"Hey baby, you don't have no choice." Succinct as he was, Cinotti was far more persuasive than DeWitt.

There was another long pause while Fiona considered the implications. She knew she was in an extremely precarious predicament, at best. Any offer was a good offer if she could save her neck, but she had to persuade these people that she would accept their lousy five thousand dollars. Despite her tenuous situation, she was amused at the thought that the numbers were improving; she would be paid for protecting two men this time.

She weighed the implications of the deal. It was certainly clever. Aside from the payment of the five thousand, if she were to ride the horse at some point she would be irrevocably locked in as a co-conspirator and less likely to reveal the fraud. She knew that this was a last ditch offer by DeWitt, and one that he could easily back out of later. She was not so gullible that she would trust him, but also knew she must stall for time, and if she were to go along with him it would take some pressure off both of them.

"Well, what do you say, can we be friends?" DeWitt urged, leaning back, eyebrows raised expectantly.

Fiona had no alternative but to agree to the deal, at least for the moment. The swine with the gun was right; she had little choice, but neither would she have any reservation about reneging at the first opportunity, no matter how it implicated her. To hell with them. If and when she got out of there, she would call the stewards, the police, the army and anyone else who would listen. And these people probably knew it, but for now she had to stall them. She had no delusions about how lethal Vince might be, and was doubtful that DeWitt would have control over him. She suspected, however, that DeWitt would try to involve her in the fraud rather than risk being implicated in a possible murder.

"All right, I'll keep quiet," she agreed. "But I want ten thousand, five of it paid now, and I will ride the horse the next time he runs."

"I said five."

At least DeWitt wanted to negotiate; maybe he believes me, Fiona thought.

"Very well, make it eight, all of it paid today. But I insist that I ride the horse in his next start."

She needed to persuade them that she accepted the offer with a lot more enthusiasm than she felt. Vince might be stupid, she speculated, but the way in which he stared at Fiona, slowly shaking his head, looking skeptical and saying nothing, didn't bring her any reassurance.

"You're tough, but it's a deal," said DeWitt, "There's one more thing, though. I need to know who you might have talked to about this horse having a name change. If there's someone else, perhaps we need to include him. Cut him in."

Cut his throat more likely, Fiona thought. Her impulse from the beginning was to tell them what Mark knew, and use him as a threat, but she quickly realized that for his safety he must not be implicated in any way. He must be protected at least until she could warn him of the danger.

"I haven't had time to talk to anyone, and besides, I didn't think it important until you made such a bloody stink about it."

DeWitt looked doubtful. "Well if you have, it will be very unfortunate for you."

"I haven't, and I won't. Why should I?" Fiona protested, she hoped with conviction. "You've made me a decent offer. I can stay out of something that is not my business."

"She won't say nothin', don't worry." Cinotti's assertion was a threat not wasted upon either Fiona or DeWitt.

There was a long pause while DeWitt studied her.

"Then we all understand each other," he said, finally. "However, there is one more condition. You'll stay here until after the race, at which time you will receive eight thousand in cash. If you decide to squeal after the race you'll be implicated as an accomplice, but in that event, I suspect Vince would have something else in mind for you anyway, wouldn't you Vince?" DeWitt looked over at him.

Cinotti stubbed out his cigarette and shifted his position from the bar. He slowly moved across the cabin, and with a hand on each arm of her chair, leaned toward Fiona, his face an inch from hers. Every movement was calculated and threatening.

"Yeah, Don, I would have all kinds of things in mind for Fiona," he said with a disingenuous grin. "But I like her."

He shrugged as he moved back to stand looking down at her. "I wouldn't want nothin' to happen to her. Maybe we can become real friends," he continued with an emphasis on the "real".

"You see, Miss Kent, Vince is pretty convincing in his own sort of way." DeWitt paused for effect.

"Now," he continued, "after the race, you shall receive the money, but there's one other little item. We're going to make sure you stay here until then, just in case you have a change of heart. Vince, why don't you arrange that?"

Cinotti left the cabin and returned moments later with several feet of light rope. He jerked Fiona out of the chair, pushing her down a long passageway and into a stateroom somewhere in the bow of the boat. She was told to lay down on a bunk, while he tied her ankles to a handhold in the leeboard. This done, he rolled her over and tied her hands behind her back. She offered no resistance. She appeared calm and resigned, but was inwardly terrified. The rope around her ankles was not excessively uncomfortable, her riding boots provided a degree of protection, but almost immediately her wrists began to burn from the rope, and the veins stood out on her hands. She knew there was little hope of releasing herself before DeWitt and Cinotti were to return after the race.

Cinotti, now that she was securely tied, leaned over her. "Just a little kiss to show we're still friends," he whispered.

Unable to resist, she turned her head away as he kissed and ran his tongue into her ear, fondling her breasts. She almost gagged as he then placed duct tape over her mouth. Any hope of calling for help was now out of the question.

13263-RUSS

DeWitt was waiting for him when he returned to the main cabin.

"Vince, I don't want her hurt. I want you to keep your hands off her," DeWitt ordered, hesitantly.

Cinotti frowned and shook his head, feigning a wounded expression. "I wouldn't hurt her," he sneered. "I just wanna scare her a little so she won't talk. She's a doll, why would I hurt her? I like her."

DeWitt knew his own situation was far from secure, and had to weigh this against possible harm to the girl. He suspected his objections were probably wasted on Cinotti, anyway. Damn her, he thought, why the hell did she have to stick her nose into something that was not her affair? If she couldn't talk, he was sure her disappearance could never be linked to the horse or DeWitt himself, so he was not going to lose a lot of sleep over that. In any event, she was now in so deep that she would just have to take her chances. At this point, there was no backing out.

"Okay," he said, "but if anything happens to her, I'm out. I don't want to know about it."

DeWitt swore to himself, that after the race, he would have fulfilled his end of the deal. There was a chance the girl was on his side and be no problem, but he would see the end of this bastard. Money was not going to be a problem in the future; he would not need Cinotti.

"Well we're all set. The horse will win," he added in a tired voice.

"So this is it, huh? When I get down it ain't no chump money," Cinotti warned. "There are a couple of bookies we want to burn, so you'd better be right."

"This is it, you can get down. There's only one horse to beat in the race and I've taken care of him," DeWitt reassured him.

Fiona had no idea when the two men had left the boat. From the cabin well forward of the main saloon, it was impossible to hear their voices, but she assumed they would have left to go to the racetrack. She could hear a radio playing that one of them had turned on, presumably to suggest that the boat was occupied and discourage anyone that was curious from coming aboard, or even to drown out any yelling that she might attempt. DeWitt and his friend would probably be gone for at least two or three hours, she guessed, which may give her enough time to break free.

She started twisting her wrists back and forth in an effort to slide her hands through the ropes, but they only cut deeper into her flesh. The pain was becoming excruciating and after several futile attempts, she gave up. She then tried, without success, to slide her feet out of her riding boots, which was always difficult under the best of conditions. In frustration, she started kicking at the leeboard to which they were tied, but that only tightened the knots in the rope. The board was too stout to break and after several minutes of exhausting struggle, she gave up, frustrated and close to tears.

She realized there was virtually no chance of anyone hearing her, but she started trying to yell, only to have an excess of saliva choke her, causing her to gag. Again she tried to loosen her ankles and wrists, but the ropes tightened even more than before.

After fifteen minutes of struggling, she finally accepted the inevitable; she was not going to get out of there until someone released her. She reflected upon the irony of having retreated to security with Mark, and after escaping every danger surrounding Adrian, she was now in the gravest peril of her life. Her time with Adrian was positively serene compared to the prospects that she now faced.

CHAPTER 21

Mark made his afternoon rounds, visiting different stables and treating horses for a variety of medical problems, many of them uniquely related to the Thoroughbred racehorse, which required his full attention. He was a little concerned that Fiona had not phoned him. He knew that she would avoid creating a problem for him if at all possible, and assumed that was probably the reason that he had not heard from her. They both wished to postpone the inevitable unpleasantness that would result in any disclosure about the identity of DeWitt's horse, but Mark was surprised that Fiona was going to wait until after the horse had run. They had decided that the insurance claim would hardly be affected by the horse racing, and could be resolved at any time. Possibly that was why Fiona was now procrastinating, he thought.

By mid afternoon, he tried to telephone her at her house, without success. He then attempted to reach her on her cell phone with the same result. The recorded message was that she was either out of the area or the phone was turned off.

After finishing his rounds, he decided to go over to the races and watch the race in which DeWitt's horse was to run, wishing without much hope that Fiona had been mistaken about its identity. It was obvious that she had been sufficiently familiar with Dantes to be able to identify him. Proof of his identity, however, would not be easy, and both Fiona and Mark were well aware that if she disclosed her suspicions to the authorities, they would almost certainly be embroiled in a long and potentially litigious investigation.

Mark pondered all of the implications as he stood unnoticed amongst the crowd surrounding the paddock. He watched with interest as Tommy Carrow saddled the horse while DeWitt hovered around, pacing nervously back and forth during the whole procedure. When the jockey came out to receive his instructions, DeWitt and Carrow joined him in a huddle at the center of the walking ring. DeWitt, when not mopping his face with a handkerchief, was otherwise animated as he offered his advice, demonstrating with his hands how the horse should be ridden and describing what he thought the jockey should do.

Mark was always fascinated by the absurdity of an anxious owner, who in all probability had never ridden a horse in his life, attempting to instruct a jockey on how he should ride a race. The jockey in this case, 'Chili' Fernandez, nicknamed for his riding style, was experienced, and was one of the leading riders in the country. He stood with arms folded, nodding his head with feigned interest and indulging the apprehensive, animated owner. Carrow said very little, and with hands stuffed into his pockets, patiently observed DeWitt's urgent remonstrations. Finally the riders were thrown up onto their horses and led out onto the track. Since Mark was not appropriately dressed for the clubhouse, he joined the surging crush of racing fans that left the paddock area, pushing and jostling as they made their way to the front of the grandstand to watch the race.

It was a warm, sunny, June afternoon, the crowd was huge, the track fast, and the money churned through the pari-mutuel windows. Optimism is nourishment for most racing fans, but beyond mere optimism, Donald DeWitt's anticipation of impending wealth, and the stress of recent events, visibly affected his behavior. His agitation was heightened by the fact that he had come to the races with fifty thousand dollars in large denomination bills to wager. Drifting through the crowd and betting at several different pari-mutuel windows to avoid drawing attention to himself, he had methodically bought fifty thousand dollars worth of tickets, all to win on Dantes. So as not to alter the odds prematurely, or any more than could be avoided, a large portion of his wager had been placed after the horses came out onto the track and while they were warming up for the race. He knew and appreciated that Cinotti had bet off-track with several bookmakers to avoid affecting the odds, and at the same time not take the risk of being identified by the racing authorities. One advantage of betting with the bookies was that they jealously guarded the identity of their clients.

It was to DeWitt's advantage that the Gateway Stakes was also being run later that day, attracting an enormous crowd. More than thirty thousand fans had come to watch Awesome Daze, the favorite for the race attempt to become the leading money winner of all time. Having already won two classics and many other stake races, only the Gateway Stakes stood in the way of the record. If he were to win, the popular chestnut and his connections would be assured of a place in history, immortalized forever in the annals of racing. Racing fans had come from far and wide in the hope of witnessing history in the making.

With large amounts of money already flowing through the pari-mutuel windows, what DeWitt wagered neither drew undue attention to him nor affected the odds to the degree that it would have on a less momentous occasion.

Aside from the irritating problem of the girl, DeWitt reflected, things were falling into place as planned. The annoying twitch in his left eye that always appeared whenever he was unduly stressed was beginning to subside with the prospect of success. The months of worry and aggravation in dealing with Cinotti would soon be behind him, and the reward for his astute management and unwavering perseverance was virtually less than two minutes away.

The horses were approaching the starting gate when DeWitt sat down in the private box next to his trainer. He had left Carrow and disappeared shortly after the horses had left the saddling paddock, and now that he had reappeared, Carrow gave him a curious look, noticing a twitch in his owner's left eye that he knew was frequently a manifestation of the poor man's anxiety.

"Where'd you go Don? It wouldn't be to make a little wager after all would it?" he teased with a wink.

DeWitt was not to be humored. "Just a small one," he lied. He still needed reassurance. "What do you think, Tom?"

Carrow picked up his binoculars and looked out across the track at the horses as they started to load into the starting gate. "He'll run awful good. Not to worry, all he's got to do is beat The Trapper, and he should have no trouble doing that. I believe he's an easy winner."

Carrow took his binoculars down as he spoke and glanced at the odds board. "B'jaisus, look at the bleedin' odds," he exclaimed. "He's gone down from sixty-to-one, and now he's thirty-five to one in a single flash. Somebody must have bet a ton o' money!"

DeWitt made no reply. He was looking intently through his binoculars, his hands visibly trembling, perspiration beading on his face, the twitch in his eye suddenly finding new energy.

The crowd fell almost silent as the announcer blared, "It is now post time!"

The two men came to their feet. DeWitt could hear his heart pounding as the gate flew open and the horses broke in a line.

The crowd noise was reduced to a grumble as over thirty thousand fans watched and listened to the announcer declaring Monte Cristo on an easy lead; the horse they believed had few credentials. By the time the field had gone half a mile he had a four-length lead, and Donald DeWitt began to relax, already enjoying the prospect of his imminent wealth.

And then something happened. Hernandez, who had been steadying his mount while maintaining an easy advantage, suddenly began urging him along. He turned his whip up and gave the horse a slap, but with no response.

"Monte Cristo is going to the whip!" the announcer blared. "The Trapper, now only three lengths back and going well, is continuing to close the gap!"

Within the next half furlong, the rest of the field had caught up and were starting to pass the now badly tiring leader. By the time the horses reached the top of the stretch, The Trapper had taken the lead while his stable-mate was rapidly fading to last place. Hernandez put away his whip, mercifully recognizing the futility of punishing his mount, and sensing that something was wrong with him. Through the stretch and coming to the finish, nothing changed. The Trapper crossed the finish line in front by several lengths, and only Donald DeWitt was in more distress than his horse.

The thought flashed through DeWitt's mind that this horse ran like the real Monte Cristo. Had he somehow made a mistake and killed Dantes instead? That was impossible; their identities had been successfully switched when they entered the country. He was certain that he had not made a mistake.

"That was a bit of a surprise," Carrow exclaimed as he put down his binoculars and turned to see DeWitt slumped in his chair, pale and visibly shaken. "Take it easy, Don, it was only a hoss race. It's too bad but the hoss lived up to his form, which wasn't very good, let's face it."

"But . . . but you said he had trained well," DeWitt stammered. "Wh . . . what happened? How could he run so badly?"

"B'jaisus, he had trained well an' all," Carrow looked puzzled. "The only thing I can think of that might have upset him was that we changed his stall yesterday morning when he came back from his gallop. But he looked well this morning when I gave him a little jog."

"You what?" DeWitt was incredulous.

"I moved him from the middle of the barn to the end stall so that he could see out a little better."

"You changed his stall?" DeWitt was on his feet and almost in shock. "You moved him to the end of the barn?"

"Sure enough. I thought he was a better hoss than The Trapper, so I switched their stalls. But that shouldn't have bothered him at all. B'jaisus, take it easy Don."

DeWitt slumped back down into his seat, removed his glasses and passed a shaking hand across his face. Nothing more was said as Carrow quietly left the box and headed down toward the winner's circle to greet the victorious and elated owners of The Trapper.

For some minutes DeWitt sat hunched over, and then, with trembling hands, pulled a stack of useless pari-mutuel tickets from his pocket. He stared dejectedly at them for several more minutes and then began to shuffle through them as if wishing them to be anything but what they were; the worthless receipts of fifty thousand dollars lost.

The roar of the crowd had long subsided to a constant murmur by the time that DeWitt, overwhelmed by the realization that he had arranged the sponging of his own horse, rose and lurched toward the exit, pallid and shaking his head as if attempting a denial, mumbling to himself. In a daze, he shuffled through the Turf Club. He was almost unaware of going down the escalator until, as he stepped off at the bottom, the last person on earth that he ever wanted to see, confronted him.

"DeWitt, that wasn't so good. We've got to talk, let's go."

"I . . . I can't, not now," DeWitt stammered.

"We've got some business to settle with the girl."

"I don't want any more to do with it," DeWitt said with far more bravado than he felt, and trying without success to side step. "If you want to give her something to shut her up, it's okay with me. I don't want to see her again, I'm out of it."

He was beyond rationalizing the implications of what he was saying, but as he spoke he felt something hard pressed against his ribs, and the arm around his shoulders, he knew, was not there out of affection. He was numb but aware enough to know that he had no chance of making an escape, or even yelling for help.

"Just walk over to your car."

DeWitt had no choice; he couldn't ignore the threat, but he was beyond being able to protest.

"We're going to the boat. You drive."

Mark watched the race with a mixture of confusion and relief. Could Fiona have been wrong? This horse bore no resemblance to the talented horse that Fiona had described and ridden in England. Perhaps he was, after all, the cheap horse, Monte Cristo.

Mark made his way through the crowd out toward his truck, again trying to phone Fiona with the same result: "The cellular customer is either out of the area," an impossibility, "or has their phone turned off," an improbability, the recording announced.

Although curious, he was yet to be alarmed. He wondered where on earth she could have gone? Even if she had gone for a sail by herself he had advised her to always take the cell phone with her in case of an emergency.

He was relieved when he watched the race with the horse finishing last after leading for only the first half-mile or so, but wanted to let Fiona know how it had turned out. She would have found him if she had been there to watch the race, Mark was sure of that. Now he was anxious to let her know that even if it were Dantes, the horse not winning the race would simplify the situation to some extent. At least it would not be necessary to go through the complicated and potentially litigious procedure of redistributing the purse money when his true identity was disclosed. If it were not Dantes that had raced but Monte Cristo, and that now looked like a very good possibility since it had run so poorly, then there would be no complications whatsoever; the insurance money would have been paid on the correct horse. Perhaps that was simply a forlorn hope, but in any event, Mark was anxious to let Fiona know how the race had turned out.

As he left the Clubhouse, Mark spotted DeWitt pushing his way through the crowd, also on his way out. He wondered if DeWitt wanted him to examine the horse back at the barn now that the race was over. But as he approached, Mark hesitated when he noticed that a tall man in a suit with his coat over his arm was forcefully prodding DeWitt from behind, with DeWitt looking extremely unhappy and quite obviously resisting. Mark was suddenly alarmed. He could hardly believe someone would have a gun, but that was certainly what it appeared to be, though barely discernable under a coat, jammed into DeWitt's ribs.

Before Mark could catch up to them, DeWitt and his companion had reached DeWitt's car where he entered from the passenger's side and slid across the seat, the other man sliding in alongside. As DeWitt drove his car out of the parking lot, Mark sprinted over to his truck, and took off after him in pursuit.

What the hell is going on, he wondered, weaving in and out of traffic to keep the other car in sight? "I don't believe this," he exclaimed out loud to himself.

He wondered if he should call the police on his cell phone. If that was a gun, and it certainly appeared to be, DeWitt would be in danger even if the police were able to catch up and find their car. And anyhow, if Mark were mistaken, which was more plausible, he would appear pretty ridiculous to have a SWAT team descend upon two friends simply going home. He decided to just follow them at a discreet distance and see what happened.

They headed north on the Cross Island Parkway before turning east onto the Long Island Expressway, with Mark following about fifty yards behind. He was anxious not to let them know that they were being followed. After all, it would be embarrassing for two perfectly amiable friends to find out they were being tailed by a paranoid acquaintance. However, the way in which they entered DeWitt's car back at the track was highly suspicious, and Mark was not going to let it go.

The chase continued for several miles, weaving erratically in and out of traffic, before DeWitt's car turned off the Expressway and proceeded north towards Port Washington. Mark knew the area fairly well since there were several good restaurants nearby where he had dined on occasion. But he also knew that DeWitt lived much farther out on Long Island, so at least it did not appear that he was going home. In an attempt to talk himself out of the pursuit, Mark reasoned that perhaps the two men were just going to stop for an early dinner. There was still plenty of opportunity for me to make an ass of myself, he thought.

They passed through the village and picked up speed on one of the country roads leading towards the north shore. Still following with a couple of cars between them, Mark's curiosity was growing by the mile, until finally the car turned onto a narrow lane.

Within a very short distance, it turned into a parking lot alongside a large motor yacht tied up to a private dock. Shadows cast by the late afternoon sun provided Mark an opportunity to stop beneath some trees without being seen.

He noted the silver convertible next to where DeWitt's car had parked. At first it did not register, but with sudden alarm, he recognized Fiona's car. It had her unmistakable rental car license plate.

As the stranger backed out of DeWitt's car, now visibly holding a gun on his prisoner, it dawned upon Mark that if Fiona was anywhere around, she could also be in danger. He looked around for help, but despite the fading light he could see that the dock was deserted, no one else was in sight.

DeWitt stepped onto the deck of the boat followed by his captor who was viciously prodding him along from behind, before both of them disappeared down a gangway that led below. Unable to hear exactly what he was saying, Mark nevertheless realized that DeWitt was protesting. There was no doubt that he was being viciously forced along at the point of a gun.

Mark could only assume that Fiona was somewhere on board and evidently entangled in the same web of events in which DeWitt had become involved. Anger and fear surged up within Mark as he jumped out of his truck and silently trotted across to the boat. He stepped on deck, careful not to make any noise, but with no clear conviction as to what his best course of action should be; he just knew he had to do something. He was not concerned too much about being heard since a radio below was blaring music, but he crept along the deck and peered through a port light into the main cabin.

Staring in shocked disbelief, Mark could see DeWitt backing away from his captor, arms outstretched before him, pleading, his eyes transfixed on the barrel of a revolver. Then, to Mark's horror, he watched a scene unfold as if in slow motion. The stranger fired. DeWitt staggered back, his hands flying to his chest, an odd look of terror and surprise upon his face. The gun fired twice more, making a popping sound above the music, as if charged by compressed air.

DeWitt staggered back two more steps, and falling back against a bulkhead with both hands to his chest, he slid to the floor, his glasses falling crookedly across his face, and blood oozing out from between his fingers. He sat, leaning slightly to one side, with more blood starting to trickle out of the corner of his mouth. His eyes were wide open, and Mark could see the vacant stare of death.

Mark turned away and leaned over the yacht's rail, trembling and sweating, his head swimming. He fought nausea, taking deep breaths in an attempt to regain control. As a veterinarian he had tried to develop a dispassionate familiarity with life and death, but he was totally unprepared to witness the murder of a human.

He was numb, shocked, on the verge of panic. My God, he thought, appalled, where was Fiona? What had happened to her? After a few moments of sheer terror, he turned back to the porthole and peered down into the cabin.

The killer had dragged DeWitt to the middle of the cabin and was unceremoniously stuffing a handkerchief into his mouth, and what appeared to be a bar towel under his shirt, presumably to stem the bleeding. The entire scene was unreal, macabre. The killer was calmly attending to a matter of housekeeping, meticulously avoiding the spilling of DeWitt's blood. Mark could see that DeWitt was lying on his back, his eyes still staring. His murderer was nothing if not methodical.

Mark watched the man push the gun into his waistband, and turning his back upon the body with apparent indifference, he went over to the bar and casually poured some whiskey into a glass. With glass in hand, he turned to consider his work, and leaning nonchalantly against the bar, he proceeded to enjoy his drink.

Mark had to tear himself away from the scene. He had to find Fiona, if she was still alive. There was a light coming from several forward ports toward the bow of the yacht. He crept forward along the deck and peered down through the first into another cabin. It

13263-RUSS

was empty, so he moved on looking into another, likewise unoccupied, until he came to the final most forward port, and peered in. Again he froze, panic almost overtaking him once again when he saw Fiona lying on a bunk. She was bound hand and foot, with duct tape over her mouth, eyes closed as if asleep, or worse, but certainly unable to see him. He knelt, looking down through the port, transfixed and impotent, feeling helpless.

CHAPTER 22

Time passed like an eternity for Mark before he realized that Fiona was breathing, but the events of the last minute were as unreal as any nightmare could possibly be. He forced himself to focus, and attempted to drag his mind back to some semblance of rational thought. There probably would not be enough time to go for help before something terrible happened to Fiona. He was compelled to act on his own no matter how inadequate he might feel. Moving silently back along the deck, he peered down into the saloon to see what the assassin was doing.

The man had finished his glass of whiskey, and while Mark watched, he proceeded down the passageway toward the stern and started up through the companionway, up the steps toward the deck. Mark retreated toward the bow and crept around to the opposite side of the deckhouse for cover, hidden from the murderer who came on deck and continued climbing up the steps onto the bridge deck. Within seconds, Mark felt the throb of powerful engines as they came to life. He assumed the boat was to be taken out from the dock, and weighed his chances of attacking the man when he came down to cast off. It would be risky, he concluded, even though it was almost dark and the man had no idea Mark was on board. Anyway, he thought, the first thing to do was to get Fiona free so that if things went wrong, she at least would have a chance to get away or at least defend herself.

He darted back toward the stern, behind the deckhouse and down the companionway as the unsuspecting murderer went forward on the other side of the boat to cast off. The engines were running now and Mark was less concerned about his own movements being heard, although at the same time being careful not make any unnecessary noise. He dashed forward through the main cabin, stepped over the prone body of DeWitt, and ran along the passageway. Quietly, he went into the cabin in which Fiona was being held captive.

Fiona turned her head at the sound of his entry, and seeing Mark, tried to speak, eyes wide.

He held a finger to his lips and shook his head. "Don't make a sound. We've got to get you out of here," he whispered.

He moved over to one side of the cabin so that he could not be seen through the port from above. He waited a minute, still indicating to Fiona not to make a sound, making sure that he had not been seen. Unhurried footsteps moved along the deck and faded as they went toward the stern of the yacht. Mark moved quickly over to the bunk, and with trembling hands, removed the tape from Fiona's mouth and untied the cord around her wrists. They were swollen and painful, but within seconds her hands were free. She threw her arms around his neck, clinging to him with a desperate strength. He kissed her, with more urgency than affection, and pulled himself free.

"Not now!" he whispered, and began to untie her ankles. The instant that they were free, she was on her feet. She followed Mark cautiously down the passageway and into the main saloon where she froze, riveted by the sight of the grotesque body of DeWitt. She put her hand to her mouth, stifling an "Oh, God." She leaned against Mark, closed her eyes to shut out the revulsion and pain, and buried her head in his shoulder.

"It's okay," he whispered. "It's okay, don't look."

He could think of nothing else to say, but he held her to him, offering protection from the horror that she had seen. Mark could feel that she was trembling violently as he held her. At least for him, the shock of witnessing the execution was past. He knew their only hope for their own survival was for him to control his emotions and act rationally.

They were standing out of sight from the companionway, but nevertheless, upon hearing footsteps going up from the main deck to the bridge, Mark closed his eyes and sighed with relief. He knew the boat had been cast off and realized that it was too late to get ashore, even if they could avoid being seen. They would be sitting ducks if they jumped into the water and tried to swim for the dock. The boat was already moving away from the dock, with its bow-thrusters pushing it out into the waterway. The throb of the powerful engines increased as it slowly gathered speed.

Mark looked around for a weapon. The killer had taken his gun with him and was now up on the bridge, presumably occupied with operating the yacht. Once again Mark considered the possibility of them jumping overboard and swimming for the shore, but again decided that would be too dangerous. They would be seen if not heard when they hit the water, even in the fading light, and probably shot before they could get halfway. The only alternative was to find a weapon, he concluded, and hopefully ambush the guy.

He calculated that sooner or later the murderer would be coming below if he were to dispose of DeWitt's body, and assumed that that was the purpose for leaving the dock. If Mark could find a weapon, this would be a good time to deal with him. He estimated that he would have at least a few minutes to calm Fiona, find a weapon, and get mentally prepared. He also realized that he would not be able to go on deck and search for a boathook or anything substantial; he would have to make the best of what he could find below decks. He had never dreamed that he would have to assault someone with a determination to injure or kill, but he was prepared to do it now. This was not going to be like roughing somebody up while playing ice hockey as he had done on occasion in his college days. The outcome of his actions would in all certainty decide whether he and Fiona would live or die; he was sure of at least that much, and there would not be any room to negotiate the penalties. He would kill if necessary, but lived at that moment in dread of the thought.

"Hang on Fi, we'll be okay, don't worry," he whispered. They held onto each other for several minutes as the yacht turned out onto Long Island Sound and continued to gather speed.

"I'm okay now." She drew a deep breath. "What do we do?"

"I want you to go forward to the cabin you were in, and wait there," he said slowly, thinking it through. "I'll jump the guy when he comes below, but if it goes wrong, he mustn't know that you're free. You'll have a second chance at him. Stand behind the door."

"Mark, I saw him this afternoon. He's got a gun."

"I know."

Mark went to the bar and handed her a full bottle of liquor. "Here take this, stand behind the door and smack him one if he comes in. Then run like hell."

Fiona knew they had few options. Anyway, she was anxious to get out of that cabin with DeWitt's staring body, so giving Mark a quick smile of encouragement, she went forward, entering the cabin in which she had been held captive. She was reluctant to leave Mark but knew that she could offer little help in the event of a fight.

She left the cabin door cracked open, and stood behind it so that she could not be seen. The bottle that Mark had given her seemed to be a pitifully inadequate weapon in her estimation. It's too bad that there was no time to be selective because if it had been anything but gin, she mused as she leaned against the bulkhead regarding her weapon, she would have taken a good pull from it for fortification. She felt weak and inadequate, but had no qualms about bouncing the bottle off Vince's head if necessary.

Mark, also with a bottle in hand, positioned himself out of sight to the side of the companionway, and waited. He thought, with grim amusement, the guy seemed to enjoy a little booze, let's see how he takes it all at once.

The assassin had cast off the dock lines, fore and aft, and gone to the bridge to navigate the boat carefully away from the dock. Even though it was almost dark, he was anxious not to draw attention to the departure of the yacht, leaving the marina at a moderate speed, taking his time. Anyway, he was in no hurry. Upon clearing the breakwater, he turned the yacht to a northeasterly heading and added power. As it gathered speed to a comfortable plane, he switched on the automatic pilot. Since there was no other traffic in sight, he calculated that the present course down Long Island Sound would be safe for fifteen minutes or so. He would have plenty of time to go below to prepare DeWitt for burial. One of the small anchors from the dinghy tied around DeWitt's neck when he went over the side would be adequate ballast. There may be people that could make a connection between him and DeWitt, and it would be a nuisance if his old friend washed up to embarrass him at some time in the future. It wouldn't take long to give old Don a proper burial.

He had to get rid of the body before he could attend to the other dilemma. The last thing he needed was a witness to murder. She almost certainly would not have heard the shots from the forward cabin, and with the body gone over the side, he may be able to convince her that he meant no harm. He still considered that she might not give him any trouble although, he admitted, that considering recent events, that was unlikely. It would be a hard sell to convince her that he was rescuing her. What he would do with her would depend upon how they got along together, but he had serious doubts about her sentiments toward him this late in the game. He was, however, prepared to be persuasive.

Whistling a happy tune to himself, he went down the steps from the bridge, onto the deck and continued on down the companionway into the main cabin.

Mark hit him hard, but a half deflected blow by a raised arm smashed the bottle, causing the man to pitch forward onto the cabin floor. He was stunned, but despite the blow his spinning brain was clear enough for him to roll to one side and pull the gun from out of his belt. Mark was standing over him with the neck of the broken bottle still in his hand, hesitating. With deliberation, the assassin leveled the gun at him. Mark kicked out making contact with the gun just as it fired.

The gun flew across the cabin, the bullet shattering a mirror on the bulkhead. As Mark turned, diving for the gun, the killer, half crawling and half running, went forward down the passageway, got onto his feet and crashed into the cabin where Fiona stood behind the door. Fiona petrified, bewildered and powerless, dropped the bottle, her only weapon.

"Adrian, what . . . .what.. . . . ?" she started. "God, Adrian . . . " she began again, in utter confusion.

Adrian hesitated only an instant and then grabbed Fiona by a wrist, spun her around, forcing her arm up behind her back and putting his other arm around her neck, choking her. He turned with her as a shield in front of him at the same moment that Mark reached the doorway of the cabin, gun in hand.

"Drop it!" Adrian snarled.

Mark hesitated, his mind racing. He had no chance for a shot without the risk of hitting Fiona.

"Drop the bloody gun or I'll break her neck!"

Fiona's face was contorted with pain, her eyes tightly shut. Adrian rammed her arm higher up her back, causing more pain to shoot through her shoulder.

"Drop the gun!"

Mark started to back up, the gun still held out in front of him. He could see Fiona was in agony, but he needed time to negotiate.

"Let her go!" Marks voice was calm. "I won't shoot if you let her go!"

As Mark was slowly backing away through the door, subconsciously taking the pressure off Fiona, Adrian saw his chance. He spun Fiona round and lunged at the door. Mark, almost into the passageway, was caught off guard, his arm extended in front of him holding the gun.

At the instant the door slammed on his wrist, in a reflex action, he pulled the trigger. The gun fired just as Adrian grabbed it, the bullet slamming harmlessly into a bulkhead. Adrian, throwing all of his weight against the door, twisted Mark's hand back to almost breaking point.

Fiona screamed, "Adrian, don't!"

Throwing her arm around Adrian's neck from behind and her knee in his back, with strength driven by terror, she heaved his head back. The gun was wrenched from Mark's hand just as it fired again. Adrian, with Fiona beneath him, crashed to the floor. In an instant, he staggered to his feet again, gun in hand, just as Mark threw the door open, re-entering the cabin.

Adrian leveled the gun at Mark's head. "You bastard!" he hissed through clenched teeth.

Mark would reflect later that it flashed through his mind, dispassionately, that he was about to die. He was simply transfixed, staring at the muzzle of the gun, the barrel of which appeared to be growing in diameter with each millisecond of his remaining life. Somewhere in the distance he heard Fiona cry, "No, Adrian . . . no!"

Adrian pulled the trigger; there was a metallic click. To Mark, it sounded like an explosion. Adrian pulled the trigger again, and again the gun misfired, its six live rounds already spent.

Mark reacted first. He lunged forward, hitting Adrian with all his strength, a vicious hook to the jaw. Adrian staggered back, tripped over Fiona and crashed to the floor. He lay on his back, groaned, and slowly raised his free hand to his chest, his eyes closed and face contorted in pain. Mark stood over him, astonished, fascinated by the blood spreading out from between Adrian's fingers, a bullet hole in his chest. Slowly, Mark reached down and took the gun from Adrian's other hand. He offered no resistance; he was dead.

13263-RUSS

CHAPTER 23

Ponderously, under floodlights, the cabin cruiser maneuvered into the dock. Ashore, a crowd of law enforcement officers, paramedics, newsreel cameras and an assortment of reporters and curious onlookers, surrounded several police cars and two ambulances, their emergency lights flashing. Overhead a television news helicopter hovered with a brilliant spotlight further illuminating the scene.

Upon the bridge deck, Fiona was huddled in the arms of Mark, with a blanket pulled around them both. Mark had carried her, sobbing and shaking uncontrollably with tears streaming down her ashen face, away from the carnage and up onto the deck. He had immediately radioed for assistance to the marine operator, with information that there had been an 'accident', and there were two people on board that had been killed. Within minutes, the Coastguard came over the radio directing Mark to turn off the boat's autopilot and heave to.

Ten minutes later, a Coastguard cutter pulled alongside and two uniformed seamen came aboard. While Mark went below to fetch a stiff whiskey and a blanket for Fiona, the crewmen from the cutter had taken control of the yacht and slowly headed it back to shore.

Even as the boat was secured to the dock, a team of paramedics in the company of two uniformed officers and a man in civilian clothes leapt on board and were directed below by the Coastguard crew. Two more uniformed officers from the County Sheriff's Department came up onto the bridge deck where Mark and Fiona were huddled.

"Is anyone injured?" one of them asked.

"Just the two down below. We're alright," Mark replied. He was reluctant to elaborate; they would find out about the extent of the injuries soon enough.

Within a minute, the plainclothes officer reappeared from below. He was tall, and although Mark was unable to see much of his features in the deep shadows cast by the spotlights, he could tell that the man was African-American, in his thirties, and powerfully built.

"I'm Lieutenant Davis," he said. "I'm with the Nassau County Sheriff's Department. Can I get your names please?"

Mark gave him the information that he required as the officer took notes on a small pad.

"You've had a bit of excitement on board this evening, I see," Davis continued. "I must ask you to come with us to the station and answer some questions."

With faces covered, Mark and Fiona pushed through the crowd of onlookers onshore and then were transported in a police car to the Nassau County Sheriff's Station. They were informed of their rights, and for the next two hours, questioned in separate rooms by police officers. The suspicion that they had murdered the two victims was removed to a large extent with the acknowledgement that they had voluntarily called the authorities for assistance. The bodies had not been thrown overboard as they in all likelihood would have been in the event of a murder. But both Fiona and Mark had difficulty in accurately and repeatedly describing the events that led to two deaths by gunshot.

"Did you know the deceased?" Fiona was asked.

"Only one of them."

"Which one?"

"The younger one in the forward cabin."

"How long have you known him?"

"About a year, I suppose."

"What was your connection with him?"

"I rode races for him in England."

"He was English?"

"Yes."

"Did you know him well?"

Fiona's eyes began to fill with tears.

"Yes, I mean, I don't know. I think so," she replied, her chin trembling.

The two detectives looked at each other.

"So this was a romantic association? He wasn't related to you?"

"No, he wasn't either. I just knew him."

"Your friend didn't kill him out of jealousy?"

"Of course not. He had taken me hostage. I had as much to do with him being killed as Mark did."

Tears were streaming down Fiona's cheeks, and she buried her face in her hands.

In another room, Mark was also being questioned. He had declined to have an attorney present, being confident that he would be capable of explaining the events without incriminating himself.

He pointed out that if the deaths were the result of either he or Fiona murdering the victims, they had ample opportunity to get rid of the bodies and return to the dock, no one being any wiser. Anyway, there was plenty of evidence to prove that there had been a fight, and Fiona's wrists still showed evidence of having been tied.

"You knew one of the deceased though?" the detectives asked.

"Only one of them. The one in the main cabin."

"Did you have a business relationship with him?"

"Yes I did, I've known him for several years and I have performed some veterinary work for him in the past."

"But you didn't shoot him?"

"No, he was killed by the other man whom I have never seen before. I can only assume that they were involved in a race-fixing scheme that went wrong."

Mark explained at length what he knew about Dantes and Monte Cristo, and how DeWitt probably masterminded an attempt to fix a race. He explained how Fiona had stumbled upon the plot and was abducted by the man called Vincent to get her out of the way.

"I don't know what went wrong, but it appears this other guy killed DeWitt possibly in retribution."

"But you didn't know the man that killed him?"

"No, I have no idea who he is, but Miss Kent said that he is not the one that abducted her. You'll have to look somewhere else for him."

"You have no idea who he is then, doctor?"

"No, but as long as he is on the loose, Miss Kent may still be in danger."

Eventually satisfied that it was not necessary to arrest and charge either of them with a crime this early in the investigation, Mark was released under his own recognizance and Fiona into his custody. They were informed that they were not to leave the State of New York, and that they would be required at a later date for additional questioning.

Shortly before midnight, Mark and Fiona were driven together back to the dock and released, and from there they drove in Mark's truck to his house. Fiona had regained much of her composure although she was pale and exhausted. She required no persuasion to stay with Mark, and with little conversation they fell into bed, Fiona clinging to him in a desperate embrace.

Newspapers and television news channels had brief coverage the next morning of the events as they knew them. There were no photographs identifying either Fiona or Mark; they had successfully covered their faces as they went ashore, and with little information forthcoming from the authorities, the story fizzled out. There was never a shortage of sordid stories about violent crimes for the media to cover.

How and when Fiona had known the assassin, troubled Mark. Her reaction to seeing him in those few moments before Adrian had been killed, was constantly weighing upon Mark's mind. She was slowly recovering from the shock of the entire episode, riding with Mark as he made his rounds at the racetrack, and refusing to leave him long enough to get on any horses in the morning or even ride a race. He was reluctant to press her about Adrian's identity, wishing to give her time to recover.

Five days passed before Mark and Fiona were summoned to FBI offices in Manhattan. Lieutenant Davis picked them up and drove them into town, not offering to discuss anything concerning the investigation of the events that had changed their lives forever, except to say that Vincent Cinotti had been identified and picked up.

From a parking lot deep within the bowels of an imposing, and to Fiona and Mark, threatening complex, their escort took them by elevator to the twenty-fifth floor. They were further ushered through a maze of thickly carpeted gray corridors, and finally ushered into a room to be greeted formally by three implacable appearing officials in civilian clothes.

Fiona, drained of most emotion was nevertheless surprised to be confronted, once again, by Inspector Mikolos. "We meet again, Miss Kent." Mikolos pursed his lips and clucked as he shook his head. "Most unhappy circumstances, no?"

A small, balding man with steel rimmed glasses, wearing the regulation dark suite and tie, stepped forward and introduced himself.

"Doctor McLennan, Miss Kent," he said shaking their hands, "I am agent Blackwell with the Federal Bureau of Investigation. Please be seated."

Blackwell retreated behind a large desk. "You have met Inspector Mikolos, Miss Kent," he continued as they all found a seat, "but Doctor, I don't believe you have had the pleasure."

Mikolos and Mark nodded their acknowledgment.

The third person in the room was an African-American woman in her twenties, wearing a navy blue suite and hair pulled tightly into a knot behind her head. She was slim and attractive, although not flattered by her severe dress. She was introduced as Agent Moorhead, also of the FBI.

The solemn group in front of him intensified Mark's nagging concern that he may yet be charged, at least, with manslaughter. "Perhaps we should be represented by an attorney. Are you intending to interrogate us?" he asked Blackwell, pointedly. "If so, you must understand that we have nothing further to say."

"You may request an attorney of course, if you wish," Blackwell replied. "But I don't think that will be necessary. As a result of our investigations we have no interest in holding either of you accountable for what happened onboard that boat."

"Well, I appreciate that," Mark replied with feeling.

"Miss Moorhead will bring you up to speed on the extent of our investigation," Blackwell continued. "And then we will let you decide if you should require an attorney to be present. We can adjourn this meeting at any time that you desire and allow you to make arrangements to engage an attorney. Miss Moorhead?"

The young woman cleared her throat, placed a pair of half-glasses upon the end of her nose and opened a file that she had been nursing.

"One of the deceased was a Donald DeWitt," she began. "According to your previous statements, he was known to both of you although he was a business associate in only a minor way to you, Doctor McLennan, and Miss Kent had only met him on one occasion. Is that correct?" she asked looking from Mark to Fiona over the top of her glasses.

Mark nodded.

"He was the registered owner of a racehorse that ran last Saturday at Gateway Park under a false name, if what you reported is correct. That issue is still under investigation. But what we do know is that a considerable amount of money, in excess of two-hundred thousand dollars, was transferred to DeWitt from the account of a Jan Mikhail Hantzen." She spelled the name before continuing.

"This money was transferred to DeWitt's bank account only two days before the time that he purchased two horses in England. We can assume that this transfer of funds was to pay for the horses, since the amount of the deposit to DeWitt's bank was exactly the same as the amount of the purchase. The money for this purchase was sent in the form of a wire transfer to the account of an Adrian Harrington in England from Donald DeWitt, and registered as an international exchange for that purpose."

"So DeWitt didn't own the horses," Mark interrupted. "This man Hantzen did, is that right?"

"We can assume that in a sense, that's correct." The young woman continued. "It has been established, however, that this person was in fact known in England as Adrian Harrington and the name Jan Mikhail Hantzen was an alias that he used in this country. They were both one and the same person."

"So that's what the initials JMH stood for on Adrian's briefcase," Fiona murmured almost imperceptibly.

"Excuse me?"

Fiona looked at Moorhead, surprised by the inquiry.

"Oh, nothing." Fiona hesitated, "I'm sorry."

The young black woman continued. "Hantzen, or Harrington, and Donald DeWitt had known each other for several months but negotiated with each other through a third party, a Vincent Cinotti. According to Miss Kent's statement, the name of the person that abducted her was also Vince or Vincent. Perhaps you can identify him from these photographs?"

She passed three photographs to Fiona. With hands shaking visibly, Fiona took a quick look and passed the photographs back, almost as if they were contagious and she had no wish to touch them.

"That's him. Yes, that's him," she said without hesitation.

Agent Moorhead took them back and continued reading from her file. "We have arrested Cinotti who will be charged with various offenses, including kidnapping. He and Hantzen had been under observation for several months due to the international aspect of their activities. And at this point, so that you know what those activities were, Inspector Mikolos will fill you in."

Up until then, Mikolos had been sitting quietly, looking rather complacent, but now he leaned forward in his chair, his elbows resting on its arms, his shoulders hunched up around his ears, giving him a pugnacious appearance. He looked directly at Fiona.

"Miss Kent," he began accusingly. "You have been involved in, or knew of, illegal activities in England, no?"

Fiona offered no acknowledgment and Mikolos continued.

"You knew that this Harrington had accepted large sums of money and when we question you, you say nothing about this. You have been under observation, and we have concluded that you did not take any payment for yourself, and we also know that, except for a meeting here in New York City, you have not seen this Harrington for several months. So we conclude that you were a dupe."

Fiona colored. "I may have been a dupe, or perhaps a dope if that's what you mean, but I can assure you that I had no intention of doing anything that would be considered illegal," she flared.

"Ah, illegal no, but evasive and foolish, yes!" Mikolos shook his finger in Fiona's direction.

Mark, hearing these revelations for the first time, stepped in. "Look here, you said there would be no charges. What the hell is that if it is not an accusation?" he protested.

"Relax, Doctor," Blackwell interrupted quietly. "There will be no formal accusations of criminal offenses or misdemeanors, even if there may have been some indiscretion concerning Miss Kent's conduct."

"Indiscrete conduct?" Mark asked.

"Miss Kent told the truth as she knew it, but she didn't divulge relevant facts during questioning. We don't consider that as illegal conduct, but considering the facts as they have evolved, such omissions were hardly prudent." Blackwell turned to Mikolos, "Continue please."

13263-RUSS

Mikolos sat back in his chair, now comfortable that he had made a point. Once again he directed his remarks to Fiona.

"Last year, Inspector Barker asked you if you recognize the photograph of a Carlo Tiriach and you say that you have seen him, but you do not tell us he is acquainted with your friend, Harrington. This Carlo is found murdered, but then we do not know who did this thing. We only know that Tiriach was the man that put a bomb in your friend's car. But I think you know who arranged Tiriach's death, even then, because you and your friend were no longer friends. Yes?"

Fiona nodded. "I didn't know; it seemed impossible. But I suppose I began to suspect." She looked over at Mark with an apologetic shrug. "I really didn't expect to see him again."

Mikolos continued. "You also tell Inspector Barker and me that your friend Harrington goes to America and we find out that he goes to Brazil, which I think you don't know. Now I will tell you why he goes to Brazil. He goes to Brazil as Adrian Harrington and there he change his passport and a Jan Mikhail Hantzen arrives in America, a different person who is the same man!" Mikolos ended by raising his voice and paused for effect.

Fiona slowly shook her head, her mind comprehending most of what she had heard. She reached over and took Mark's hand, seeking reassurance.

Mark was only beginning to understand the connection between Harrington and Fiona. "If Harrington was in fact this man Hantzen, why would he buy his own horse?" he asked.

"Because, Doctor, he want to make American dollars into English pounds. He use the horse buying to, how do you say, wash money?" Mikolos explained, smiling a stage smile and rubbing his fingers and thumb together as if he were actually feeling the money. "It is very difficult to smuggle money into England and when he buys his own horse, well, it was so easy, no?"

"Now, Miss Kent," he continued. "You do not know why your friend does these things, yes? You do not know his business?"

"I have no idea, I thought he worked for the British government," Fiona replied in bewilderment, slowly shaking her head.

"He did work for a government. He worked for British MI-5 but he knew many people in many governments, did this Adrian Harrington. He grew up with contacts in many governments, yes he did. His father was an important man. But this Adrian worked for his government, and also illegal organizations in other governments. He bought arms, weapons you see, and sold them illegally to the KLA, the Kosovo Liberation Army, and the Irish Republican Army, the IRA. Because of that, many innocent people die!"

Mikolos spat out the last few words, his voice rising again. He paused, and after thrusting himself forward for emphasis throughout the discourse, he slowly leaned back in his chair surveying the room for approval before continuing.

"This man Carlo Tiriach, a Yugoslavian, was killed by your friend Harrington's friend, Max Molter, an English. We know this Molter and your friend have a business illegally selling weapons. And now Scotland Yard arrests this man Molter for murdering the Yugoslavian, Tiriach, who attempted to blow up your friend. You see, the Yugoslavian, he wanted to stop weapons going to the Kosovo Liberation Army," Mikolos explained in a slightly less impassioned voice.

"This Max Molter was arrested with a pistol that ballistics say is the one used to shoot Tiriach. Because Tiriach was an intelligence agent for Yugoslavia, your friend Harrington had Molter get rid of him."

"I wish you wouldn't refer to him as my friend," protested Fiona, at least willing to challenge upon that point. "I will concede that I was a friend once, and probably used by him, but I ended our friendship a long time ago."

Blackwell had been sitting impassively behind his desk, intensely watching Fiona. "Perhaps it was Harrington's friendship for you that saved your life," he said quietly. "You see, according to Vincent Cinotti, when Harrington found out that you were tied up on the boat, he decided not to let Cinotti go back onboard. Cinotti was quick to disclose this to us, denying any complicity in the murder of DeWitt. Harrington went to the boat himself, knowing you were onboard, possibly intending to protect you. I don't know, of course, that Harrington would not have killed you, he may have. Cinotti certainly would have."

"It is hard to believe that of Adrian," Fiona said quietly. "But I suppose I really never knew him."

"DeWitt was killed," Blackwell continued, "because in an investigation about the horse, he almost certainly would have revealed Harrington's identity. I'm sure Harrington was afraid DeWitt would bail out and expose him. Harrington was very dangerous. But if he had disposed of DeWitt's body before he released you, you might never have known he was a murderer, and he may not have thought it necessary to kill you. That's pure speculation. There was a slight chance that you would have believed that he had rescued you, in which case, you might have survived."

"Miss Kent did know about the insurance fraud on the horse," offered Mark, more willing than Fiona to accept the fact that Adrian was a murderer. "Of course she knew the true identity of the horse and obviously Harrington wasn't going to be happy about that. I doubt if he would have let her live with that information."

"I suppose my meeting him in New York for lunch could have been to find out if I knew anything about Dantes," Fiona suggested. "Since both the horse and I were in New York, he may have been concerned. I remember asking him about the horse, so he could have reasonably assumed at that point that I knew nothing."

"It would not have made any difference," Blackwell argued. "Cinotti told him later that you did know about the horse's identity."

"I saw him kill DeWitt," Mark interjected. "The guy was absolutely ruthless and showed no remorse whatsoever. I have no doubt he would have killed Fiona too."

"That's probably true, you're probably correct." Blackwell stood up and came from behind his desk. "We will be staying in touch with you as the investigation progresses," he continued, "and we would like you to inform us if you know of any other acquaintances of the deceased persons, but in the meantime, you are of course free to go."

The meeting was over, and with a sense of profound relief for Fiona, Mark reached over and squeezed her hand.

She turned to him with a weak smile. "I'm so sorry Mark. At some point I would have told you what I knew about Adrian, but he seemed so insignificant until now."

EPILOGUE

A gentle breeze dried the crystal beads of seawater that clung to Fiona's naked body as she lay upon a beach towel. Mark reclined beside her on the deck of their chartered boat, only a towel around his waist and a drink in his hand. The early morning sun that was climbing into the cobalt Aegean sky, cast long shadows from the surrounding hills out to where they were anchored. Their yacht, standing just off the beach of an isolated cove, rocked gently upon the placid sea.

The two-week honeymoon was almost over, and the events of the summer seemed far away in the past. Now that they were sailing alone off the Greek Islands, Fiona had finally wanted to talk about their terrible ordeal.

"Mark, you can't blame yourself. You didn't kill anyone. You couldn't have prevented the deaths of either of those people."

"I know Fi, but I can't help wondering what I might have done differently."

"Adrian killed himself wrestling the gun away from you. You know you would never have shot him in any event, but he certainly would have shot you."

"You really believe that?"

"Absolutely. I know that."

She sat up pulled him towards her and kissed him. He held her and ran his fingers through her damp hair.

"That was something that we could never imagine could touch our lives," he said, shaking his head slowly, still finding it too incredulous. He leaned back against the lifelines of the yacht, and took a sip of his drink.

"Fortunately, the insurance company has made a claim against the estate of DeWitt, you know," he continued. "So they will get their money back in full on the fraudulent claim. His farm will be sold for much more than that."

"Well, since they're going to hold you blameless, will they continue to employ you?"

"They said that they would."

"Is that an important part of your business?"

Mark reflected for a moment before answering. "Oh, not that important, but you're wondering if I would relocate and start a practice in England, aren't you?"

"Would you?" she smiled, tracing his mouth with a forefinger.

"The answer is, I would consider it, dear heart. I love you and England." He looked earnestly into her eyes. "I mean it. I could practice in England quite happily. I could move there if that's what you want."

"You almost went to jail for me," she said with a laugh.

She leaned back and stretched out once more on the towel, thoughtfully gazing into the sky. "You know, Mark, Mikolos found it hard to believe that you hadn't murdered Adrian in some sort of love triangle."

"Maybe I would have," he chuckled quietly.

"Did they ever find out who owned the boat?"

"It was registered to Jan Mikhail Hantzen, Harrington's alias. The United States Treasury Department is selling it because it was used in the commission of a crime. They ought to sink it."

After a while, Fiona sat up and took a sip from his drink. "I feel sorry for Dantes. What will become of him?" she asked.

"He'll be all right, don't worry. When I did the exam a couple of days after the race and discovered the sponges, his nasal passages were clean. I was surprised that there was no damage or infection. He was lucky."

"By the way," he added as an afterthought, "Tommy called just before we left and said he was training great."

After a while, Fiona with a quizzical frown, asked, "Will he be allowed to race again?"

"Possibly. The stewards are considering the fact that since he finished last in the name of another horse, a horse that is deceased and never ran in America, there may be no harm in expunging that race from his record and permitting him to run in his own name. But as of now, he may only run under National Hunt rules, steeple-chasing, which means he really has a much reduced value."

"Well I think he's valuable, God bless him."

"In the meantime," Mark continued, "he doesn't have an owner and is being sold by the Justice Department, probably for next to nothing. They're accepting sealed bids for him."

"Wouldn't it be lovely to own him?" Fiona mused, wistfully, staring off into the distance. She was reflecting upon the happier times when she had ridden him in England.

It was early in the afternoon that they sat in the cockpit, enjoying the warm air and a lunch of lobster salad, fresh mango and a bottle of Greek wine.

The ship to shore radio crackled to life. "Odette, Odette. This is the marine operator, do you read me?"

Mark went below to answer it.

"This is the yacht, Odette. Go ahead."

"We have a message from the United States for you, sir. Over."

"Go ahead."

"The message reads: 'Your bid was successful, congratulations. Signed, Tommy'. Do you copy? Over."

"Yes I have that, thank you. Is that all? Over."

"That is all, sir. Do you wish to reply?"

"No reply. Message understood, thank you. Out."

Mark came up through the companionway with a broad grin. Fiona looked at him, not sure but suspecting what had transpired.

"Dear Fiona, you've just got another wedding present. You now own Dantes!" he sang.

"Oh Mark, I can't believe it. You did do it. You bought him. You're so clever!" She threw her arms around him.

With a whoop of sheer exuberance, he pulled her arms from around his neck, threw off his towel, danced around the deck and dived into the sea. She dived in behind him and came up with her arms and legs wrapped around him, their naked bodies locked together.

"Let go!" he spluttered. "You'll drown me!"

"We'll drown together then. I'll never let you go!" she laughed.

Printed in the United States
5927